i

The Pitch

Hank Owens

Pocol Press
Clifton, VA

POCOL PRESS

Published in the United States of America
by Pocol Press.
6023 Pocol Drive
Clifton, VA 20124
http://www.pocolpress.com

Publisher's Cataloguing-in-Publication

Owens, Hank 1967-

    The pitch / Hank Owens. – 1st ed. – Clifton, VA :
Pocol Press, 2011.

        p. ; cm.

        ISBN-13: 978-1-929763-47-4
        ISBN-10: 1-929763-47-6

        1. Baseball–United States–Fiction. 2. Baseball
stories. I. Title.

PS3563.W46 P58 2011
813.6–dc22   1104

Dedication

To K, my muse, my partner, and an even bigger Cubs fan.

The Lineup:

M:	Orval Sheckerd
C:	Sam "Speedy" Killefer
1B:	Hack Hendrix
2B:	Chuck "Smokey" Dubuc
3B:	Rollie "Gunner" Thomas
SS:	Everett "Ee-Yah" Hollocher
LF:	Dode "Hoops" Hooper
CF:	Amos "Pantyhose" Paskert
RF:	Fred "Stuffy" Flack
P:	Harry "Hot Rod" Barber
P:	Phil "Preacher" Bush
P:	Joe "Moose" Mays
P:	Freddie "Fresh" McInnis
P:	Rube Tyler
IF:	Norm "Footsie" Snodgrass
IF:	Wally Zeider
IF:	Turner Agnew
OF:	Solly Stivetts
OF:	Charlie Schang
Bench:	Hobie Beaumont
Pi:	Brickyard Bransfield
FirstCo	Deacon LaChance

The League:

Keokuk Westerns
Red Wing Red Wings
Winona Wolverines
Rochester Athletics
Dubuque Browns
Clinton Colts
Burlington Bees
Galesburg Spiders
Quincy Giants
Hannibal Robins

Batting Practice

The year it rained horseflies on opening day I knew it was going to be a weird, *weird* summer. Two outs in the top of the fifth, we're up 2-0, and all of a sudden the skies open up. Thousands, or hell, I don't know, *millions* of the things, maybe. They start fallin' from the sky like we're getting bombed. First just a few. One hits Hack Hendrix, our first baseman, on the back of the neck. That was the first I saw of them. Hack swats at it. *Smack.* Then our pitcher gets one, hits him on the hand and when he sees it he brushes it off, but he looks at it and it's huge, the size of a nickel and he rears back a bit. Then pretty soon everyone's getting hit. Fans start shoutin' and the sky gets dark—the sky gets *dark* with 'em—and then it's a madhouse. There're big, ugly horseflies everywhere, fallin' from the sky, stingin' people—and I ain't never heard of no Goddamned *stingin'* horsefly before, usually they just bug you but these were *stingin'* people left and right. The umps stop play 'cuz the batter's too worried about the damned flies, not that this meat couldn't of hit ol' Hot Rod fuckin' *blind*, mind, but the ump wasn't going to be able to call the damned balls and strikes anyway, what with the flies fallin' from the sky. So he calls time and then no one's watchin' the field and everyone at the park looks *up* and it looks like the Goddamned apocalypse, the sky is just black with flies and they're all headin' right for us and lookin' for blood. The buggers get in the dugout and they swarm up to the concrete roof where it's warm and then when that fills up they start swarmin' at *face* level and that's when it goes from bein' weird to scaring the hell out of me, cuz' we're all breathin the damn things and that's about when Speedy Killefer huffs off the field sayin' he's getting the hell *out* and all of us head for the tunnel trailin' a couple million blood-suckin' horseflies behind us. The Keokuk Westerns get in the locker room and slam the door and we're all in there swattin' at the flies that came in with us, killin' as many as we can while they're stickin' us for blood, and then we hear the umps poundin' on the door sayin' "LET US THE HELL IN, YOU COCKSUCKERS! WE'RE GETTIN' KILLED OUT HERE" and since we was leadin' at the time of the fly delay, I figure what the hell, maybe if we're nice to 'em these guys'll call the game and we open the door wide enough to let their fat asses in the locker room along with another armada of mutant flies.

We sit in there for a while and realize that we ain't got no way of knowin' what the hell's happenin' outside, whether our fans are getting eaten up or whether they've all said the hell with it and gotten out of there. "What the hell are we gonna do now, ump?" I says, and the crew chief looks at me and says "I got no Goddamned idea, Orval. The rulebook don't say nothin' about Goddamned *flies* anywheres in it" and we all think this is pretty funny and laugh while he swats a few stragglers that are feasting on his thick neck. Hoops says he reckons this is some sort of invasion and we tell him to shut up, this is just what you get when you build a ballfield in the Goddamned swamp next to the river. A few of the guys who are spending their second or third year in Keokuk—waiting for the call that ain't, believe me, *ain't* ever gonna come—reckon that this happens every year, and it does, we get hellacious flies every April, but nothing like this. Nothing like this. Anyway, once flies start comin' in the fresh air vent we all look at each other like, *holy shit*, we don't wanna get eaten to death in a Goddamned sixty-year old single-A locker room on opening day. So I say "Let's get the hell outta here" and I open the door a crack and then they're *gone*, just as fast as they came the things are *gone* and I look up the tunnel and see the sunlight and the grass of the infield and think that we're OK and that we can all come out. I lean back in and say to the fat boy "Hey, ump, I reckon we're back on" and he says "the hell we are, Orval. That's my call, not yours" and he gets up and squeezes by me to take a look. And sure enough, he says "OK boys, we're back on" and the Westerns get up and head back on out and get screwed 8-2 off a couple of Red Wing home runs and a shitty call at the plate in the eighth. The fans had mostly gone home after the flies, but about a dozen stick it out to see the carnage and when Gunner strikes out to end the game, off a ball that was practically in the Goddamned dirt, the rest of them pick up their kids and leave their beer cups and head out into the Iowa night, crunching flies under their flip flops as they head down the bleacher seats. We hear 'em yellin' when they get to their cars and realize they left the Goddamned windows open and now their cars are full of the fuckin' things.

Now, normally the flies would be the weirdest thing of the summer, but this is single-A ball and you're gonna see some shit every year that you don't quite believe. I been in the game forty years and I spent fifteen of them managing down here and hoping that my kids get the call that sends them up to Peoria and hoping even more that I get the call that gets me *out* of Keokuk and on to somewheres where they don't have killer horseflies every April. Some of my kids get that call, and I even had a couple that ended up in Chicago playin' at Wrigley, one of 'em a pitcher and another that was a catcher, but I been stuck in this place ever since I been managing and I figured I was probably here another ten years till they retire me or till I got run over by the team bus. I wasn't angry, at least not yet, I sure wished things had turned out different but I was getting paid to manage a ball club and there's plenty worse. Anyway, like I was sayin', down here you get a good player every now and then, but they don't hang around long, a couple of 400 foot taters, or a couple of complete games, or even a few stolen bases and the organization moves 'em on up. So the ones you get to know are the ones that are hopeless, that the organization don't want, but don't necessarily want to get rid of. If you start two seasons as a Westerner, you might as well start learnin' to ask whether you want fries with that burger, because you ain't goin' nowhere but Keokuk in baseball. So with that kind of lineup I seen all kinds a weirdness on and off the field. I seen a triple play once when there was already an out, since the umps we got here are also single-A and some of them ain't goin' nowheres else, neither. I seen two inside the park grand slams, and believe me that takes some original fielding when the deepest part of the field ain't no more than 390 feet. But believe me, I also seen some baserunnin' that turned what should have been an inside the park home run into an easy out at second, and I seen three guys standin' on a base once lookin' at each other like they woke up in bed together wonderin' what the hell happened.

Alright, so you see it all in single-A and the horseflies were just one more weird-assed piece of shit that I gotta deal with. So after the game we get all the bases pulled up and the equipment put away and the kids go off home to shower up, since we ain't got no working plumbing in the Goddamned locker room till they turn the pipes on, and I sit down with Hobie and Brickyard and we put our heads in our hands and wonder how we're going to survive this season without the organization noticin' that we're going to lose about sixty games again. And we talk about the new kids, some of 'em straight from the rookie season which started a couple weeks early and peein' their pants on account of the seventy-five

3

mile-an-hour crap that these A-ball pitchers are mincin' by 'em and we wonder how any scout ever thought these pansies were going to be ballplayers someday when they just about burst into tears after striking out on big fat donut pitches. Fat donut pitches that would have been hit so hard in triple-A that they wouldn't have ever come the hell *down*. And we finish up the scouting report for tomorrow night's game, which is easy because we still don't know a Goddamned thing about Red Wing except they got a third baseman who can't handle bad hops and a left fielder who ain't gonna be bothering us much longer if he keeps hitting shots out into the river like he did to us tonight. Then I pull out my little helper from the bottom drawer and we all have a couple of shots and figure that we'll manage somehow with this bunch of kids and here's to a new beginning and all that and maybe just one more shot of hooch and we'll call it a night.

Leaving the locker room I reckon maybe I've had one too many, though, because I see this guy who ain't on the team but dressed like he is. He's got the Keokuk jersey on, with the Cubs hat since we don't make enough money to get our own damn logo on our hats anymore, and he's got on baseball pants that are too tight with cleats and a glove that looks like it could've been Cy Young's. I'm thinkin' to myself, "oh shit, no, this ain't one of ours come to talk to me about his girlfriend or his meth problem or some crap like that, not now" and then I realize that this guy is also wearin' Goddamned prescription glasses and a butt-nuzzling mustache and I think oh, holy crap this is sad if he's waiting for autographs at a single-A game and then I realize that the team's all gone home and I realize that he's lookin' at me, like he's been waitin' for me.

"I help you?" I say.

Guy sticks out his hand, the one with the Goddamned glove on it, then he realizes he's made a bad first impression, shakes the glove off and sticks his hand out again.

"Rube Tyler," he says. "I'm a pitcher."

"The hell you are," I say. "You look forty Goddamned years old. What do you want?"

"I been working on a pitch," he says, and my eyes just glaze over.

"Yeah, you and every other outta shape beer hound in Keokuk," I say. I'm not tryin' to be mean, and I appreciate that some folks just can't let go of their dream, but even I realized when I hit thirty-five that I wasn't going to be catchin' fly balls in Wrigley's outfield. Ever. I like to think that I let it go graciously, that I found a way to stay involved, to keep going with a game I loved with some measure of dignity and self-respect, and that losers like this guy are making the rest of us aging guys

4

look bad. But as I open the door to my 1988 Plymouth Valiant I realize that everything's relative, and the hangdog look on Rube Tyler's face makes me feel bad, like I've just told a younger version of myself *go fuck yourself. That 24 home runs that you hit in high school is the best you're ever gonna do. And in a few years you're gonna have a heart condition, your stomach's gonna hurt every day and you're gonna have trouble peein'. And all you're going to have to show for it is a career in crappy little small town ballparks. On your tombstone it's going to say "A-ball." Get used to it.* And so I stop being a manager for one minute and feel a little sympathy for Rube Tyler and I move my hand from my car to my hip and, no, just be patient, this is his dream and you've gotta let him down gently. And I take a deep breath and I say "Look, I get guys comin' up to me all the time thinkin' they got a pitch, or they got some magic strategy, or they been workin' out and they lead their damned softball league in home runs. You know, that's great that you been workin' at it. But this here is a kids' game, y'understand? I got no pull with the organization, they don't move my players up because I say so. So there ain't nothin' I can talk to you about. The oldest kid on my team is twenty-four, and he's ridin' out the twilight of his career with the organization. I love the game, too, and I like takin' bee-pee with my boys and pretendin' I'm eighteen years old again. But I ain't, and you ain't, and you probably got better things to do with your time than think about how you're gonna play ball again because you got some magic pitch."

The guy looks right at me and there's a long silence like I just drank his last beer and I think he's gonna *cry* but then I realize that he ain't and I just seen his crossed eyes through his inch-thick glasses and it just *always* looks, maybe, like he's gonna cry.

"I know, sir. But I been workin' on a really *good* pitch."

"Look, Carter"

"Tyler, sir, Rube Tyler."

"Tyler, whatever. I said my piece. I ain't a scout. I'm a manager. I can't help you. It's late, and my team got eaten up by killer horseflies tonight and I just want to get home and take a shower and have a beer and go the hell to bed. I'm sorry, but it ain't even my job to look for pitchers and to be honest you ain't what my bosses think of when they're scoutin' players."

Rube blinks two times, three times. He breathes kinda slow and firm like he knew this was comin' and he's sorry to waste both of our time. But then he starts in again.

"Please, sir, just let me show you this pitch. I don't think anyone can hit it, I been workin' on it for years and I finally got it so that it moves real good."

My hand moves back to my car door. "Son, have a good night. We all got a pitch somewhere, but that don't mean we're all pitchers."

I open the car door and get in. Rube stands there. I start the car and he turns away and winds up, like he's gonna show me the pitch no matter what. My ass crunches a couple dozen dead horseflies. I left the Goddamned window open too and I'm cleanin' the flies out of my crotch so I ain't lookin' at Rube when he delivers.

Thunk

As I pull out, Rube's thrown his pitch at the side of the grandstand and it's hit the wooden siding. I know that sound. It's the sound of a sixty-mile-an-hour fastball. A sixty-mile-an-hour fastball would make even a crappy A-ball hitter look like Ted Williams. Keep throwin', Rube, I think, but quit dreaming.

I drive out of the parking lot and drive home. The smell of dead horseflies smashed under my ass sticks with me the whole drive and I think that all of us have got that miracle that we think's gonna pull us out of the crappy ball season ahead of us and into something else. Someone's gonna win the lottery and trade in their Plymouth Valiant for a Hummer. Someone else is gonna get on TV singing and move from East Jesus, Iowa to Hollywood. Rube's gonna add thirty miles an hour to his fastball—or, really, his straightball—and cash in his factory job for sixteen-million a year in Chicago's starting lineup. And then there's me. I'm gonna somehow what, win seventy games for the organization and get the call up to yet another crappy little ballclub and start my march up to Wrigley, too?

Bullshit, I think. See you there, Rube.

1st Inning

That year, the year we had the flies, the Westerns were trying to live down one of our worst seasons ever. We had finished at the bottom of the River League for the second year in a row, but we had done it in style, thirty-five games out, which is quite an achievement considering that we only played eighty-two Goddamned games. Hannibal had finished on top, and they kicked our asses in the nine games we played against them, but we didn't do much better against the rest of the league and the organization stopped calling me about prospects by the first of August. We were considerably on our own and they let us finish out the season without much fanfare and then the kids all went back to their jobs at the Wal-Mart or wherever else and not all of them came back this year. The organization sent us six new kids after rookie ball and we got a couple of new faces since there wasn't too much room in double-A, on account of the big league team sucked so bad that they demoted a bunch of guys and replaced them with castoffs from other, smarter teams.

Usually I like the first few practices of the season, but that year I was deeply troubled. When you've been managing suck-ass ballplayers as long as I have, you get to be something of a connoisseur of God-awful fielding and weak-ass hitting. I figure I've coached some of the worst outfielders ever to get paid for wearing a glove, and I've gotten pretty good at knowing which ones are worth spending time on and which ones you just have to endure. I've watched enough kids whiff at cheap-assed junk that I myself have thrown at them to know that hitting ain't easy, and I know from experience that even mediocre hitting is something is a thing you don't see every day. Or even every year in single-A. The River League is the bottom of the barrel, and most of our kids make about six-hundred bucks a month during the summer. They'll spend a couple of years in single-A, bouncing around or—worse—staying with the same team for a couple of years before they figure out that they aren't going anywhere. So I'm used to watching shitty ball and I'm used to seeing eighteen-year-old lunkheads who think they're the next Willie Mays get up there and discover real fast that another career is in order.

But this team, Jesus Christ, this team was bad. I got them together that first day of practice and I looked out over them and I looked at Hobie, my bench coach and we both thought to ourselves that we were going to earn our fuckin' salaries this year. We had a few standouts from the year before, like Hack Hendrix, our first baseman who had hit .230

7

with seventeen home runs and sallied around like he'd be up in Davenport anyday, and Stuffy Flack, our right fielder who had set the River League record for errors in a season with forty-two. Footsie Snodgrass had been our designated pine-rider, but we got him into a few games in the late innings and he managed to finish the season with a run batted in and an invitation from the organization to loaf around in the dugout at our expense for another Goddamned year. And there was Harry "Hot Rod" Barber, the all-time Westerns leader in hit batsmen who'd told me on the mound during one game that he wasn't hurt, he was just drunk, and if we left him in he'd figure it out. We did, but he didn't and the next Galesburg Spider ended up getting knocked on his ass by Hot Rod's patented Jack Daniels curve ball.

And those three, along with our lump of a backstop, Speedy Killefer, Hoops Hooper, our left fielder who almost choked to death on bubble gum in one game, and Solly Stivetts, a retread who had made it as far as triple-A for a week before blowing out his arm and then not taking a single hint as the organization sent him down the ladder for three Goddamned years, were the ones that *made* it back to the team that year. I don't need to explain much more about the ones who got let go, other than to say that they are now, so much as they can be, *otherwise employed*. When Hobie and I looked at the *new* faces, well, our jaws just about dropped. It turned out one of them had a prison record for stealin' panties, one had just finished a stint as a missionary in New Guinea or some damned place like that and had played a couple weeks of community college ball before some drunk-assed scout figured he'd be the next big thing, and a third had been drafted something like four years ago but had gotten called up by his National Guard unit and was just now getting back to the States, expectin' the organization to live up to its Goddamned contract and therefore being placed unceremoniously in my care.

So we had a team of half-talented, occasionally drunk, mostly ignorant and basically inept shitheads. Now, if this were some Hollywood novel, I'd tell you that, golly gee, we *never* expected to win the championship that season and boy are you in for a wild story, but this ain't that Hollywood novel, and nothing like that happened. We sucked that whole season, the one of the horseflies, but we didn't end up sucking as bad as the year before and you probably already guessed why, but believe me you don't know the half of it. Hobie, Brickyard, and I put those kids to work that first day of practice and it was a sight to behold, a team full of greenhorns chasing little white balls all over the field, and all over the strike zone, with little success in either category. We put'em through their drills, God help us, and we pitched 'em bee-pee for hours at a time, but they were rookie ball when they walked into that first practice and they were rookie ball when we showed up for our first game. We clocked Speedy running the bases at just over thirty seconds at top speed, and we watched Stuffy chase down flies and tried not to laugh or cry when he missed them, and we watched Hack prance around the field with the ego of a major leaguer and the bat speed of a slug's right ass. Hot Rod showed up late for every single Goddamned practice, sometimes being dropped off by some middle-aged woman in an AMC Pacer and just about always stinking of warm tequila and truckstop perfume. And meanwhile Hobie, Brickyard, and I looked out at the field, and looked at each other, and all thought we were too Goddamned old for this and maybe it was time to hang it up and go work at the True Value downtown and sell nails and paint and toilets instead of crapping our pants watching these guys turn the game of ball into a Goddamned three-ring circus. The morning that Speedy missed a pitch in bee-pee and spun himself around twice and then fell down and rolled halfway to the backstop Hobie came over and told me I wasn't payin' him enough and I told him to fuck himself that *I* wasn't getting paid enough and we shook our heads at each other and that night got drunk at the Frog in the Hole and he told me that we needed a Goddamned miracle or we were going to finish forty games out. I told him he was about right and then we ordered a round of shots and he puked on the drive home.

As opening day got closer we thought there were a couple of rays of hope. Our new shortstop, Everett Hollecher, turned a couple of sweet-assed double plays in practice and smoked a few line drives in bee-pee that nearly killed Brickyard. His infield partner, Smokey Dubuc, ended up bein' a solid enough hitter and he turned out to be pretty quick, too, except that he was dumb as a box of stupid rocks and we figured we had our work cut out with teachin' him what the signals were and ended up just yellin' "RUN!" at him when the outfielders fucked up the relay, which, believe me, was most of the time. And we had one, *one* bright spot on the mound in the form of Freddie McInnis, an eighteen year old kid who actually had what looked like at least a double-A fastball.

But boy howdy we were not ready that first night. I went home each night after practice goin' over the lineup in my head and wonderin' how the Goddamned hell I was goin' to squeeze a season's worth of runs out of this team and not embarrass myself and keep fans showin' up in the wooden bleacher seats behind home plate. I remember thinkin' at one point that maybe my job wasn't so bad, that maybe the assholes in the office that was wedged under those bleachers had it worse, that Josie in marketing maybe had the worst Goddamned job of all seein' as how she had to convince people to pay $3.50 to get into the ballpark—$5.00 if

9

you wanted a seat with a back on it—to watch the Westerns swing away at shitty pitching and still manage to finish dead last in the worst damned A-ball league in the country. Josie had it bad, but then there was Buddy Brison who had to not only sit through every home game but actually *call it*, actually make sense of this to the accumulated fans, and keep track of every error, figure out how to score the wild-ass plays that we managed to come up with, and cue up Kool and the Gang on the $49.99 CD player that was hooked up to the loudspeakers on those rare occasions when the Gods smiled on us and we actually won a game. Buddy sat up in the press box, a tin shed on top of the wood grandstand that baked in the summer sun, and he sweat so Goddamned much that he shorted out the PA once, but for some reason he loved his job and he lived and died with the Westerns. He could still name you the lineup from ten years ago, the last year we topped the division and went to the A-ball playoffs, and he hauled his fat ass up to the top of the grandstand every home game an hour before bee-pee and started laying out his scorecards and the info on the opposing team. And there was Harry Hulbert, of course, the poor bastard who owned the team. Harry also owned the paper cup manufacturing plant outside of town and the marina up the river, both of which seemed to do rather well, which made all of us wonder just how drunk he'd been when he bought the Westerns back in the eighties. What he owned, of course, was the stadium and the merchandising rights. The organization held all the contracts and charged Harry for the privilege of having their players call themselves Westerns for a couple of years. No one could figure out why Harry still owned the team, and when he showed up for home games he always had this look on his face like he'd walked into an operating room where something was going horribly wrong. He'd take me and Hobie out for dinner at the start of every season, and at the end of every season, and tell us he was real proud of the team we put out there and that the community just loved this team and how he was real pleased to be part of such an organization, but the truth was that he couldn't do dick about the weak-assed salaries we got from the organization to babysit their little twinkie-eatin' rookies on the off chance that one of them would put asses in the seats up in Wrigley some year down the road. I always thought Harry still owned the team because no one else was stupid enough to take it off his hands.

So as opening day closed in on us we were lookin' forward to another five months of this shit. Five months of showin' up at the ballpark at two o'clock for a seven PM game, or worse, showing up at ten o'clock for an afternoon matinee. And those were on good days. Away games we had to load up an old Keokuk School District bus with all the bats and uniforms and equipment and then bake on the yellow

10

sonofabitch all the way to Red Wing or Quincy or some other little town in the River League. I knew all the roads up and down the river by that year, knew which turns would mess up the driver, where all the Steak & Shake's were that we'd stop at to load up on milkshakes and burgers, knew every shitty little motel in each of the towns where we held court and slept three to a room each night and kept track of which players snored and which snuck in at 6:30 in the morning and who jerked off in the showers and who read the bible to themselves to go to sleep each night and tried to assign roommates accordingly. The River League's got ten crappy ballparks in ten little towns all up and down the Mississippi and each of them's got a manager like me, who holds their team together as best they can and suffers come September when the kids who've proved themselves get bumped up to double-A or at least up to a single-A league that's got a Goddamned working toilet in their clubhouse.

Most opening days are full of the crap that the writers love about baseball, all the high hopes for a winning season, the fresh spring grass and the kids who take their first professional swings and see nothing ahead but fast cars and pussy by the barrel. But I been around long enough that opening day is a pain in the ass, when nothin' works right and kids forget the signs and it's usually colder than hell especially if we open up in Rochester or Red Wing and it basically means my winter is over and now I got to work every day. This year hadn't been no different, but once the horseflies came I figured it was some kind of omen even if it weren't no invasion and that this season was going to try my soul in ways that the indignities of the school bus and the shit-filled toilet in our clubhouse couldn't even begin to. I had weird premonitions during the last weeks of practice. Brickyard jokin' about how the pitchers couldn't hit the side of a barn didn't make me laugh like it had the previous ten years and when I couldn't sleep and drove back to the ballpark at three in the morning to just breathe that air and think a little bit one night there was heat lightning off in one corner of the sky that lit up the field like day. I thought to myself then that baseball's an innocent game but that the lines between winnin' and losin' are so fine that somethin' else has to play a role. You can run the numbers all you want, and your players can run their asses off and hit bee-pee an extra hour a day and all that but then when the game starts things are so close and tight that something else takes over and wins or loses the game. I ain't much on the spirit world and I don't buy crap about the game's ghosts or curses but I do think you can only control so much and then you just have to take your hands off the Goddamned wheel sometimes and let things happen the way they're going to happen. And that heat lightning just unsettled the hell out of me, like someone was tellin' me that this season

11

in particular wasn't going to be in my hands and I was along for the ride, but Jesus H. Christ I had no idea what the hell was going to happen and how much I'd realize by October about what the game really meant to some folks and how little I could actually do to control it.

So after the flies showed up I figured it was just part of a demon-wracked season and we'd better just get on with it and I'd take my hands off that wheel when I thought it was time but hell, yes, I'd do my best with what the baseball Gods and the organization give me. The next day I showed up at the ballpark an hour early and watched the grounds crew clean up the field, suckin' up dead flies with the rider mower that Harry had bought for 'em a couple of years ago and rakin' 'em out of the infield into big hefty sacks. Hobie came up behind me since he showed up early too.

"Hell, they oughta send those to the concession stand and fry 'em up. Deep fried flies, I reckon they could sell 'em for a buck a bucket, put 'em in those chicken finger boxes and sauce 'em up."

I chuckled. "It'd beat what they got now. I don't reckon those fingers came off chickens."

Hobie laughed but we was both still pretty freaked out by the whole thing.

"Never seen anything like that, Orval. I remember they postponed a game in Toronto once 'cuz of bugs but they wasn't breathin' em in like we was last night. Shit, I was pullin' em outta my pants last night when I got home."

"I can still taste 'em."

We headed back to the office and filled out the lineup on the metal 1940s Army surplus desk. Kids started comin' in and getting ready for bee-pee while we was finishin' up and Preacher Bush comes in and asks us, standin' there in his boxers, whether he can lead a prayer circle before each game.

"Son, if it helps that weak-assed slider you can do any Goddamned thing you want."

Bush gives me that wide open stare and it takes me a minute to realize what the hell I've said and then it hits me and I don't know whether to chuckle or apologize, so I don't do either, just give him the stare right back and keep him mystified. Half of leadership is keepin' these kids on their toes, I reckon and this strikes me as a good thing to do to a kid who reckons every answer comes outta that book.

Anyway, it ain't Bush throwin' that night, not that he'd of thrown any better, but Moose Mays, who's on his way down the ladder but ain't given up yet. This was Moose's second year in Keokuk and I reckon most of him knew that there wasn't no logical reason for him to be

12

flailin' away in the boy's league down here for a couple hundred a week but these were the only hitters he could strike out anymore and at the advanced age of twenty-six Moose wasn't ready to be a has-been yet. He comes in on time, gets out to the field and starts tossin' balls around with Brickyard and I get out onto the field and watch him and the boys warmin' up.

The stands fill up with a few dozen fans, and I see ol' Buddy in the press box goin' over the scoresheet and the lineups for the night. I'd forgotten about the flies by then. Hobie and Deacon were hittin' fungoes to the outfield as the kids trickled out of the dugout and took a few short breaths of the cold April air. We got the batting cage in place and pretty soon they's all lined up for bee-pee and Brickyard gets behind the chain link protector and starts throwin' soft stuff to build their confidence up and they're hittin' balls all over the place, out off the plywood in the outfield and foulin' 'em back into the backstop and then the PA starts playin' old classic rock tunes and now it feels like the season's started a bit, that it ain't openin' day no more but we're all there doing our Goddamned day jobs. When we head back into the clubhouse before the Red Wings start practicin' ol' Preacher calls out that he wants to get his circle of church ladies together and most of the team looks at each other and looks at Preacher and then about three of 'em get together and bow their heads while the rest of the team starts makin' smart remarks. Moose tells 'em to knock it off, that they got the right and we oughta leave 'em be, and everyone gets changed from their warm-ups into their unis and sits around waiting for the Red Wings to get done on our field. Fresh McInnes pulls out his boom box and starts playin' it and that gets Pantyhose Paskert all pissed off.

"Turn that shit down, asshole."

"Screw you, pantyhead." McInnes turns it up.

"I said turn that shit down."

Both of them are nervous. They don't want to beat the crap out of each other, really, but now they got it started. I heard it before, every opening homestand. It's always two rookies, two rookies that ain't sure of how long they're going to be here but who gotta make an impression somehow. I look up at Brickyard and he takes the hint.

"Turn it down, McInnes. Paskert gets his dibs tomorrow night. Y'all are on the same damned team, start acting like it."

McInnes slams his hand down on the box and ices Paskert with a long stare. Paskert looks back at him with a grin.

"Hell, I was just messin' around. Y'all too uptight."

It's like a damned Marine landing craft in the locker room in the early season. Kids in there who never know from night to night if

13

they're going to find that pitcher who knows where they're weak, who's gonna throw that one magic bullet that they, for the first time in their lives, can't hit. Everyone's takin' up more room than they need to, everyone's into each other's space and into each other's junk. Pre-game goes on forever and Brickyard and Hobie and I are more playin' camp counselors than anything else, keepin' our boys from killin' each other so they can go out and beat up on some other bunch of nervous boy-men who reckon they can play ball.

"Come on boys. 6:45. Time to earn those paychecks. Scouts are here looking for fresh meat. Turn it up tonight if you want to get out of Keokuk."

So we head out into Veteran's Stadium to the cheers of the assembled dozens and we throw it around out there. I take the lineup card out and Lefty Papowski, the Red Wings' manager, shakes hands with me and says "Nice place you got here. Any flies on the lineup card tonite?" and I says back "Nope. Just on your trainin' table. Stir fried." And the ump chuckles too but he looks at me with them tired eyes that say he, too, has seen everything and a half in this league and he don't want to get locked out again if the flies come tonight. Anyways I jog back to the dugout and I'm shootin' shit with Hobie and Brickyard and then we all stand up on the top step while some junior high girl in a spandex pantsuit belts out the Star Spangled Banner while the Westerns and the River Rats stand there in their cheap-assed uniforms and some even sing along.

"Man," says Hobie, "I hate it when they do the Banner all messed up like 'at. How long is this gonna take tonight?"

I hear him, but I don't say nothing. I hate it too, some white girl out there singing like she's raised in a gospel choir. I read once that no other country plays their national anthem before normal games of soccer or whatever and I don't know whether that makes me proud or not. But I don't say nothing. Hobie takes his Banner seriously and his eyes roll when the girl in the pantsuit misses the high note.

"Damn. She shouldn't be wearin' that tight suit, neither."

This one I can't resist and out of the corner of my mouth I mumble "Maybe if that suit was tighter she'd have hit that note" and Hobie chuckles but then Preacher turns around and gives us the hairy eyeball and we shut the hell up 'cuz who knows who's watchin' us from the stands.

Moose took the mound that night and threw a couple of decent innings. He struck out two Red Wings in the first and gave up one hit and one fly ball, and in the second he walked two but got the other three to ground out. We couldn't get nothin' going on offense though, on

14

account of the Red Wings' pitcher was throwin' serious shit. Brickyard looked over at me in the third and said he thought Moose had somethin' going tonight but then he walked a couple more and gave up a long double and suddenly we was down 2-0 and I figured it was going to be another long night, horseflies or not. After we got a run in the fourth Moose settled down again, but by the sixth he'd given up a couple of taters and we'd dropped an easy throw and now he's on the losin' end of 6-1. Brickyard and I headed out there after he loaded them up in the seventh and he was pissed 'cuz he knew he was running out of chances and every second on that holy mound of dirt might be his last.

"Come on, coach. I know I gave up a couple of them longballs but I got my rhythm back."

"Fuck that, son. You never had no rhythm. You pitched OK, time to give it to the firemen."

"Firemen my ass. We need the Goddamned National Guard to get out of this one." Brickyard ain't a finesse kind of guy and he ain't recovered from last night.

"Damn."

"Alright, Moose. Grab a seat and we'll talk after." He knows what that means and he walks back to the dugout slow, his head hung way down and something in his heart fallin' to pieces.

Our relievers ain't shit, either, and the only bright spot we got to add to the night is a Hack Hendrix two-run shot that adds some respectability in the home ninth. Still, a 9-3 game ain't so hot and there's only about fifteen people in the ballpark when the Red Wings finally shoot our asses to put us out of our misery, and at least eight of 'em are high school kids who just come to sit in the top row and smoke weed. So now we's 0-2 and I can't even blame this one on fat boy since they called the game OK, just the game they called was one where we just barely showed up. Hobie chews the Westerns' collective asses out good while they's changing. He loves doin' this, yellin' at 'em while they're naked and vulnerable. He reckons this is when they're "psychologically open" to new ways of thinkin' and his sports management degree starts to come out in unusual ways.

"How the FUCK you ever gonna get out of Keokuk when you're swingin' at low cornball crap from a single-A pitcher? We looked like SHIT out there tonight, ladies. S-H-I-T. How many of you want to keep workin' them winter jobs? Goddamn. We work on this crap all spring and some pansy-assed pitcher throws low heat at y'all and y'all just about crap your Goddamn pants. Motherfucker! Hooper, you struck out *three Goddamned times* tonight. How many pitches that sumbitch throw you? Huh?"

Hooper's bare-assed naked. He don't want to be here, in this moment, right now. But he shrugs and gives his best answer.

"Iuhno, coach. Twelve?"

Hobie stands up straight. His face is good and red by now and he's just warmin' up. I reckon watchin' this is like watchin' Picasso in his studio, or watchin' Hemingway write. It is a rare privilege to watch a true artist at work and Hobie tearin' some suck-ass ballplayer a new asshole is about as finely crafted as you can get. It is his calling, and we are now getting to see him practice his trade.

"TWELVE? TWELVE PITCHES? YOU THINK THAT MOTHERFUCKER THREW TWELVE PITCHES AT YOU? WHERE THE FUCK DID YOU LEARN TO COUNT? OR DID YOU BOTHER TO COUNT THEM PITCHES? GODDAMIT, HE STRUCK YOU OUT THREE GODDAMN TIMES ON *NINE* GODDAMN PITCHES! YOU SWUNG AT EVERY GODDAMNED MEATBALL HE THREW AT YOU AND I RECKON YOU MISSED EVERY ONE! JESUS H. FUCKIN' CHRIST! YOU'RE GONNA BE ON HIS HIGHLIGHT REEL WHEN HIS ORGANIZATION MOVES HIM UP! HE'S GONNA SEND YOU A GODDAMNED CHRISTMAS CARD EVERY YEAR FOR THE REST OF HIS MAJOR LEAGUE CAREER WHILE YOU'RE SWINGIN' AT LOW HEAT FROM EVERY PUSSY-WHIPPED FUDGE SLINGER IN THE GODDAMNED RIVER LEAGUE!"

By my count, that's seven Goddamns and four fucks in five seconds. Hooper's too dumb to do anything but stare back at Hobie while Hobie's in his face, spit flying, pointing out the finer details on how to not swing at crappy pitches but it's just Hoops' night, cuz that Red Wing boy had it all over us and it maybe wasn't that we sucked so bad, just that we were up against a boy who was going to the show someday. I eased around the back wall, lettin' Hobie be the bad cop, and there's Moose in the office waitin' for what I know he thinks is another ass-chewin' session, but I ain't got that in me. You wouldn't cuss out a dyin' man, and Moose the Ballplayer is a dyin' man, someday soon to be reborn, as the organization sees fit, as a taxpayin' member of society.

"Hey, Moose."

"Coach, I felt alright tonight. I was just missing pitches. I had a few good innings and it was just a few bad locations that they got around on."

I look at him straight, but I turn around and open my mini-fridge and pull out two cans of Old Style.

16

"Hell, Moose. I know. Your first two innings were fine. You got your fastball by those boys alright." I crack both cans and put one in front of him. He knows what this talk is about and I can see that he's doin' everything he can to keep from bawlin' his eyes out.

"But we play more than two innings, son. The second time those boys got up they knew what to look for and it wasn't anything for them to get around. After a dozen pitches your speed's down in the high 70s."

"I can work more finesse stuff, coach. You saw my curve tonight, it moved pretty good? Brickyard's been working on it with me and it just needs a bit more motion and it's droppin' fast."

Hobies' still goin' strong outside and I get up and shut the door.

"Look, man. Brickyard's been doin' good work with you. And your curve's getting better. But it ain't ever goin' to be major league. And I ain't doin' you any favors if I tell you that you're going to be major league. You've had a good run. You've gotten paid to play ball for a few summers now. That's a hell of a lot more than most guys ever get, and someday—someday soon—you're going to have to come around to the fact that it's over and that you better be lookin' ahead at what you're going to do with the next fifty years of your life, son, because pitchin' ain't gonna be it."

Moose looks at me kinda funny. "Soon. You mean I ain't getting cut tonight."

"Not tonight, Moose. Not tonight. I don't want to cut you. You been around long enough that you're leadin' this team. These kids respect you. But more and more they respect you like a coach, not like a player. I want to keep you around, have you keep these thumbsuckers from killin' each other or themselves this summer. But the organization is gonna need to make room at some point."

"I can pitch relief. I can throw bee-pee. Anything to not show up at the hardware store this summer."

"Moose, I'll keep you as long as I can. But as a coach, I gotta let you know that your career is done. Soon."

"I know. But I can stay?"

"For a while. I'm gonna move you into the bullpen. I'm gonna ask you to work with our new kids. I'm gonna give you a few innings every now and then. But when we need to make room, you gotta understand that the organization's gonna have to make some hard decisions." Which is bullshit, because Moose here ain't gonna be a hard decision at all if he keeps throwin' like that.

Moose nods. He looks down into his beer. He ain't cryin'. He's happy to hear that he's gonna play another day, another week. Maybe the organization will forget about Keokuk and he'll be here in August.

17

Or maybe he'll be at the True Value, makin' more money but dying inside every day.

"OK, Coach." He and I drink our beers without sayin' anything.

"...*GODDAMNED MOTHERFUCKIN' WEAK-ASSED FIRST BALL SWINGIN' SHITHEADS! WE'RE GONNA LOSE SIXTY GODDAMNED GAMES THIS YEAR IF Y'ALL KEEP GIVIN' PITCHERS THOSE CHEAP-ASSED STRIKEOUTS!*"

"I ain't gonna miss that, coach."

"Oh, you will. You'll miss getting your ass chewed by a coach, especially when you're getting your ass chewed by some punk-assed teenaged store manager."

He smiles, but it's more of a grimace. He knows.

And that's the way the season goes for the first couple of weeks. We get our asses kicked all up and down the Mississippi River. Pantyhose Paskert busted up his hand getting in the way of a Hannibal fastball and we put in a new kid in centerfield and we still couldn't hit nothin'. We beat Dubuque twice at their ballpark, though, which felt pretty good, and Hack hit a couple of taters that would have been out in any big league field. Two weeks on the road, though, and we came back to Keokuk with a balls-up 4-10 record, ass rash from the bus, and me and Hobie wonderin' again what the point of all this was.

Give you an idea of what we were playin' like, against Clinton we threw Hot Rod Barber at 'em and he had a shutout goin' into the sixth. Then he gave up a hit, knocked their ninth batter in the head with a fastball, and pitched a gopherball at Speedy Knute, their hitless wonder of a leadoff who can steal anything in the park but can't ever get on base. A home run from him is front page Goddamned material, but we managed it. Brickyard and I went out there and Brickyard goes "you alright?" and Hot Rod goes "sure, coach, that one just got away" and I says "you're done today, Hot Rod, you pitched a hell of a game but you lost it," and he looks right at me and says "what choice you got, coach, you gonna put Moose in?" and I says "what the fuck, give me the damn ball" but as Hot Rod is walking off the field Brickyard chuckles and reminds me that our relief corps has pitched most of the innings out there on this road trip and I think aw, nuts, we're probably better off with Hot Rod in there after all. And I was right 'cuz from there on we worked real hard at taking a 3-2 game and turning it into a 15-3 display of Clinton Colt hitting. Moose was a good sport about it, but we just didn't have anyone out there who could throw the ball anymore and he just pitched whatever he had and watched as those balls just popped off their bats and out over the fence. Three Goddamned innings, they hit around in two and each time we got the third out the Clinton fans gave

18

us a nice round of applause. That hurt, but we played the game and when Stuffy Flack singled to bring in a lumbering Smokey Dubuc from third in the ninth they gave us a standing O and the Colts' bullpen even pretended to warm up. Our boys took that hard but I had to admit it was pretty funny.

We get back to the friendly confines of Keokuk Veterans Stadium on a Wednesday night and Brickyard and Hobie and I hit the Frog in the Hole for a nightcap. The Chicago team had started out pretty hot and they're on TV and we're suckin' down our Old Styles and shootin' shit with each other.

"Helluva trip," says Hobie.

"We gotta learn these boys some ball," says Brickyard.

Hobie shakes his head. "We're missin' cutoff men, swingin' at cheap-ass shit down and away, and we ain't playin' small ball. It's a Goddamned train wreck out there."

"Fundamentals. They ain't got the fundamentals. These kids come up through high school and all they do is swing the bat well and suddenly they got scouts all over 'em and those Goddamned scouts ain't lookin' at defense. Right now the guy we need, the fast shortstop with glue in his glove is stockin' shelves at Safeway 'cause he couldn't hit back in 12th grade."

I suck down the last warm backwash of an Oldie. "We'll give 'em hell tomorrow. Get 'em in early on Friday and spend an hour or two after the game. They'll get it."

"I sure as hell hope so. I can't take another trip like that."

We all sighed and looked around at each other and at the salubrious atmosphere of the bar. "I'm too old for this," says Hobie. "I'm too Goddamned old."

The next day we get practice going at about 2:00 and boy, Hobie gives 'em shit for the better part of an hour about how they's lettin' the game down, they's lettin' themselves down, hell, they're lettin' *Hobie* down, Goddamnit, and he didn't spend thirty years in the game to watch them fuck it up with wild hacks at circle-jerk pitches down and away. The boys' heads were hung pretty low and I reckon they knew everything Hobie was tellin' 'em, on account of by the time we was pitchin' pre-game bee-pee to 'em they at least looked like they was workin'. Even Stuffy Flack was workin' hard at catchin' pop flies, a sight to behold. Hack Hendrix looked pissed in the batter's box facin' Brickyard and he took some big swings and even connected on a few of 'em.

When we come out of the locker room for the anthem the crowd is well into the high two-digits. We're standing there on the top step for

19

the anthem and my eyes scan the seats. There's what's-his-name, Rube? That's it, Rube. Rube's sittin' in the top row with his glove and his full uniform, lookin' at the field with what I can recognize from across the park as an acute sense of longing. Now I love every fan that's willin' to pay a couple of bucks to watch this three-ring circus of a ballclub fight the forces of chaos and disaster for nine innings, but some guys, you know, they got to get a life, for chrissake, and realize that they ain't ever goin' to be the ones on the field. They're gonna be the ones in the stands, and that's just the way it is. Not every dream gets fulfilled, you know?

Anyways, we didn't do half bad that evening, pullin' out a real heart-stopper in the last inning when Hendrix, who was still fumin' at his getting his lazy ass called out by Hobie, managed to work out his anger on a Haitian Hoppy ball and put it over the fence into the river with two outs, two strikes, and a man on. Never mind that we'd given up eight runs that afternoon, we scored nine and while our defense just about had me and Hobie pissin' our pants all afternoon, hell, we won the game and sent somewhere south of a hundred folks home happy.

Well, almost all of them. I was finishin' up in the office and just stubbin' out my smoke and lookin' forward to a late evening of TV and Old Style when ol' Hobie pokes his head in the door and says "Orval, you wanna come take a look at this" and I says "what" and he says "you just want to come take a look a this" and I get my fat ass up off the chair and walk with him out to the parking lot and he's just shakin' his head, a look on his face that's half serious and half just smilin' like crazy and I says "what the hell's goin' on out here" and he says "just wait" and then we get out the door and *he is standin' there in his uniform and his glasses and his dumb-ass hick mustache.* I says "Hobie, you're out of your mind" and I start to rear back to let this guy have it, the same guy who's sittin' in the stands earlier in the day, the same guy I done told off a couple of weeks ago, he's *still in my parkin' lot* thinking I'm gonna spend my beer hour coachin' him on some pitch.

"Howdy, Mr. Sheckerd. I's hopin' you'd take just one look at this pitch I got…"

And then I sees that Brickyard is there, too, and Brickyard is shakin' his head and lookin at the ground.

"Rube, sir. Rube Tyler. We met after that first game this year and I was just…"

"Goddamn, boy, you're persistent, I'll give you that. But I reckon I told you that I don't…"

"Orval, just take a look at this," says Hobie, and he says it like he means it. And I'm standin' out there in my stocking feet, in a gravel parking lot with the big yellow lights just a few minutes away from getting turned off, and the flies off the river just startin' to ease up, and the stars and moon all out shining over Keokuk, Iowa and environs, and ladies and gentlemen, what I saw that night might have beat the second coming, because it changed my life and how I think about ball, forever. I saw Rube Tyler throw a ball for the first time that night, and brother, I don't ever want to see something like that again, because what happened after that would shake up everything I know about physics and God and baseball and no one ought to get all that messed around in their heads more than once.

2nd Inning

"All right, then, son. I've been coaching with these two for a hell of a long time and if they say I ought to watch you pitch, then I'll watch you pitch. But make it fast, on account of I've got a six-pack sittin' at home waitin' for me."

"Yes, sir. Won't take but a second, sir."

Brickyard says "throw it at that letter 'e' in 'Westerns' there on the sign again just like you did before..."

"Yes, sir. Here it is, sir..."

Rube got set and picked up his left leg. He lifted up his hands over his head and reared his right arm back and I swear you could hear the gristle in all of his joints creak as he did it. Then he started forward and brought his arm over the top, his gut hangin' out of his old uniform shirt the whole time, and he let the ball go and all of our lives changed.

Now y'all have heard of a knuckleball before, I'm sure, and there's a load of scientists and aerodynamic guys and engineers who would tell you everything you ever wanted to know about how it works but here's the God's honest truth: the knuckleball, when thrown right, is a treason against time and space. When a knuckler throws his pitch he lets it go without any spin. Any spin at all, or it don't work. And then what happens is that instead of corkscrewing its way to the plate, it just hammers ahead like a freight train with a gigantic flat plate on its front and instead of cuttin' the air it pushes the air out of the way, and when it does that the air pushes *back*, and then the *ball* gets out of the way of the *air*, and then all hell breaks loose. The ball goes in about ten different directions at once—it goes down, it goes up, it goes left, right slower, faster, everywhere but where the batter reckons it's gonna be. And so if you decide to swing at a knuckleball, you're just guessin', because that ball could be *anywhere* in the ballpark by the time your bat gets from your shoulder to out over the plate and its about one in five odds that you'll connect with it, and one in a million that you'll connect in a way that won't pop up, or ground out, or foul it all over the park. If you *do* hit it right, of course, there's no tellin' where it'll land, but it'll more than likely be somewhere real far, because by the time that ball has got to you it's slowed way the hell down. But you more than likely *ain't* gonna hit it right.

Throwin' one of these sumbitches ain't easy, or we'd all do it. Hell, I used to work on one when I played, but I could only get it right about one out of five times, and that ain't good enough, 'cuz the other four times that ball just went straight and slow and it would have been blood to any shark in the box. Knuckleballers have all kinds of techniques they won't tell you about—they trim their nails, they push the ball with their fingertips, if they can get away with it they'll put motor oil, or Vaseline, or lube on their fingers to make the ball slip out of their hands without spinning. It's hard to do once, and it's harder to do it twice, and it's harder than *that* to do it two times in a row, much less do it a hundred or whatever over the course of a game. But if you can do it every time, you'll do fine, since there's no sense throwin' it hard, so you can stay out there all day squeezin' the ball out of your fingers and prayin' you've done it right and watchin' hitters flail around lookin' for it and finally you get one wrong and you see the look in their eyes and you don't *have* to see where the ball landed then, cuz' it's just gone.

Anyway. When that ball left Rube's hand, it did everything. It was the most beautiful, wrongest-headed, baddest-*assed* knuckler I'd ever seen. It went up and down at what looked like the same time, then it veered left and looked like it was goin' to miss the wall of the stadium entirely, and then it came back right and it didn't hit that letter "e", but that don't matter cuz' it sure *looked* for a minute like it *was* gonna hit that damn letter and hell, I woulda swung at it, but then it goes back *right* and hits the crossbar of the "t". Two whole letters of motion in its last, dying moments. *Thwock.*

Brickyard just breathed out real slow. Rube looks over at me.

"Alright, son, you got a knuckler there. But anyone can get one of those to work once." I lied. "Show me that again."

"Yes, sir…here you go sir…"

He winds up and lets another one go. Same Goddamned thing. All over the map, then for a split second it hones in on the strike zone, and then it hits the top of the "W". *Thwock.*

"Again."

S. *Thwock.*

"Again."

T again. *Thwock.*

I didn't ask him no more. He just kept pickin' up balls out of the bucket and sendin' them on their random journey as if all the air molecules and all the microbreezes and all the random variations of all that were things he could see and sense.

E. *Thwock.* Aha, you're thinkin'. There's that pitch that's out of the park. The knuckleball killer. There's where it all falls apart. Sure, except that on its way to E it headed for W. And S. And T. And the gravel in the parking lot *and* that big moon over Keokuk.

He keeps goin' like this 'till he's almost out of balls. A couple dozen pitches, all of them covering much more ground than sixty and a half feet once you account for the side trips. Then he just stands there, holdin' on to the last ball in the bucket, blinkin', waitin' for us to say somethin'.

I leave Brickyard to make the first move. "Well Goddamn, boy. I gotta say you got some pretty good motion on that knuckler. How long you been workin' on that?"

"All my life, sir."

Hobie just shakes his head. He ain't gonna say it, and *I* ain't gonna say it, but what we've just seen is baseball perfection. 26 perfectly thrown, utterly unpredictable, bat-defying bits of eyewitness evidence that the laws of physics are more complex and beautiful and just stranger than the average person will ever know.

"Well, Tyler, I reckon that's a pretty impressive demonstration." I lied, because it was just Goddamned... *awesome* is what it was. "But there's all kinds of reasons we can't just pick up someone off the street and give 'em a uniform and let 'em pitch for the organization, you know..."

He just looks at me, blinkin' behind his coke-bottle glasses. Brickyard's tryin' like hell to keep a straight face, tryin' to help me out as I hedge my bets but we's both thinkin' how bad we'd rather see these crazy knuckleballs flyin' up and down the league than the shit that Moose and Hot Rod are throwin'.

He's still lookin' at me. I'm tryin' to figure out what the hell to tell 'im. And I'm pissin' my pants thinkin' about them pitches.

"Where you work now, Rube?"

"Out at the plastics plant."

"That big ass factory on 218? What the hell do you do there?"

"Yes, sir. I work one of the injection molders."

"How long you been doin' that?"

"'Bout twenty years, sir."

"And they ain't moved you up at all? You still workin' plant machinery after twenty years?"

"Yes, sir."

"That don't speak too well to your motivation, now, does it?"

He just stands there. He's rollin' the ball around in his fingers, lookin' down at the ground. Now I feel pretty bad for the guy. Twenty fuckin' years working in that craphole out at the edge of Keokuk. He's got the look of a man who's spent most of his nights workin' on that one pitch and tryin' to forget about most of his days.

"You play ball in high school?"

"Yes, sir."

"You pitch?"

"No, sir. Third base. I hit .328 my last year."

"You play any college ball? Semi-pro? American Legion?"

"No, sir. I never made it to college. And I just started right in at the plant. I had to make some money. I played a lot of softball, but I ain't played organized hardball in, um, I guess about nineteen years."

I'm sizin' him up. He's out of shape. He ain't got any muscle in his upper arms, but he's got some forearms. He's about 5'-10", about 200 pounds. He'd puke if I put him through one of our conditioning drills. Hell, he might die. Still, you ain't gotta have strength to throw a knuckleball. You just gotta caress that ball and let it go just right every time. Goddammit, I think, now I'm actually thinking about what this beer-bellied middle-aged knuckle chucker might be able to do on the field. I've lost my mind. I'm supposed to be workin' with 18 year olds—boys who were just born when ol' Rube here was startin' work at that damned plastics plant. How the hell does this even work, I think. Do I fill out a scouting report on this guy and just forget his age?

And then Rube grips the ball behind his glove. I can tell he's keen to show me one more time this physics-defyin', rollercoaster pitch. He looks at me, and I squint back at him, like we're negotiatin' already. He blinks again. I don't. But I nod, and he turns, and winds up and the ball floats out of his hand like it's on strings, and this time it just arcs slowly toward the wall and at the last minute it goes from bein' a 63-mile and hour gopher ball over the fat part of the plate to flickin' up near the ghost batter's head, a little kick at the end of its travels that would have had the batter swinging for the fences while divin' for cover. A thing of absolute, unparalleled beauty. A pitch that would win ballgames. A pitch that would have batters breakin' their Goddamn bats after every up, cursin' the laws of aerodynamics that were suddenly takin' a holiday over Keokuk Veterans. Brickyard breathes out real slow, like he's steadyin' himself, or like he's at some titty bar with a pair of perfect ones right in his face and he's thinkin' about how he wants that pitch but he can't touch that pitch right now but *damn* what he'd do if he had that pitch in his lineup.

Blink.

"Tell you what. Show up here tomorrow before the game. We'll see how you do throwin' beepee to our boys. Then I'll make a few calls and see if I can get a scout or two here. I ain't promisin' nothing, but if you can do that a hundred times in an evening I reckon you might be of some use."

And then Rube Tyler stares at me, and he says the words that's gonna haunt me the rest of my life, 'cuz I didn't know just what this meant then, but I did later on and that's when it near about killed me.

"Thank you, sir," he says, "You got no idea how much this means to me. To get a chance, I mean. To show you my pitch."

"Don't get your hopes up, Rube. But that is a pretty sweet lookin' pitch."

"Yes sir. I'll see you tomorrow, sir." Blink.

So then me and Brickyard and Hobie sat around the office til' late talkin' about what the hell we'd just seen. Brickyard reckoned we'd just seen the equal of the Mona Lisa painted in the parking lot of Keokuk Veterans Stadium, and Hobie said bullshit, because when you paint you can sit and think about every bit of paint you're puttin' on a canvas, but what we just saw was the human mind *willing* a ball to do things a ball ain't ever done before, and that's something else, because you only got a second to do what you're gonna do to a baseball before you let it go out into the world and then it ain't in your control anymore. No, he says, what you just saw was God's own creation out there. And then *I* says bullshit, we didn't see no art or no religious act of creation, we just saw a guy who's spent way too much of his life figurin' out how to throw a knuckleball, and yes, it was a damn fine knuckleball, but we ain't in the business of draftin' forty year old plastic molder operators and what the hell's goin' to happen when he's fielding, for instance, and you two might just recall that the big club's in the National Goddamned League, right? We ain't seen him hit.

"Damn, Orval," says Brickyard. "You seen what passes for hittin' on our field this year?"

Hobie pipes up. "Orval, That ain't no knuckleball we just seen tonight. I don't know what the hell that is—a knuckleball, a gyroball, a Goddmanned monkeyball, whatever. But it wasn't hittable. I know that. I ain't ever seen a pitch like that before, much less have one just dropped in my lap. We gotta get a scout out here."

So that's how it all started. I made a couple of calls that night and the Peoria guy said sure, he'd come by later in the week but he had a shortstop at some high school in Putnam County he had to check out first and oh, how old did you say this kid was? And I cleared my throat and said I didn't know but he was a little older it looked like to me, and sure, I'd find out for him.

I woke up the next morning knowin' something special was going to happen that day. Drivin' my truck to the stadium the sky was a radiant blue, the sun was beatin' down on things and all the greens of the Keokuk suburbs seemed to harmonize with each other. Hell, we'd squeaked by them Galesburg boys last night and we just might do it again tonight. A sudden turnaround seemed like part of the grand cosmic plan as I parked in the gravel lot outside the clubhouse and walked past the rotting concrete and plywood signs and smelled last night's beer and walking tacos and God knows what else.

So practice gets started with me still kind of smilin' inside, for the first time in a while, and we's out on the field and Brickyard pipes up.

"Tyler, over here!"

And I look and there he is, at the foot of the stands just over the dugout. He paid to get in, it looks like, and I chuckle about that. He gets up and steps from the stands on to the field, kinda wonderin' whether this is okay or not, and sort of jogs over to us. Brickyard walks out to meet him and I look around and everyone on the team is lookin'. Moose is lookin', too, and he seemed to know things were occurring that were gonna affect him, and he stood there with his hands on his hips wonderin', like everyone else, what this was all about.

Tyler and Brickyard shake hands and then Tyler just sorta stands there. Blinkin'.

"Alright," I says. "I want to see that messed up pitch again. Can you throw a little beepeee?"

"Sure, coach. Yes, sir. I can throw all the beepee you want."

"You need to warm up?"

"No, sir. I got that pitch ready to go."

"Alright, then. That there in the box is Footsie Snodgrass. Give him your best stuff."

"Yep. I know him."

Deacon's been throwin', and he steps off the mound. He ain't seen what we seen, and he's lookin' at me like he ain't in on some big joke. Footsie's in the box and he's chucklin', seein' big ol' Rube Tyler and his portly frame and big glasses and mustache ascending the mound.

"This here's Rube Tyler," I say out loud. "He might be helpin' us out with some coachin'" I say, makin' things up as I go along.

He nods at everyone. The team starts scratchin' their heads, wonderin' what the hell's goin' on.

"You tryin' to build up our confidence or somethin'?" Footsie yells out from the batter's box, "Tryin' to give us a false sense of self-esteem?" Everyone chuckles at this. "Cuz yesterday y'all weren't too worried about our collective sense of, um, *self-worth*." More laughin'.

27

"No, boys," I say. "Rube here's a pitcher from back in the day."
I don't tell 'em how far back. "Don't worry about holdin' up on him,
Footsie, you just swing away at whatever he's got."

Footsie's got a big grin on his face now, and he's lookin' across
the river at Illinois and thinkin' he's about to plant a good dozen practice
balls between the fence and over there. "Alright, coach. Whatever you
say. Gimme your best shot, there, Uncle Rube."

I nod at Rube. He nods back. He winds up and lets one go, and
I'm watchin' Footsie, and for the first twenty feet or so of the pitch he's
got that shit-eatin' grin plastered wide across his face and he's rearin'
back thinkin' he knows where that ball's gonna be when it gets to him,
and part of him is thinkin' about where it's gonna be shortly *after* it gets
to him. And then for the second twenty feet he's got a slightly more
concerned look on his face, like that ball isn't goin' where he *thought* it
was goin', and actually it looks like it's goin' over *there*, away from the
plate a bit, but that *can't* be, because just a split second ago that ball was
headin' *here*, and now it's headin' *there*, and now he can't decide
whether he oughta keep swingin', or hold up, or wait just a split second
longer knowin' he'd be late on the pitch but maybe he could poke it
anyway, because God*damn* it ain't movin' that *fast*, that's for sure. And
then for the last twenty he's thinking *AW, JEESUS* because now instead
of goin' to the *outside* that ball's comin' *inside* and he's swingin' with
all his might now thinkin' he's gonna push it to the opposite field and
now it's comin' in on his wrists and that last millisecond of time his
mind is tellin' him three different things: *swing* at that fat outside pitch,
don't swing at that pitch 'cuz you don't know where it's goin', and *get
out of the way* because that pitch is gonna bounce right off where your
wrists are set up thinkin' it's an outside pitch.

Footsie ends up swingin' *and* getting out of the way. He whiffs.
And falls, all twisted up because he was swingin' big as he was goin'
down. The ball ends up at the backstop, having successfully avoided
Footsie's bat, Footsie's flailing body, and the catcher.

"Boy HOWDY!" yells Hack Hendrix from first. "What the hell
you swingin' at, Footsie?" The whole team starts yellin' at 'im, holdin'
their sides from laughin', and Foosie looks at me, looks at Tyler all
mean, and he picks himself up mad as hell.

"Throw me that SHIT again, asshole!"

Tyler looks like he's worried about getting his nose caved in.

"Don't worry, Tyler, you just throw another one of those and let
Foostie paste it."

Tyler winds up. His pudgy, mustachioed frame builds up all the
momentum it can, and he floats the ball out into space again. Footsie's

28

ready for anything now, but you can't be ready for what can't happen, and he swings again, hoping to put the ball into the river. It hits the backstop again and the field erupts one more time in big waves of laughter but this time there's a nervous edge to it, 'cause no hitter out there wants to think about the implications of what they just saw. It ain't karmic to laugh at the bullet what's got your name on it, after all.

"Jesus tapdancing Christ," sez Hobie. "That fooled Footsie pretty good. THROW ANOTHER ONE, RUBE!"

Now Footsie's pissed. He's seen something that he cain't hit, no matter how hard he tries, and he's seen it come from a donut of a man, standing out on the mound, no expression on his face except blank, nervous concentration. Tyler's been waitin' his whole life for this, I realize. This is the debut of his lifetime project. And it's all happenin' in Keokuk, Iowa.

Tyler winds up a third time and he lets fly but this time Footsie ain't swingin' at shit. He's decided that there ain't no sense in trying to make contact, he'll just wait for the random trajectory of the ball to take it out of the strike zone and out of his peace of mind, and the ball goes all over the place again, but Footsie's thought too damned much this time, and the ball ends up zeroing in at crotch level and finding the catcher's mitt full on after another wild ride through time and space. Perfect strike.

"MotherFUCKER!" yells Footsie. "What do you got, there, pie boy, some kinda trick ball? What the FUCK is going on? GodDAMNIT!"

There's no laughter this time. Them boys see what me and Hobie was seein' last night. They're seein' the pitch that cain't be hit. They're seein' a genuine, true blood baseball miracle.

Tyler throws another one. Footsie tries to beat hell out of it again and corkscrews himself into the dirt. It's about now that I look around in the stands and see that folks is startin' to notice. They're seein' Tyler on the mound, and they're seein' Footsie getting more and more pissed, but they are just startin' to put two and two together. They ain't seein' what we're seein' yet, and something in the back of my mind makes me think that maybe it ain't time to let this out just yet. I poke Hobie and tell him to go tell Rube to let Footsie have somethin' that ain't a knuckler, and he runs out to the mound and jaws with Tyler for a bit and Tyler looks confused as hell. Hobie runs back and sez to me "I told him to let Footsie win."

Tyler rears back again, but this time the ball comes out straight and slow. Footsie leans back, winds his bat back off his shoulder, and

29

hits the holy crap out of it, pullin' it over the right field fence and into the wild blue beyond. It's still risin' when he yells at Tyler.

"Beat your ass there, didn't I? What, did you finally throw a real baseball?"

Tyler's still watchin' the ball pay out distance. *Sploosh.*

"WHOO-EE! Nice hit, Foots!"

"Alright, folks," I says, "Tyler, that looked pretty good. Come on in and let Hobie finish up beepee." Tyler jogs over and looks at me all quizzical.

"Was that alright, Coach?" he sez.

"Hell yeah, boy," I sez. That was real fine. Footsie can't hit curves for shit, though. I want to see what you can do, but I don't…um…wanna embarrass my team in front of payin' customers, if you get my meanin'."

"Sure,   Coach.   So,   was   that   a   real   tryout?"

"Hell, no. You gotta show one of the club's scouts
what you got, boy, before you pitch for me."

"But you'll talk to them—you'll get a scout to see my knuckler sometime?"

"Thursday, I reckon, Rube."

And then, for the first time since I met him, Rube cracks a smile, a big, grin full of bad teeth and high hopes. He reaches into his pocket and pulls out a single work glove and quick puts it on his pitchin' hand.

"Gotta protect this guy. He might be my meal ticket."

I chuckle. "Don't know as I'd go that far, boy," I says, "but you do what you gotta do. You wanna sit on the bench for the game?"

"Yes, sir. That'd be real nice."

"Alright. I can't have you in that…uniform. Go change into your street clothes."

"OK, sir." He turns. "Um, sir?"

"Yeah, boy?"

"Do I have to pay to get in again? No pass outs, you know."

"Boy," I said, laughin' to myself, "you come in the team entrance. I'll leave your name with the girl there."

"Alright, sir. I'll be back in a little while. And thank you, sir. I really appreciate it."

"No problem, Rube," I says. "Anyone can throw a knuckler like that deserves a look."

After our beepee I walk into the locker room and call a team meeting. I give 'em the usual shit about watchin' fundamentals, hittin' the Goddamn cutoff man and sittin' on the first pitch every so often and at the end Gunner looks up from the back of the pack and raises his hand.

"What is it Gunner?"

"Coach, all due respect, but what the hell was that out there during beepee?"

"What are you talkin' about, Gunner?" I says.

"That fat dude pitchin' to Footsie. Who was that, and what the hell was he throwin'?"

A murmur runs through the room. Tyler bugged these guys. Footsie spits a big looger in disgust.

"Boys," I say, "That fat man was one Rube Tyler, local resident and longtime Westerns' fan. Rube's been workin' on that pitch you saw for a while, and we reckoned we'd give him a chance to show what he's got."

"What he's got fooled the beejeezus out of Snodgrass," Hot Rod says.

"What he's got makes your pitchin' look like shit," says Footsie. Hot Rod smirks and shakes his head.

"Ain't no fat boy can throw better than me," he says.

I pause for a moment and look at him. "That fat boy put them pitches right by one of our better hitters. That fat boy wants to play ball, and he wants it pretty bad, and I reckon he'd put all y'all in shit creek if I let him throw a full round of beepee.

Footsie speaks up. "Bullshit, coach. I hit the snot out of that last pitch. That asshole's full of it."

Hobie starts laughin'. "That weak-assed pitch was his fastball," I says, "and if he ever throws that shit again I'm gonna personally kick his ass. Sometimes all you need is one pitch, and that boy's got it."

Footsie spits again.

"Anyways," I says. "Scout's comin' Thursday. I reckon Tyler's pitch puts him on the hot seat. The rest of you better pull your heads out of your asses."

So that afternoon Rube Tyler gets his first wish, settin' on the pine with the team watchin' the Westerns lose 8-2 to the Spiders. For the first few inning's the team's sittin' far away from him, still not sure what to make of this guy, a portly, mustachioed guy with a freak pitch, but pretty soon some of the guys are talkin' to him and startin' to ask him what in the hell he was throwin' out there, and can he show *them* how to throw it, and he's showin' 'em the mechanics, showin' 'em how the ball's supposed to slip out, unmolested by friction or spin, from their knuckles. And it's about this time that I notice the black work glove

31

he's put on his left hand, his throwin' hand, and some of the boys are givin' him a hard time about it, and he says somethin' that later on will come back and hit my like a ton of bricks.

"Can't take it off, boys. Not till it's time to throw. Gotta keep the magic on the inside."

Well. The team thinks that's pretty funny, and it's the first time I see ol' Rube relax even just a little bit, and now I can't wait till Thursday when the scout comes and we find out whether this is for real or just plain ol' crazy.

The next day or two Brickyard works with Rube in the bullpen while the team's warmin' up, and every so often I look over there and see that he's got Speedy Killefer catchin', or I should say *blockin'* ol' Rube's throws, because they're goin' everywhere but the plate, but they're goin' there in interestin' ways, one might even say *productive* ways. Brickyard got his own radar gun out and told me later it was worthless because he couldn't so much as point the gun in the right direction when Rube threw, but one time he caught just the tail end of one pitch and it hit a whopping 53 miles per hour, enough to get ticketed in a residential zone but not really enough to arouse much interest. But then Brickyard told me somethin' interesting.

"You know, these are old police surplus guns we got."

"Hell, yes, Brickyard, I know we ain't got the best equipment, but I'm workin' on it…"

"No, coach, what I mean is that these guns tell you which direction the target's comin', whether it's goin' by you, or comin' toward you, or goin' away from you."

"Yeah, Brickyard, so what?"

"So I'm standing behind Speedy tryin' to get a God-damned *bead* on this thing, and you know what it tells me? It tells me that Tyler's pitch is goin' that 53 miles per hour, but it's goin' that *across the beam*. That pitch was goin' *left to right* when I got a piece of it, it wasn't *comin' at me*. You understand that? Rube threw that fuckin' thing *sideways*."

And I just chuckled, because I realized what this meant. You can't hit a pitch that suddenly turns right. Or up.

We split the next two games, the last of the Spiders we'd see at home for awhile, thank christ, and Thursday morning Brickyard and I went over our plan to introduce Tyler to the Big Club's scouting organization. We figured we couldn't do things normal—introduce the prospect and the scout, find out what the guy wanted to see, all the usual stuff, because the moment anyone laid eyes on Rube the tryout would be *over*, and by this point Brickyard and I were relishin' the thought of

32

getting Rube a place on the team, because we'd both worked out that his knuckleball was so gravity and air-defying that he'd probably be worth a handful of wins on his own in what was left of the season. Not to mention that we were lettin' him throw beepee during warm-ups and Brickyard told everyone that anyone who could hit one of Tyler's knucklers would get fifty bucks, cash, on the spot and that pissed off Hobie good because it wiped out a month or two of him tellin' 'em to slow down and watch the pitches closer and now they were just shuttin' their eyes and lettin' their bats fly through space toward some random spot, hopin' like hell that Tyler's pitch would be where their bat was at some point during their swing. Mostly, it wasn't.

Anyway, that Thursday mornin' we arranged things so that Tyler'd get his fair look. Brickyard and I met the guy when he came in and we convinced Moose Mays to go along with the ruse, tellin' the scout that here was that pitcher we's tellin' you about and why don't we go up and get you set up down the foul line where the bullpens are, since we're tryin' like hell to get some hittin' out of our seven through nine hitters and so they're up hittin' beepee right now. And the scout is all pissed about this, since he's not used to drivin' out to Keokuk anyway and now we ain't even givin' him the backstop, but he grumbles and heads out with Brickyard to the stands while Moose goes out and starts warmin' up, like he's done for scouts the last few years, knowin' it ain't gonna mean anything this time, neither. Meanwhile, I get Hobie to set up his hitters and to put Tyler out on the mound, and I run out there first thing and tell Tyler to start throwin' nothin' but crazy-assed knuckleballs to his heart's content. Then I run over back to the stands to go set with the scout and talk up Moose real good, layin' on the bullshit thick and heavy.

"See, look right there—that slider's got some real potential, there."

Scout hits his radar gun on its side. "Hmmp. Didn't see much movement on that. Give me another one."

Moose gives it everything he's got.

"Orval, what was that? That was about an 82-mile per hour gopher ball."

"Aw, give him a minute."

Meanwhile I look out the corner of my eye. Tyler's got his stuff together, and he's throwin' pitches with hummingbird-like jump on 'em. Stuffy Flack's up there hackin' away and about to drill himself into the dirt. Moose lofts another one.

33

"Alright, I seen enough. I don't know what you think you got here, Orval, but the big club's got enough shitty pitchers to last 'em a couple dozen years. Y'all have a nice day."

I give the hittin' crew the signal, takin' off my hat and standin' up.

"Well where are you runnin' off to so fast? Moose here is just gettin' started?"

"Look, I leave now, I can be in Danville by dinner. Thanks for everything, Orval, have a good summer."

"JESUS SHIT ON A SHINGLE!" comes from around the batting cage. Scout looks up but keeps packin'.

"SOOOO-EEE! HOW THE HELL WE SUPPOSED TO HIT THAT, COACH?" Scout sees the commotion around the batting cage and watches as Tyler rears back and lets float. While he's lookin' at the pitch, I'm lookin' at him, and as that ball made its way majestically, slowly, randomly toward the plate, I saw what I knew I'd see. His brow furrowed briefly, then he blinked as if he was tryin' to normalize what had just happened. And then he straightened up, starin' out at the infield. Stuffy uncoiled himself again and swore like hell again, makin' sure we could hear down the first base line.

"GODAMMIT COACH, GET HOBIE BACK IN THERE PITCHIN', YOU KNOW WE CAN'T HIT THIS GUY'S JUICE!" Stuffy's playin' his role perfect, right on target. Tyler winds again and another pitch with wings and an ornery mind starts dippin' and divin' toward the plate.

This time, scout sees the whole thing, beginning to end, and the look on his face is one of wonderment and concern. His jaw opens just a bit, like it would if you'd been trained your whole life to be skeptical and suddenly you saw, right before your eyes, a God-given miracle.

"What..." he says quietly, "what...the...*hell*...is...that..."

"Oh, what's that, I see Hobie's got that local boy throwin' at our boys for fun again. Kid's got somethin' of a knuckler and Hobie's tryin to get 'em to watch for...

Scout is now walkin', slowly, past me and Brickyard, his radar gun at his side. "Whadaya mean, local boy," he says, "throwin' a knuckleball like that?" Tyler gets a tailing strike past Flack that ends up risin' into the backstop over the catcher's head.

"Yeah, it's pretty funny to watch. Course, that kid ain't in any kinda shape, and he's a bit older, but it sure is he-*lar*ious to see our boys tryin' to hit that shit." We're followin' him now, watchin' him, and watchin Tyler, and lookin' at each other, tryin' to see whether this is gonna go where we hope it's gonna go.

34

"He throws like this all the time?"

"Yep. Like clockwork. Wild-ass knuckleballs, perfect lack of location and speed. Good for our boys to try and…"

"Orval," he interrupts, "that guy is throwin' one hell of a knuckler…I know your team can't hit for shit, but I ain't seen 'em even make *contact* yet…you mean to tell me you just found this guy on the street? And he's throwin' you beepee?"

"Well," I says, "I know it's a bit…*unusual*, and all, but we can use all the help we can get…"

"Sweet Mary Mother on a moped," he says, reachin' for his radar gun. Tyler lets fly another one, and scout has the same problem Brickyard had. The ball just don't show up, there ain't nothin' to point at. Scout sits down and doesn't say anything for a while, just sits there, slack-jawed, watchin' Tyler put on an aerodynamic display of unhittable loveliness. Flack takes a couple more cuts, then Hack Hendrix gets up and he flails away for ten minutes or so, and each pitch seems better, more bizarre than the last, and finally scout gets a reading and he takes off his cap and runs his fingers through his hair and lets out a long, slow, cleansing breath.

"How long have you had this guy around?"

"Oh, just a few days, really, I know I shoulda cleared it with the organization, but it's just so damned funny to watch…"

"Any of your boys ever hit him?"

"Only when he tries to throw a fastball."

"Get his ass over here." I stand up and wave at Hobie and he and Tyler jog over. Tyler's already got his work glove on by the time they're over to the stands.

"Son," scout starts in, "I been watchin' you throw for a while, and I got to say I ain't ever seen anyone make a baseball do what you're makin' it do. When'd you learn to throw a knuckleball?"

Tyler tells him the same story he told me the other night. I can see scout sizin' him up and down, getting more and more nervous as he figures out that he's lookin' at a pitchin' sensation that's twice the age of every other player out on that field.

Scout looks at me. "Orval, what do you think?"

I play it cool. "Oh, Rube here has got some mean stuff, that's for sure."

"No, I mean what do you think about him pitchin' for a livin'?"

"Oh, now I ain't no scout. Rube here's what, thirty years old?" I cut ten off to try to seal the deal. "I mean, he ain't really in our demographic in terms of huntin' for new meat. But hell, fans love a knuckler and he might help us win a couple of…"

35

"Goddamn, Orval, I ain't interested in helpin' you win games here in Goddamned Keokuk. I reckon that's a major league knuckleball right there. What do you think," he cleared his throat, "about what those pitches would do against big hitters?"

No one said anything for a few minutes. I sat there pretending to ponder it, but I knew there wasn't a hitter on earth who could smack one of those pitches and tell you where it was going to end up. I wasn't sure, at that point, there was a hitter on earth who could even make contact. Brickyard finally broke the silence.

"I'd sure as hell like to find out."

So that's how Rube Tyler, at age forty, became a professional ballplayer. Scout went back and wrote up a careful but glowing report, and authorized us to sign him for a 21-day evaluation contract, at the princely sum of thirty-five hundred dollars. Rube got him some vacation time from the plastics plant, we got him an extra-husky uniform and we penciled him in for a road start against Winona on April 25. Scout told us he'd tell the club he thought there was a prospect with immediate potential, and we oughta expect some attention when we came back for our homestand the week afterwards. I sat Rube down in my office the next day and I explained the contract to him. He seemed overwhelmed by it all, but he was happy to get the chance to play ball. When we got to the part about the physical, though, he got all tense at the thought of the team sending in their medical staff to check him out.

"I got a real thing about doctors, Coach," he said. "Bad experience when I was a kid."

"Well come on, Rube," I said, "it can't be so bad it's a deal breaker."

Rube shook his head. "I just don't want any needles," he said. I reckoned that would work OK, at least for the contract we were gonna have with him.

"Alright, then, son," I told him. "If you'd told me I'd be signin' a contract with you a couple of weeks ago in the parking lot, I'd have said you were out of your mind. But here we go. Sign right there and you'll be, for the next three weeks, a real-life Keokuk Western."

He did. He signed his name in his big, third-grade scrawl, a signature that, I thought, wouldn't look right on some baseball on a kid's bedroom shelf somewhere. Rube's pitch needed nothing; it was perfect. Everything else about Rube, it seemed, was gonna need work.

3rd Inning

So we had a couple more games before we left for Winona, against Dubuque, and we split them and there was some good hittin' but some lousy-assed pitchin', and my mind wasn't on those games so much, 'cuz each of 'em I was thinkin' about what I'd seen in practice beforehand. We got Rube out on the field a couple hours before game time, before anyone seriously showed up in the stands, 'cuz the big club didn't think they wanted anyone on to the forty-year old comeback kid just yet. We had him throw some beepee to the boys, but figured we'd quit that because it was screwin' up their timing something awful. They'd swing like hell at Rube's sixty-mile an hour knuckler, and then step up to the plate against the Browns and be late on every single pitch. The first game of that series the Browns was no-hittin' us until the sixth inning and their poor sorry-assed pitcher was sittin' there thinkin' he'd finally got his shit together until Stuffy Flack closed his eyes and waited an extra half second before swingin' and he smacked a line drive triple that started a big inning for us and their pitcher got pulled out of the game wonderin' what the hell had happened after watchin' his brief dream of double-A disappear down the left field line a few times.

As good a pitcher as he was, though, Rube Tyler was a God-damned crappy fielder. He had no range of motion, his reflexes were shot after twenty years of beer drinkin', and as wild as he could throw off the mound, he was even worse tryin' to get the ball to first base. Ol' Hack Hendrix reckoned he maybe better git a bigger glove, and he asked Rube whether he could ever *stop* throwin' that knuckleball, and then even when it went straight it seemed like it took for-Goddamned-*ever* to get across the infield. Them drills were tough to watch, and we set to work tryin' to get some flexibility into Rube's portly frame. That wasn't easy. He'd do some stretching and practically fall over, and after a few minutes of throwin' he'd set there with his hands on his knees wheezin' pretty good.

"You alright, Rube?" I asked him. "Yeah, Coach, I just ain't used to movin' around so much. (puff). Out at the plant I'm mostly just settin' on my ass all day. (pant)."

"Well, shit, boy, we gotta get you into shape."

"I know, Coach. I can do it. It's just gonna take a bit."

It turned out that Tyler smoked two packs a day. He drank a six pack of cheap beer every night, and he ate like a garbage truck. The

37

concession stand at the Keokuk Veterans had a nacho plate special they called the Coronary. And Rube had made it a habit to eat one of those every game. With a couple of beers to wash it down. That had left him kind of doughy, and he was carrying around an extra forty pounds or so.

"You got a woman to cook for you?" I asked him.

"Naw, coach. I ain't what you'd call marryin' material. I just mostly make some mac'n'cheese at night, or get a pizza or maybe some tacos."

So we decided we had to get him on some kind of diet. We got him the first bag of apples maybe that he'd ever seen and I sent Hobie over to clean out his fridge and put in some stuff that would give him some energy. Hobie came back a bit glazed over after he'd seen the contents of Rube's trailer. It was mostly beer, I guess, with some old frozen pizzas and some cans of cheese spread, but he also mentioned a few cartons of cheap cigs and enough porn to choke a horse. So in addition to workin' on his pitch, we had some lifestyle adjustments to make, too. Hobie reckoned we needed to get him a date, but I thought that might be more trouble than it was worth.

Anyways, the Rube Tyler who got on that bus to Winona wasn't no different than the guy who showed up to throw against the side of the stadium a couple weeks beforehand, except he had a new suit that we sent him out to get with Speedy Killefer, who we reckoned was the best dresser on the team, but for the $150 we had in petty cash they couldn't find much at the local men's store and there hadn't been time to tailor it, so he got on the bus lookin' just a bit out of place, and he even got himself a nice leather drivin' glove for his pitchin' hand, and we headed out of Keokuk on a warm April morning to meet Rube's destiny in his professional debut.

Now, the team bus in single-A is never a pretty time, but that morning everyone was pretty quiet. We left early, so most of the boys was nappin' anyways, but us coaches up in the front was all feelin' just a bit reflective. Rube was settin' next to Footsie and they was talkin' a bit, but by the time we got to Rock Island Footsie had fallen asleep and Rube was left to stare out the window at the newly turned dirt fields and the river as it rolled down the other way past us. By the time we were up to Clinton, Hoops had a poker game started and Rube turned out to be a hell of a player. Brickyard and Hobie and I sat up front hearin' Rube pick up a few bucks from everyone and we noticed he kept the glove on the whole damn time, even when he's dealin' cards.

I asked Brickyard what he thought about our new rookie and he said he was worried after seein' him in practice, that his pitchin' looked fine but it was all the other stuff that bothered him. Our league played the DH, so Rube wasn't gonna have to hit yet, thank God, but keepin' his head about him on the field was going to be hard enough.

"Well hell, Brickyard," I said, "he'll just have to keep everyone off base."

"That's the thing, Orval," Brickyard said, "I ain't worried about him one on one with a batter. It's what happens once someone's on. He's got this one skill, and that's gonna strike plenty of batters out, but I don't know that it's gonna win us any games."

We stopped for lunch at some truck stop up north and I made Hobie stick with Rube and not let him get a double haystack or nothin' like that and Rube complained a bit, but then Hobie let him sneak a couple of smokes outside and that seemed to placate him. Gettin' back on the bus I smacked him on the back and asked him how we was doin', and he took a deep breath and told me he was alright but he was gettin' a bit nervous, and I told him to just sit back and take in the first game that night, to watch Preacher Bush, who was startin' that one, and to just take it all in. Then we'd take care of him the day of his game and it would all go fine. Rube scraped the gravel of the parking lot with his sneaker (and I was just noticin' that we needed to buy him some Goddamned wing tips to go with the suit), and let out a deep sigh and said "I just don't want to embarrass myself or the team, coach. I just want to get this done and pitch a good game."

"Pretty Goddamned tough to embarrass this bunch," I said.

So we pulled into Winona mid-afternoon and got ourselves checked into the local Motel 6. I made Rube and Speedy Killefer roommates so that Speedy could talk to him about some of the finer points of the battery and bond a little bit. We all got changed into our uniforms and got back on the bus, and headed over to the Winona stadium to start practice. Speedy was busy warmin' up Preacher, so Hobie and I threw around with Rube for a while and kept him as loose as we could, but he couldn't stop thinkin' about the next day's game and you could tell he was getting nervous about it.

Preacher pitched a pretty bad game that night, he gave up two runs in the second and then couldn't find the strike zone for another couple of innings. I had to put Moose in to relieve him in the sixth, and even after a couple of taters by Hack and Smokey we ended up on the wrong end of a 7-3 score. By this point I was tired of yellin' at the boys, so we just packed it in, headed to the local Denny's for a late team dinner and made sure everyone got back to the motel instead of samplin' the local wildlife that evening. Hobie had a strict curfew of 11:00 the night before afternoon games, after one real bad outing by Hot Rod that came after he ended up spendin' the night at some seventeen-year-old jailbait's house in Galesburg, and you could tell that Rube needed him a drink but I reckoned he needed a good night's sleep before anything else.

So his big day opened up cold, with a ray of sunshine and a cup of motel coffee. I stepped out on the motel balcony in my long johns and watched the steam from my breath wrap around itself in the cold Minnesota air. I got dressed and then we all went to the Denny's down the road and got breakfast and Speedy came up to me and said he didn't think Rube got much sleep the night before and I said "how do you know?" and he said that the only sleep *he'd* had all night was when Rube was awake and wasn't snorin', which he did pretty loud, and Gunner and Smokey in the room next to their's said yeah, the snorin' had woken them up but then it had quit enough for them to get a good night's rest.

After brunch I walked up to Rube and asked him how he was doin', and he said "pretty nervous, Coach," and that he hadn't eaten too much but he felt pretty sick from gettin' all worked up about the game. When we got back to the hotel, Speedy told me later, Tyler had the shits pretty bad, and then he puked right before we left for the ballpark. He looked like hell on the bus, and I told him not to worry about it, that we was all behind him and he forced a weak smile, but you could tell he was wonderin' whether this had all been a big mistake on his part.

"Hell, Rube," said Hobie, "Even if you just go out there and spill your guts all over the mound, you got a free bus ride to Winona out of all this, now, didn't you?"

Rube chuckled a bit and then he just sat and looked out the window at the town goin' by as we headed out to the park.

Now, no one—not a soul—had said anything about Rube Tyler's magical knuckleball to the press, or to the other teams, or to the commissioner of the River League. The big club didn't really give a damn just yet, and our signin' a 40-year old chain-smokin' plastics assembly line worker didn't even raise an eyebrow with the other clubs. They must've just figured we was as desperate as ever. When Buddy back in the Keokuk press box had asked me about the new guy I just kinda shrugged and said somethin' about how the management reckoned we could use a backup pitcher for a few weeks and that was that. So when we pulled up to the Winona stadium we didn't expect to see no one there and sure as hell we didn't. Their groundskeeper undid the padlock and we walked into the clubhouse in the dark, flipped on the lights ourselves, threw our stuff in our lockers and trotted out to start practice. The stands was empty and only the scorer was in the box, so we had the place to ourselves. The team just trotted out but not Rube, he

40

stood on the top step of the dugout and took it all in, the patchy grass outfield, the rotting concrete of Winona's 500-seat 1930s WPA stadium, the smell of last night's beer and the nearby cheese plant mixin' with the river out back, and with a look of desperate trepidation he shuffled on out and jogged a few steps till he was out by Brickyard and then they started just tossin' back and forth and I thought maybe things was gonna be alright.

But of course they weren't. Rube hadn't never been in the spotlight like this. He'd played ball in high school, sure, but there weren't no expectations then, I reckon. No one was lookin' at him playin' and wonderin' whether he'd had any business out on that field then, that's for sure. Now, though, he'd been sittin' at home, or sittin' on his ass at the plastics factory and I would hazard a guess that ain't nobody noticed that man for one minute except when he turned in his time card or bought someone a beer after work or messed up something on the line. Nobody noticed, I'm pretty sure. He'd had more than twenty years of doin' his job, punchin' buttons and haulin' his sorry ass to work in his beat-up old car and goin' home and fixin' somethin' out of a can and washin' it down with a cheap beer and then watchin' late night TV until he was tired enough to go to sleep. I reckoned that just about summed up Rube Tyler's life to that point, except for one thing. Every so often, Rube had a flash of ambition, just a bit more than most, that made him go out back with his Johnny Bench Batter-Up and his glove and an old ball and work on that sweet-assed knuckleball. Most men, given that life situation, would just say the hell with it and pack it in and see how much porn and beer they could get in before they stroked out or drove their pickup drunk into the side of a bridge or just drank or smoked themselves into a soft, quiet oblivion. But not Rube. He'd tried something, something with a million-to-one shot, and here he was. His life's ambition had landed him in a third-rate ballpark in Winona, Minnesota, ready to pitch his first game on just about the bottom rung in professional baseball.

And I am sure, just as I'm standin' here tellin' this story, that Rube Tyler was thinkin' the same thing, thinkin' that this was probably just about as far as he could ever hope to have gotten, that standin' here tossin' with Brickyard was probably about as much as he could have asked out of his life's ambition and that was pretty alright. That was what had given him the shits after we got back from Denny's, I reckon, realizin' that for all practical purposes all that time in the back yard pitchin' had gotten him here, and now what the hell was he gonna do with it?

41

People trickled in to the early afternoon sunshine still wrapped up in their coats and mittens as we was finishin' up practice. Mostly old folks, grandparents with their kids, a typical weekday afternoon crowd. I surveyed them all and wondered how many of them would really understand what they were about to see, wondered if they realized what acts of extraordinary physics and ball control were about to happen in their little ballpark. But then just as I was startin' to choke up a bit the umps showed up and there was lineup cards to fill out, and Buzz, the Wolverines' manager, to shake hands with and say how're you doin' this season, and what's up with that left fielder that got busted for weed last year, and who the Goddamned *hell* is this guy you're warmin' up in the bullpen and how desperate are you all for pitchin'? By this point Brickyard had Rube in the bullpen but he wasn't lettin' him throw no knuckleballs, just soft pitches down the middle, waitin' for the big moment to surprise the hell out of the opposing batters. Rube was in the groove, but he still didn't look like he totally wanted to be there. I left them alone, not wantin' to add to the pressure, but after they played an eight-track recording of the anthem I gathered him and the team in the dugout and told 'em that I wanted them all behind Rube, that he was gonna need plenty of backup out there and to keep talkin' to him and not let him get worked up or nervous. This was a big day, I said to them, for Rube, for all of you, for me. So let's get some hits, let's play some tight defense, and let's give Rube a win in his debut. The team they was all for it, and Stuffy Flack patted Rube on the belly and said to give it his all and Preacher Bush said a little prayer and then Gunner picked up his bat and waltzed on out to the batter's box and Rube ran back into the clubhouse and puked his guts out for most of the top half of the first inning.

The boys gave him somethin' to work with. Gunner managed a walk and then he took second after their catcher dropped an easy slider. Hack singled him home and then the middle of the lineup went out in sequence and suddenly it was time. Rube had been sittin' on the bench with his leg shakin' up and down since he got back from blowin' his donuts and now I went over and thumped him on the arm and said "get out there and show 'em that bad-assed shit you got, tiger," and he looked up at me a bit uncertain through his glasses and then he stood up and shuffled out of the dugout. I'd told Speedy to warm him up slow, to just let him chuck a few soft pitches for the Wolverines to feast their eyes on, and to wait until batter up to let him throw the knuckleball. They didn't need no signs or nothin', Rube knew what he was supposed to do and that was to just throw that floating queerball till he couldn't no more or until there was 27 outs, and to stay out there all day if he could, restin'

Moose or at least avoidin' the possibility that Moose would need to offer up any type of pitch to their hitters.

"BATTER UP!" yelled the ump and brother, it was on. I looked out at Rube and I caught his eye and I yelled "go get 'em, Tyler!" and the boys on the bench yelled too and they couldn't wait to see some other sumbitches try to hit his knuckler after they'd been flailin' away at 'em. I looked out at Speedy and he gave me a nod and then he looked out at Rube and flashed him some bullshit sign and nodded real good, and the Wolverine's leadoff hitter, a shrimp of a second baseman named Schmutz or somethin' like that, he got in the batter's box and he sized up Rube real good, he had a grin on his face like he was about to get a big-assed plate of dinner served up to him and he swung a couple of times and squinted and spit a wad of sunflower seeds out. Rube nodded at Speedy, he wound up, picked the ball up into the air, kicked and spun toward home...

...and the ball came out of his hands spinnin' like an old jukebox record, straight as an arrow right at home plate and doin' well under the local speed limit. Speedy looked like someone had just shot his dog and Schmutz just reared back and beat the hell out of that ball and sent it flyin' over the right field fence like he'd launched it from a mortar. I swear to God it whistled as it went out, and the crack his bat made on that cheap-assed piece of shit pitch echoed off the hills out past the outfield fence and came back at me, at Brickyard, at Speedy, and at Rube like the baseball Gods was just laughin' at our best laid plans. Schmutz just stood there, like a major league slugger watchin' that thing play out, then he clapped his hands twice and trotted around the diamond like he owned it while the half-full grandstand stood and applauded what must have been the easiest home run of his career. There's Rube, standin' with his hands on his knees, lookin' at the ground all ready to puke one more time, and there's Schmutz, high-fivin' his teammates at home plate, and there's the geek behind the scoreboard puttin' up a big yellow "1." Winona 1, Keokuk 0. Rube Tyler, lifetime ERA, ∞. Holy fuckin' shit, I thought to myself, what the Goddamned hell have we done?

"That's alright, Rube," Brickyard yelled, "Let it go, son."

"Yeah, Rube, get the next one! They can't hit your good shit!"

Rube looked up at the sky. Speedy came out to talk him down. I could see him askin' Rube was he alright, and I could see Rube nod without the slightest shred of conviction. Speedy gave him a new ball and ran back behind the plate and Rube took a deep breath and looked over at me and Brickyard and both of us were clappin' and sayin' he could do it, and just settle down and get that ball dancin'.

43

Rube came set, and pretended to shake Speedy off a couple of times before he nodded and brought the ball up to his chest. He wound up and this time the ball broke just a little bit, spinnin' a bit less and fallin' off right at the end. Slow as it was, the batter knew better than to chase it and it ended up bouncin' off the plate into Speedy's glove.

"BALL ONE!" yelled the ump and now Brickyard looked at me and he was genuinely worried about what he'd just seen. Rube's miracle pitch had just evaporated, it had disappeared, and now he was just another keg softball player up there against kids who could actually beat the hell out of even a reasonably quick fastball. Speedy chucked the ball back and he looked over toward us to see what the hell we thought we oughta do, and we both looked back at him with practiced looks of confidence.

"COME ON, RUBE," Brickyard shouted. "YOU CAN DO IT, BOY!"

Another deep breath on the mound. Rube looks in at Speedy, wipes his hand on his shirt and winds up and this one ain't hittable, because it's in the dirt five feet in front of home plate. Speedy blocks it and the ump give him a new ball and shakes his head because he realizes it's gonna be a long afternoon in Winona.

Two deep breaths this time. Set. Windup. Floater, high and inside. *Crack.* Just over Gunner Thomas' head down the third base line, fair ball and almost getting past Hoops Hooper in left field. Hoops came runnin' over and grabbed it and managed to hold the runner at first. Now everyone is lookin' at me, and they're lookin' at Rube, and ladies and gentlemen we are in deep, deep crap if this keeps up.

"Shit," Brickyard says. "You reckon I need to go out there?"

I look out at Rube, and he's just starin' at his shoes, shakin' his head.

"Let's give it a minute, see if he pulls this thing together on his own."

Low and outside. 1-0. No spin. Bounces off the plate, past Speedy, and runner gets to second. Behind the batter's head, all the way to the backstop, runner takes third. Then, instead of just chuckin' ball four, Rube just plunks the guy on the ankle. Two men on now, seven pitches in, and their number three hitter comes up. Brickyard's lookin' at me out the corner of his eye, and the boys out in the field are tryin' like hell to get Rube in the zone.

Next batter's no different for the first two pitches. Then Rube grooves one and the batter comes around wicked late and fouls it out of the park in right field.

"ALRIGHT, RUBE! STRIKE ONE, BABY! GET US ANOTHER LIKE THAT!" This is the loudest anyone's ever cheered for a Goddamned foul ball, but it's a strike all the same.

Another low ball, then a high outside one that the batter chases, I figure cause he's bored. He tomahawks it foul the other way and now we got us a full count. But it don't matter, 'cuz Rube throws the next one so far outside that Speedy prostrates himself chasin' it, and he stops it but just barely, and now we got a full count (two full counts!) and the Wolverine's cleanup hitter lickin' his chops.

Speedy jogs up to the mound, probably tellin' Rube to pitch around this guy a bit, and Brickyard asks me if I want to walk him and waste one run instead of four. I say "Let's go see what's up" and the two of us jog out to the mound.

"Sorry, Coach," Tyler says. "I don't know what's wrong. I can't get the knuckler goin' all of a sudden."

Brickyard lights up.

"Well this is a HELL OF A TIME to lose that pitch, son! I reckon you better find it or we're gonna be out of this game before it starts."

Rube starts, but I cut him off.

"What the hell you doin' different?" I say, which is stupid, but I think I gotta figure out what's goin' wrong here.

"I don't know, sir. I just can't relax and just throw it. Maybe you'd better take me out. I'm blowin' it, I know. I'm sorry. I'm just…"

I cross my arms and spit a sunflower husk onto the mound.

"The hell I'm gonna take your sorry ass out. I ain't gonna sit here and watch Moose chuck nine innings of gopherball. You're our man, Tyler. You got a job to do here. A God-damned *job*."

He blinks.

"This is your *job* right now, son. *This is your job.*"

Speedy looks behind us. The ump is comin' to bust things up. I start turnin' to go, but Brickyard calls me back.

"Time, gentlemen," the ump says.

"Just a sec," Brickyard says. "Look, Rube. Forget these guys on base. Just concentrate on your hand. Focus on the ball. Focus on gettin' that ball to slip out of those fingers. Come on."

Rube glances around at the bases, and this gives me an idea.

"Son," I say, "give yourself a clean start. Groove one to this guy here."

"What, sir?" he says.

45

"This guy's second in the league in slugging," I say. "The way you're pitchin', you ain't gonna strike him out anyway. Throw something straight. Give him a fastball and let him clear the bases. It's only four runs, and then let's just start from scratch. Go ahead. Chuck him the biggest gopherball you ever threw. I'm not kiddin', let's just get this over with and then get you pitchin' that good stuff."

Blink. Tyler looks at Brickyard, and Brickyard sees what I'm doin'. I ain't tryin' to win a game here. I'm tryin' to get him to *let go*. I'm thinkin' long term here, you see. I tell him to stop focusin' on what he can't do, and to focus on what he can. This is a little thing I picked up from some sports shrink years ago. Eliminate your distractions and focus on what you can do.

"Go on," Brickyard says. "Get these guys off the bases and let's start over."

"OK, Coach. I'm real sorry…"

"Son," I say. "Quit apologizing. Do what I tell you to do and then we'll talk about gettin' things goin' again."

We walk back to the dugout and Brickyard looks at me and says "crazy-assed day, I hope you know what you're doin'" and I say "I don't."

Now Rube's lookin' down at the ball, and he winds up and floats one down the pike, maybe not a strike, but close enough, and it flies off the bat and into the cool afternoon sky and doesn't ever come down, at least not that we can see, and it's 4-0 with no outs and we trot out to the mound again.

"That's what you told me to do, right, Coach?" Rube says.

"That was just fine, Rube," I say, chuckling. "Look. It's just a game. Let me worry about those four runs and gettin' 'em back. All we've talked about is how your pitch works and we ain't talked about why. So here's the thing. You're overthinkin'. You're worryin' about everything but what you gotta worry about. So don't think about the big stuff when you're out here. Just sweat the small stuff. Don't even think about the batter. Just get your pitch floating out here. Alright?"

"Alright, sir."

"Alright." I smack the ball back into his hand. "Fuck 'em up."

Rube looks down at his hand, and the ball, and says "the small stuff. Got it."

I smack him on the ass and we head back to the dugout.

Now what happened next happened slowly. The next batter smacked a triple down the line, but he smacked it the wrong way—he'd swung late, but the ball wasn't quite where he expected it and he took off out of the box pretty confused about what he'd just hit. Then Rube got his first out, a pop up that Speedy himself caught about halfway down the third base line. The crowd gave him a polite cheer, and Brickyard turned to me and said "a hundred and eight," which was now Rube's lifetime ERA.

But Speedy looked in at us after making the catch and gave us a knowin' grin. Rube was settlin' down, and as he was settlin' down them pitches was gettin' just a bit riled up. That pop up had been a home run swing, and it was deadly accurate, right where the sweet spot should have been. But it wasn't. The ball didn't go where it was supposed to, and just by maybe an eighth of an inch. But that's all it takes, that's the difference between a 400 foot home run and a weak pop up in the infield, the difference between a million bucks a week at Wrigley and a warm six pack out in the cornfields.

Smack. Single down the right field line. Run scores. 5-0, one out, runner on. Now we're into the bottom of their lineup, but any one of these guys could take Rube's pitchin' for a ride if it ain't movin' like it's supposed to. Next pitch is high and inside, brushin' the batter back, but at the last possible second, meanin' that he hadn't seen it comin', quite, and on the next pitch Rube wound up, let loose, and threw that perfect hummingbird, a pitch that hovered, dove, arced down and then seemed to rise up at the last minute. The batter swung and instead of hittin' the center of the ball he hit the top of the ball, and instead of a line drive over the shortstop's head it was a cheap ground ball and Hollocher picked it up, chucked it to Smokey on second and back to Hack Hendrix on first. A double play, the third out, and a damn fine pitch. We was down 5-0, but somehow that last pitch had me and Brickyard smackin' each other on the back and thinkin' things was maybe gonna turn out alright.

Rube shuffled back in to the dugout and the boys was real good about it, hittin' him on the back and tellin' him "that's alright, Rube, you'll get 'em next inning" and sayin' to not get down on himself. I put my hand on his shoulder and said don't worry, that things will calm down and that just might be the worst inning you'll throw all year, so just relax and remember what I told you. He kinda nodded and pulled that dumbassed work glove on his hand for good luck. But then I went and found Speedy and took him aside down at one end of the dugout and said "OK, what did you see out there," and Speedy smiled a bit.

"Well, Coach, it was horseshit until that last pitch, but that one was all over the place. It's a good thing that kid hit it or I might have missed it completely. He's gonna be alright."

"OK, Speedy. I trust you. Let's keep him in the game. Your job is keepin' him off the ledge out there."

47

Winona's pitchin' was pretty good and we ended up out of the top of the second with one walk, two strikeouts, and a pop fly that got snagged at the wall to end it. Rube watched all of this quietly, sittin' down at the end of the bench and fiddlin' with a ball between his fingers, and when that third out came I went over and I just told him "get out there and do what you know how to do" and out he went.

His warmup pitches were the same dumb, slow hangers that he'd thrown before, but when the batter stepped in I could have sworn it got a bit brighter over the ballpark. Rube looked over at me and Brickyard in the dugout and he smiled a little bit, and then he reared back and chucked one of them monkey balls that took hours, maybe days to reach the plate, but that tied up the hitter, Speedy, and the ump all at once, all three of 'em lookin' twice to see where the ball ended up and the batter all coiled around after slugging the piece of air that should have held a baseball as hard as he possibly could. I swear you could hear the crowd suck in their breath at what they saw, and the batter two-stepped his way out of the box and then just sat there and stared a ray through Rube as if he was tryin' to figure out what the hell had just happened and how this sad sack on the mound had just got him to look so Goddamned bad swingin' at a pitch that *wasn't even there*.

"STRIKE!"

"ALRIGHT, RUBE!" Brickyard yelled, and the boys in the field chimed in real good, too.

"THAT'S THE PITCH! THROW ANOTHER ONE LIKE THAT, RUBE!"

Now he wound up again, lookin' just a bit more confident. This one came out spinnin' a bit, but it broke to one side as it zeroed in. The batter swung again, knowin' it was a mistake before he was all the way around.

"STRIKE TWO!"

I could hear the batter mutter as the ump called it. The crowd, which had already been silent, got even quieter.

"ONE MORE PITCH, TYLER! GO GET 'EM!"

Now Rube reared back again and this time the ball slipped out of his fingers perfectly. The pitch ambled on toward the plate, dippin, and bobbin', and weavin' its way toward Speedy. Then it headed toward the on deck circle, and the dugout, and then it changed its mind and headed back toward the plate, and the batter just laid the heck off this one and it just hopped over the plate right down the middle for a called third strike.

"YERROUUT!"

"WOOO! ATTABOY, RUBE! GET 'EM OUTTA HERE!"

"Shit," said Brickyard. "That was purdy right there. Maybe the boy's got it back after all."

"Maybe," I said. "I ain't seen three game pitches like that in a row ever. Sweet stuff."

"SUMBITCH" said their hitter, slammin' his bat in the dirt on his way back to the bench.

Three straight pitches. Three Goddamned beautiful pitches. Three pitches Rube had been watin' to throw his whole damned life, and here they were, enshrined in the box score against the Winona Wolverines. Three pitches that I didn't know it, but I'd been waitin' my whole career for. Three of the best knuckleballs I'd ever seen, maybe the three best ones ever, never mind in a row, and one poor single-A batter who just stood there in the box, with no idea what the hell had just happened to him. An inning before this pitcher had been chucking meatballs, and now he'd just blown the hitter away with absolutely unhittable stuff. The crowd just sat there, not moving, not cheering anyone on, wondering what had just happened.

Now we was up at the top of their order again, and Schmutz walked out a little tentative, like he wasn't quite sure it was such a good idea this time around. Rube didn't crack a smile—not yet. He was still plenty nervous, though his eyes were just a little more focused now and he didn't look quite so much like he was gonna puke again. This time he missed on a couple of pitches first, ran up the count 2-0, but then the ball started findin' the plate, and I mean findin', like it wandered around that sixty-and-a-half feet not sure where it was goin', and then suddenly realized it was supposed to go *over there*, by that thing on the ground and into the waiting, friendly glove behind it. The batter got a piece of it on 3-2, but it was a weak grounder to Gunner over at third and Rube had himself another quick out. The next batter just sat there, and Rube's pitches had a little trouble getting there and he walked him after goin' to another full count. But then, their third hitter just lost it, swingin' at everything Rube chucked and bein' behind, ahead, high, low, and underneath everything, sometimes all on the same pitch. Third strike, and we got out of the inning completely unscathed.

Rube almost couldn't get back into the dugout after that. The boys mobbed him up and slugged him between the shoulder blades and high-fived him like he'd just won game seven of the Series. Rube let just a little bit of tension go out of himself, grabbin' his lucky glove out of the back of the dugout and slidin' it onto his hand right away, and then catchin' my eye as I was comin' over and sayin' "how was that, Coach?"

"That's what we're lookin' for, son," I said. "That's the shit right there. What'd you do to get that pitch back, anyway?"

"I just stopped thinkin' for a minute. I put my mind in view of a cold six pack and just let go. I just pitched."

"Atta boy, Rube," I said. "Atta boy. Keep loose and let's get another inning like that."

Now our hittin' wasn't much that afternoon, but we started clawin' our way back from 5-0. Hack got lucky and hit one out in the fourth, and we put together a little rally in the sixth, stole a couple of bases, and got three runs in after a wild pitch and Stuffy Flack takin' one on the ass and Gunner strokin' a nice triple down the right field line.

But no one—no one—in the stands or in either dugout that afternoon gave a damn what we were hittin'. Rube Tyler set the next five hitters down in a row, with them swingin' at every Goddamned pitch and either missin' 'em or poppin' 'em up or hittin' weak fouls either way. Rube started gettin' focused, and his pitch just got crazier, and the batters started just losin' their cool and flailin' away desperately and all mad and tryin' like hell to prove that this *just could not happen*, that this tub out on the mound could not, conceivably, have a pitch that did all this to them. This, every one of their angry swings seemed to say, *will not stand*. It *cannot happen like this, after all the time we spent groveling up the ladder and takin' beepee and workin' to get to this point*. This *is bullshit*. And big ol' Rube just stood there flutterin' that pitch by 'em and getting more and more confident with every pitch and beginnin' to think of himself as more than just the guy at the plastics plant with the six-pack and the backyard hobby.

They picked him up in the sixth, though, getting a man on and then, with Rube pitchin' from the stretch and thinkin' too Goddamned much, hittin' another gopherball deep into the Minnesota sky. But then, with the bases empty, he regained his composure and laid out the last eight hitters with only one walk and a freak double that the hitter got because he just closed his eyes and guessed. Rube went the whole game, threw about 120 pitches and he was huffin' pretty good by the end, but he survived. A near as damnit complete game to start his professional career, Brickyard never even called Moose out to the bullpen, Rube looked so damned good by the late innings. He lost the game, but he lost it honest, and if it hadn't been for that first inning he would have won it, and won it pretty much honest, too. His final box score didn't look like much, but the story behind it was pretty damned something:

	IP	R	ER	H	SO	BB
Tyler	8.0	6	6	7	9	5

Back in the clubhouse you woulda thought we'd won the Goddamned game goin' away, what with all the shoutin' and the clubbin' of poor Rube on the back. I gave Brickyard the last-out ball to give to Rube in front of all the guys and everyone gave him a big shout and a round of applause. He looked a little stunned, like this was something he hadn't never expected to happen, and kinda like the dog that catches up to that car he's been chasin' all afternoon he didn't have any clue at all what to do with it.

"Way to go, Tyler," I said. "Those were eight fine innings. The whole team backed you up, and I wish we'd got a bit more offense for you, but that's the best losing effort I've seen in a long time. We'll get that first inning out of the game plan next."

That night Brickyard and Hobie and I took Rube out to the local watering hole after we'd all ate and we got him good and drunk. Hobie gave him all kinds of crap 'cuz he was still wearin' that Goddamned work glove on his pitchin' hand. He just laughed and said hey, so long as it worked he was keepin' it on. And then Rube asked me if I thought he'd pitch past his three week contract and I looked him in the eye and I said "I don't know if you'll be pitchin' for us, but you keep that shit up and you'll be pitchin' somewhere all the way to October."

I was gonna be right about that, too.

4th Inning

Losin' that game 6-3 was the high point of the set in Winona. They kicked our asses the next night, shut us right out after Hot Rod showed up late and only got a few throws in before game time. He was pretty damned hung over and he was suddenly pissed off that this new kid, who of course was twice his age, but nonetheless this new kid, had shown him up so bad and apparently he and Hack had gone out and had this discussion over several bottles of loudmouth soup and Hack had said he didn't see what the problem was, Tyler was 0-1 and Hot Rod was what, 2-4? So who's got the better percentage, he'd said, and then after a few more drinks they got thrown out for hittin' on the local girls a bit too hard and Hot Rod ended up back at the motel with a fifth of cheap bourbon and that's why he'd slept all fuckin' day and why he was a bit slow on his feet once game time rolled around. Then the next night we kept pace pretty good but Moose gave up a two-run walkoff homer in the bottom of the ninth after he came in relievin' Preacher, who'd pitched a pretty damn good game but still gave up two runs and we'd only scored three so we ended up headin' out of there getting swept.

But Rube got his name in the paper and he was pretty damn proud of that, and I've still got a clippin' from the *Winona Daily News* with the headline "Wolverines Win It in First" sayin' that the Keokuk Westerns had debuted a new knuckleballer who didn't look like much and had a rough start, but who threw some pretty good stuff after he settled down and if he kept pitchin' like that he was bound to make some noise in the River League for the rest of the season.

We had a day off to get back down to Dubuque, where we won the first game 8-5, raisin' our record to a league-trailin' 5-9, and the bus ride down was pretty gloomy except that the boys got a pretty wild poker game goin' and Rube kicked their butts pretty good. That night in Dubuque Brickyard and Hobie and I went out for some beers after we all ate at the local Steak'n'Shake and Brickyard said he had to send a note up the ladder about what we saw outta Rube and what should he say? I told him to say that he survived his first game but we didn't have much to look at yet, and I was a bit worried about what was gonna happen if he turned out to be as good as he'd looked in those last few innings up at Winona. There wasn't nothin' in the manager's handbook about this. What do you do with a guy who's twice the age of anyone else on the team and he's maybe gonna be the linchpin that makes this bunch of greenhorn, girl-happy, junk-swinging sonsabitches win a few games? Because at this point I had three scenarios mapped out. One was that Rube was gonna tear a ligament, probably in his knee before his elbow, and he was never gonna finish out that evaluation contract. The other was that we was gonna get to the end of the three weeks and he was gonna get a contract to finish out the season with us and maybe we'd win a few extra games and he'd be a good influence on our players, maybe teach one or two how to pitch that crazy queer shit and hang on as a volunteer coach or somethin'. But there was a third possibility that I didn't want to think about all of a sudden, and that was that he might even get called *up* just as he was startin' to pull this crapaholic Westerns team out of the Goddamned basement.

"Tell 'em we ain't seen enough yet to give 'em an honest answer."

"Holy Goddamned crap, Orval, you see the same game I saw?"

"Yeah, I saw it, but I don't want anyone getting excited. Or even interested. Not yet, anyway. That guy ain't even pitched but one game. It was a lulu, but maybe it was a freak. Or maybe he gets through the league the first time and kids is just swingin' away and shit, and by the time he gets through the league a second time they've figgered him out and it ain't so special anymore. Just don't say anything. Be noncommittal. No one'll give a damn at this point, anyway."

That was true. All up the Cubs ladder, at Peoria and out in North Carolina and up in Des Moines, they had other things to worry about. The big club had started the season like a rocket, bringing along the hopes of northsiders everywhere. They were a remarkable 10-3, with some good baserunning, ground ball pitchers, and just enough power to keep the ballhawks on Waveland Avenue busy. We'd all got a memo just before we left for Winona that gave us the farm strategy for the season, though this never really meant anything when you were as far upstream as we were, but it was clear that they was expectin' to be in the postseason, and they was lookin' to find players that could back up the big club as and when someone got hurt or wasn't producin'.

After the next day's game against the Browns, though, we wasn't no 10-3. We was 5-10 and I was wonderin' if we was ever gonna win another game that whole damn season. I stood up in the clubhouse afterwards and tore everyone's ass up, especially Smokey, who'd muffed a couple of real easy grounders and stunk up a double play that would've gotten us out of the sixth with only a run in, and instead the next three batters reached and we'd given up four and that was all Dubuque needed to drop us down from a crappy winning percentage to only a decent hitting percentage. I told them boys that the organization would just as

53

soon cut anyone who wasn't playin' 100% and they could finish up the season slingin' lumber out at the hardware store for all I cared. The big boys is winnin', I told 'em, and they want winners. They don't want guys who're lookin' in the stands for road beef, or showin' up pissin' whiskey, or settin' out in the field with their heads down between pitches. They want winners, and right now I told 'em none of you qualify and I ain't keepin' anyone I don't think can move up later this season and so you can walk out right now and hitchhike your way back down the river to Keokuk. Goddamnit.

Rube had the ball the next day, and I was actually kinda relaxed knowin' he was gonna throw. No reason I shoulda been, since he very easily could have blown up in the first inning again. But he had acquired a sort of calm demeanor about him after getting through his professional debut. That night he was settin' outside of his and Speedy's motel room on one of the plastic pool chairs and he had his six pack of lite beer and he was just leanin' back and starin' up at the moon.

"How you doin', Rube," I asked him.

"I'm alright, coach. I'm a little nervous about tomorrow, but I ain't throwin' up and I reckon a couple of beers in me and I'll sleep just fine this time."

"Well, shit, that ain't our usual trainin' regimen, but if it works for you then whatever floats your boat, son," I said back.

We sat there for a minute and then it occurred to me to ask him whether he was happy he'd tried out, whether he'd show me that pitch again after gettin' through one game.

"Sure. Yeah. I mean, if you'd asked me in the middle of that first inning up there I'd of said somethin' different, but I'm glad to have a chance like this. I'm sittin' here with a cold beer and tomorrow all I gotta do is throw the ball a hundred times or so instead of spendin' eight hours inside that factory, and so yeah, I reckon this beats hell outta workin', anyway."

And he was right. I thought that all the time. That no matter how bad the game was goin', no matter how pissed off I was at the boys, no matter how I was getting fucked over by the big club over some player or my penny ante salary or the fact that we didn't have no toilet paper in the clubhouse, I was getting paid to play—or hell, not even play—I was gettin' paid to watch this beautiful game. Sometimes—more often than not—it pissed me off, but it wasn't like real jobs pissed real people off, you know?

"You want a beer, Coach?"

"Hell, yeah, Rube," I said and I pulled up another chair from the pool deck. We sat and sipped them Oldies and watched the clouds roll

54

past the moon and watched Hot Rod head out with some local jailbait in an El Camino and Footsie and Hoops head out in their best nightclub clothes lookin' for the public bus, and it was pretty alright settin' there in the cool Dubuque evening knowin' that Rube Tyler had done himself proud, no matter what happened from here. I finished the last of my beer and stood up.

"Alright, son. Get some sleep. And take off that stupid glove, will you?"

"No way, Coach. This glove's got the magic in it tonight. I swear."

"We'll see about that tomorrow, son."

"Sure as hell we will."

The next day broke cloudy. Lookin' at the sky I would have guessed we'd be rained out, but we had an early practice scheduled at midday and then we'd see, I guessed. I got up and met Hobie for breakfast at the diner across the highway from the motel and I couldn't quite put my finger on it but somethin' in the clouds and the air that mornin' felt damn special, I couldn't decide whether it was good special or not but either way the hairs on the back of my neck was all stood up.

When we got to the field for practice it was still gloomy, and our boys was movin' pretty slow. I got beepee started and then I headed out to the bullpen to see how Rube was handlin' things. And what I saw was just fearsome. Rube had his motion, alright. He didn't look nervous or nothin', in fact he looked like a man possessed. He was slippin' that ball out of his fingers like it was greased up, and that ball wasn't spinnin' *at all* when it left his hand, and once it did it was like it couldn't decide which way to go. Rube had his shit, alright, and Speedy was tryin' like hell to catch him and Brickyard was standin' there with his hands on his knees and his mouth hangin' open, watchin' pitch after pitch corkscrew through the damp air like a drunk college kid tryin' to get home on a Friday night. I let them do their thing for a few pitches, then I asked Rube how he felt, and he looked at me and cracked a wicked shit-eatin' grin and said "I'm alright today, I reckon, Coach. I'm alright today."

That evening the Dubuque crowd filed in not knowin' if they were goin' to see a game or not, the skies were so heavy and rain seemed so imminent. But it hadn't let loose when game time came around, and the folks that gambled on it stayin' dry got somethin' in return, I reckon. When I handed in the lineup card the ump looked at me and asked who the lunkhead pitchin' for us was, was he new and what the hell were we doin' scoutin' up AARP for startin' pitchin'? Hell, he said, he woulda come down to Keokuk if he'd known we was hirin' senior citizens, and the Dubuque manager thought that was pretty funny and asked if he

55

could get a startin' slot, too, and I just spit a sunflower husk out and said that they could both have a job if they could throw like our boy Rube.

We went three and out in the top of the first, and when Rube shuffled out to take the mound he had an air of confidence and presence that I reckoned he hadn't had in himself since maybe high school prom night. Brickyard hit him on the ass on the way out of the dugout and said "go get 'im, Tyler," and the boys takin' the field all rubbed his beer gut for good luck. He went through his warmup pitches playin' it totally straight, chuckin' those 60 mile an hour warm Velveeta pitches and makin' the Browns' hitters wet their pants waitin' for their turn to hack away. But when the ump yelled "BATTER UP," Rube got quiet. He looked out at the outfield and saw them boys smilin' back at him and he just smiled back, and right then I reckoned we were about to see somethin' pretty. He hunkered down on the mound and didn't even bother to mess around shakin' off Speedy's imaginary pitches. No, friends, Rube Tyler went right the hell to work. He grabbed that ball lovingly between his index and pinky fingers, wound up, and just lightly flicked that sucker with his other two, lettin' the momentum of his arm carry the ball in the general direction of home plate and lettin' the thick evening air and the laws of physics and chaos theory and the great pantheon of baseball Gods guide that ball around the infield and eventually show it the way in to Speedy's waitin' glove. That first Dubuque hitter swung twice, missin' everything, then waited back on the third pitch and watched it graze his elbow and still make it across the middle of the plate, belt high. He yelled like hell when the ump called "STRIKE THREE!" but he knew, and the ump knew, and everyone in the ballpark knew, but most importantly Rube knew, that there had probably not been three more devastating pitches in the history of minor league ball. Speedy threw the ball back to Rube, and the ump stood up and looked over at our bench, and I caught his eye and I could see him mouthin' the words at me, the words I'd wanted to say for a couple weeks now. "What," he said silently, "what…the…fuck?"

That second Browns batter stepped up a bit unsure, and Rube just set his ass down with three more pitches. He waited on one, then realized he'd better swing at somethin', and he fouled off the next one and then looked like he swung three times at the last one. Two out on six pitches. I looked over at Brickyard and he didn't say nothin'. He didn't have to. He just crossed his arms and eased back onto the bench and slowly nodded his head.

I looked out at the crowd. They were curious by this point at the spectacle on the mound, but I don't think they realized yet what was happenin'. The Browns bench, on the other hand, had just received reports from those first two batters and they were all at the edge of the dugout, lookin' out at this pitcher and wonderin' what the hell was up, and tryin' to figure out just what he was throwin'. Their third hitter stepped up, Joe Schmoltz, leadin' the league thus far in hits and batting average, hittin' .430 and probably not long for the riverside stadium in good ol' Dubuque. He stepped up confident, sure he could solve this mystery on the mound, and took a few warmup swings. Rube sized him up, just for show, really, and then let fly. Schmoltz watched it come in and took a mighty swing and tipped the underside of the ball just right, and the full power of his swing ended up wedging the ball just about straight up into the sky, and it just hung there for a while and he just stared at it, wonderin' how in hell it had moved from bein' right on the bat's centerline and a sure thing home run to bein' off by just that eighth of an inch, a eighth of an inch that made all the difference between .436 and .424 that evening. Just like we'd taught him Rube got the hell out of the way and let Gunner come in and make the catch. Gunner had the best glove on the infield except maybe Hack, but we figured that Hack might not be able to make it all the way across the infield on flies like this and so in practice we'd decided that Gunner would be the designated rescue squad if it ever looked like Rube was gonna have to make a play. And he did, the ball settled right into his glove and now it was seven pitches, three outs, and at this rate not only was Rube gonna have a shutout, but he was gonna do it on less than seventy pitches.

"ATTABOY, RUBE," Brickyard yelled, and all the boys in the field high fived him on their way back in. "Nice catch, Gunner," Hobie told him, and the boys was suddenly just a bit excited that maybe they weren't gonna lose this one, or at least they weren't maybe going to have to work quite so hard if Rube could keep pitchin' like this.

"Alright, boys," I said, "let's play some small ball and get Rube a run or two right here." I told Hack to get out there and do whatever it took to get on base, and maybe we'd be able to move him around. And he did, he stuck his elbow out over the plate and took a pitch for the team, and the Dubuque boys was real steamed about that and their manager came runnin' out and so I got up too and listened to him give the ump hell about it. The ump turned to me and I said "my boy just got hit on the arm and I'm a little pissed about it and I reckon you oughta warn their asses," and the ump just rolled his eyes and told me he better not see me puttin' our players in harms' way because someone was likely to get a busted elbow doin' that and I winked at 'em both and said shit, I'd never do that and I ran back to the dugout knowin' full well that the other dugout was callin' me an ass behind my back. Still, Hollocher managed a clean single and then with him on first and Hack on third Speedy popped up to right and there it was, we had our run. The bottom of the lineup washed out, though, and so that was all we got in the second.

Rube kept it up that inning. Nine pitches, three outs, two of them strikeouts and one lazy ground ball to first. The Browns' hitters were pissed as hell now and they was yellin' when they went down and sayin' how that pitch was bullshit and our boy was throwin' spitballs and they could hit any legal pitch ump, what the hell was that? Rube just started chucklin' on the mound and he looked like he was about eight years old all of a sudden, laughin' and goofin' around between hitters like he owned the damn place. His infield was totally behind him now, seein' what he was like when he was full on and now that he had some confidence in him. After that second he came over to me and he said "now, THAT's what I can do, coach, with this pitch" and I told him to keep doin' it, and brother, he did.

Rube pitched the rest of the game like he was on fire, except of course he wasn't pitchin' smoke, he was more pitchin' soft lard. But he was all pepped up and he started pumpin' his fist a bit when he got them batters out, and that kept on happenin', and happenin' fast, real fast. He got through the third and fourth in twelve pitches each, now that the batters were startin' to lay off just a little, and he ran the count full for the first time in the fifth. But no one had gotten on base yet, and the crowd now started thinkin' that maybe they was seein' somethin' just a bit special, and they started inchin' forward on their seats and not worryin' about the clouds overhead anymore, and after a while they started not carin' that they was losin', though it was still only 1-0 and a single wrong pitch coulda tied it all up, they found themselves startin' to cheer inside for the history, for the no-hitter or the perfect game. And that, of course, started to get on everyone's mind in our dugout, too, and no one mentioned it to Rube and by the fifth inning they weren't even talkin' to him, just lettin' him sit alone in the dugout 'cause no one wanted to be the one to jinx it. Rube understood what was goin' on, and he just sat there, kinda smilin' to himself and I could tell that he was still just so Goddamned happy not to be runnin' the injection molder down at the plant that it wasn't sinkin' in what he was doin' here in his second professional game. He was mowin' 'em down, mowin' everyone down, one after the other, with that unhittable sweetness slidin' out of his hand. But that didn't matter so much to him, I reckon, as it did that he was outside on a day when lots of people he knew were inside, that he was getting paid, not much admittedly, but he was getting paid, to chuck a baseball in a tidy ballpark on a weekday. It almost didn't matter to him what he was doin', what mattered was that he was doin' it.

The Browns' announcer tried his best to jinx things in the sixth, pointin' out how Rube Tyler was *throwin' a perfect game here in the bottom of the sixth* and the last perfect game in the River League had been six years ago by a Red Wings pitcher name of Juice Johnson, who'd gone on to an historic career in double-A, and yes folks, a *Perfect Game* goin' on right here and let's see if he can keep it up through this inning against the Browns' as the bottom of their lineup comes around for a second time.

"Asshole," Brickyard muttered, and I chuckled a bit thinkin' that ol' Rube was kind of a superstitious type, with that glove on his hand, but he didn't seem to get bent outta shape at all by the announcer, he just kept flickin' that ball out of his hand and sendin' it on its merry way, and bein' pleased with the result when it twisted some hitter around in a knot there at the plate. The ump had gotten into it by this point too, makin' big gestures on strike three and lettin' the crowd know that he, too, was pretty damned impressed by what he was seein'.

Sure enough, Rube lost the perfecto that inning, plunking their ninth pitcher on the ear with a ball that wandered just a bit too much after strikin' out the first hitter. The crowd let out a big sigh, kinda happy their guy got on but let down that they weren't gonna see a perfect game.

"Tyler's STILL got a no-hitter goin', though, folks, through six, and it's been two years since Dubuque has gone down without a hit, so let's cheer them on!"

Tyler looked over at us in the dugout and we just looked somewheres else, wonderin' what counted as a jinx and what didn't. I had to admit that I really, really wanted him to get it, wanted him to put a gem of a game into his back pocket here in Dubuque on the road and see what the hell people would make of it when we got back to Keokuk, but I also wanted pretty bad to be careful and to not look like an overeager ass when I had to fill out my scouting report.

Speedy let the next pitch by him, and the runner took second, which seemed to take a bit of the wind out of Rube's sails. Still, two out, man on, up by one, he looked like he was in control more or less and there wasn't nothin' to worry about. The runner was distractin' him, though, and he walked their leadoff hitter on five pitches. I nodded to Brickyard and we wandered out to see what was up.

"Hey, Rube, you're fine, son. Don't even think about those baserunners, just focus on the batter. Get the ball to Speedy, just get it there and let it wander like you've been doin' all game."

Tyler nodded, took a deep breath, and said "Damn, I wish I hadn't hit that first one," and I said "you ain't got time right now to worry about how many men are on," meanin' don't give a shit about the no-hitter or the perfect game, but of course I couldn't say that, "you just gotta worry about the guy at the plate."

He nodded again, fast, and fiddled with the ball for a bit. Brickyard patted him on the ass and said "alright, come on now and get this guy out," and we headed back to the dugout.

"He's a fragile one. We gotta keep his head level when things ain't goin' his way."

"Uh-huh," I said.

"One crack is all it's gonna take with him, I reckon."

Pitchers is funny that way, their moods swing like a weathervane and what's a fine game, a perfecto one minute might be a four run disaster a few pitches later. I've seen that happen all the time, and it was occurrin' to me that we were gonna have to find a way to get some perspective into Rube's pitchin'.

"STRIKE ONE," the ump rang out after Rube danced one past the next hitter. "That's it, Rube," Smokey yelled, breaking two innings of silence. "Strike this weak assed hitter out. He ain't got nothin'."

Rube reared back and heaved the next one and missed just a bit, but the hitter was still wicked late and ended up groundin' to third. Smokey picked it up and tagged the bag, then threw over to Hollocher coverin' second and that was it. He was out of the inning on a beautiful double play.

"ALRIGHT BOYS," Hobie yelled, "Way to play up to your pitcher's level," and we all clapped but still no one said nothin' to Rube even though now he looked a bit tired and he had flop sweat comin' off the back of his cap like a waterfall. I didn't even look over at him, I just clapped and smacked Smokey on the ass and told him that was a nice play and way to work for your pitcher and I reckoned that would do the job for Rube.

Miracle of miracles, Stuffy Flack hit a freak pop fly in the seventh that landed out over the right field fence, and we was up 2-0, and Hobie said "alright, way to get your pitcher some cushion" and then everyone got pretty nervous with the Browns comin' up for the third time through the lineup and wonderin' whether they was gonna figure Rube's pitchin' out or not. As it turned out, they got somethin' on him in terms of timin', but in terms of location he was still all over them and they had nothin', absolutely nothin' to tell them where the hell the ball was gonna be. Two batters chipped a couple of pitches, but they skittered off the bat and back into the stands harmlessly. The third batter in the seventh hit him cleanly, but just a bit too soon, and the ball soared up into the air toward right and everyone watched it goin' out there and Stuffy went runnin' to the wall and waited there to see if he was gonna have to jump or just wait there while it sailed over. That was the first piece of work the outfield had all day, but as it turned out he didn't even have to jump, it just drilled down into his glove in front of him and me and Brickyard just sat there not breathin', and then the crowd let out with some polite applause lettin' Rube know that they wasn't rootin' for him, not yet, but they understood the gravity of the situation, and respected the ass-tearin' he was givin' their beloved Browns ballclub.

"How many times you see that," Hobie shouted as the team came back in. "Gets the home run in the top and makes the star play in the bottom. Way to go, Stuffy." Rube bounded down into the dugout a little sheepish, and he just picked up a bag of sunflower seeds and chucked it toward his right fielder without sayin' a word and Stuffy just grinned back.

Them last two innings only took twenty minutes by the clock, but for me and Brickyard and Hobie and the team and especially Rube they went on for Goddamned hours. He walked two to lead off the eighth, and here go Brickyard and I out to the mound again to see was he alright and he said yeah, sure, he was fine but he had just let his concentration slip just a bit and he'd get back on it. And the next batter popped the first pitch back behind the plate but then he swung at three straight that he didn't come close to hittin, and the last one to him he swung at even while he was duckin' his head tryin' to get out of its way.

The next two batters both went down fast, the first strikin' out but hittin' one long, long foul ball down the right field line that scared the hell out of all of us. Rube came back in and everyone just stayed the hell away from him and I looked over at him and gave him a shrug, like you got somethin' you want to tell me or that we need to talk about? And he looked back and shook me off, just like he'd been shakin' off those bullshit signals from Speedy the whole game. Now he had the whole half bench to himself, seein' as how every one of his teammates was tryin' to stay as far away from him as they could, and as a result they was all over each other like it was a slumber party. But Rube just sat there tuggin' at the end of that stupid work glove on his pitchin' hand, not a single intelligible look on his face and I looked over at Brickyard and I said what do you think, should we get Moose up just in case, and Brickyard reckoned we oughta, but don't let Tyler see that and so I nodded over toward Moose and he slithered out of the dugout and headed out down the right field foul territory to toss a few.

Now we went three and out, too, to start off the ninth, and here it was. Rube was three outs away from makin' a hell of an impression, halvin' that awful ERA and makin' a lot of scouts up and down the River League, and probably up and down the organization, scratch their heads

61

and wonder what the hell was happenin', and how long would it last. I just looked down at the floor as Rube headed out to take the field and the boys they avoided him like he had the stomach flu, and he warmed up with Speedy and here it was, Ladies and Gentlemen, the Westerns are gonna try to no-hit our Browns and let's give them hitters some support!

Rube did look a bit tired by now. He hadn't been throwin' fast, but you could tell he'd been concentratin' pretty hard and that was takin' somethin' out of him mentally if not physically, but just standin' out there for two and a half hours was probably more than his husky frame was used to, too, and so I was just a bit worried about what was going to happen here. He wound up, though, and he slithered one in there and the Browns hitter took a giant swing at it and *crack*, off it went like a shot, but up more than out and Pantyhose Paskert chased it down toward the wall and made the catch. One down.

Speedy went out to the mound before the next hitter came up, and I could see Speedy give Rube a little pep talk, tellin' him to just look at this batter, don't think any bigger than that, just do the small stuff this time. Rube now had that puke look on his face and he looked out at where Paskert had caught that ball and I was thinkin' *a long fly ball is still an out, Rube, right now it's just as good as a strikeout. I don't care how the hell you do it, just get this fucker out.*

Speedy ran back to the plate and Rube thunked the ball in his glove a few times. The crowd gave a sort of half-hearted cheer as the next Browns hitter stepped in. Rube stared him down and I saw that he was sweatin' something good now, even though it was still clammy and pretty cool out.

Nod.

Blink.

Wind up. Throw, flick, and squeeze. This one floated toward the plate movin' all over the map and the Browns' hitter laid off just as it sunk down out of the strike zone. Ball one.

Next pitch. Bounced off the dirt in front of home plate. Ball two. Sweet Lord, here we go. Rube breathed real deep as he caught the throw back from Speedy. Hobie broke ranks and shouted out "COME ON, RUBE, YOU CAN GET HIM!" and everyone looked at him like he'd just crapped his pants in church.

"Shut up, Hobie," Brickyard said, and Hobie just looked out at the field, chewin' on his lip and tryin' not to wet his pants.

Rube's next pitch ended up in the strike zone, and the hitter swung at it but it popped up out of play. 2-1. He looked up at the sky like he was hopin' for some kind of divine intervention.

The Browns' batter got totally fooled on the next pitch, swingin' like hell at it and spinnin' almost all the way around while the ball ended up rollin' across the plate. 2-2.

"Shit," Brickyard said, "I can't take this."

Now Rube bore down and stared at the hitter like he was tryin' to take his lunch from him. The batter stared back, ready to end this *right here, right now. Throw that weak-assed pitch again and let me show you a Goddamned laser show. Sixty-five miles an hour coming in? A hundred and two goin' out. Bring it on.*

Rube wound up and flitted one high. Still high halfway to the plate and not movin', and then all at once, just as the hitter started windin' himself up, it broke huge, without warning, cuttin' down across the plate just half an inch too low. *Smack* and the ball bounced up toward Rube. Gunner came over but not soon enough, and Rube threw his glove up in front of his face, knockin' it down. Hack was comin' in, too, so Smokey headed over to first. Rube reached down for it and winged it over to first, off the line, but not far enough that Smokey couldn't reel it in and reach back to put his foot on the bag. Two out.

"FUCK YEAH!" Hot Rod said from the bench, and the crowd gave a round of polite applause. *One more, Lord, one more. Just let this happen. Let this beautiful thing happen. I'll cut down on beer, I'll stop downloadin' porn, just please please please give Rube Tyler this one thing.*

Speedy ran out to the mound and smacked Rube on the ass and I figured he was tellin' him to just do his job, just float another three pitches where no one could get at 'em, and then he jogged back and it was dead silent in the stands and I reckoned some of them Dubuque fans were thinkin' the same thing as I was, wantin' to see somethin' special from this big lunk out there on the mound with the ghost pitch.

Rube threw a beaut to start things off and the batter just laid back and it went right in the zone. 0-1. Some applause in the stands, some hollerin' on the bench and a big fist pump from Smokey as Rube turned around with the ball.

Pitch two. Low, but hittable, and the hitter tries to tear into it. Total whiff. 0-2. Now Rube steps off the mound walks around a little bit. The whole stadium stands up slowly, not wantin' to discourage their own batters but wantin' this last pitch to go into history, and everyone on the bench starts moving forward, not standin' yet but doin' more than sittin. No one says a Goddamned word.

Rube looks in. He winds up, and he bounces one three feet in front of the plate. 1-2. Brickyard pokes me in the ribs.

"I think that batter was getting ready to swing anyway."

The Announcer says "And now we're going to do it one more time. Rube Tyler and the Keokuk Westerns, one pitch away from a no-hitter, folks!"

Rube chuckles when he hears that, he steps off the mound again and rolls the ball around in his hand a bit. He walks behind the mound, looks out at his fielders, and climbs back up. He shakes his shoulders out, breathes out hard, and stares down Speedy.

Come on, son. Get the job done.

He winds up, and this seems to take minutes. The crowd is standing now, staring down Rube Tyler, forty years old, the oldest pitcher to start a River League game in three decades and in a few seconds maybe, just maybe, the oldest one to throw a no-hitter. The ball leaves Rube's hand, and everyone sees that this one isn't any good, that it's rollin' like hell and cuttin' through the air all wrong. It heads to the plate straight as an arrow and not goin' fast enough, and the Browns' hitter rears back and tags it full strength, and it's a line drive off the sweet spot of the bat headin' to right field and getting there in a hurry. In a split second the entire stadium sucks in its breath, Rube's head whips around to follow the ball, Speedy jumps up out of his crouch, Brickyard and I grab each other around the shoulders and we ain't even got time to say nothin', and at the same time Smokey, who'd been playin' just two steps out of position, dives and sticks his right hand out over his body and he's thinkin' he's gonna knock it down and we hear it hit leather and he crashes to the infield dirt, slidin' an extra foot or so and diggin' up a big cloud, and time just stops for a second as we're all lookin' at Smokey and lookin' for the ball and the Browns' hitter goes flyin' past first and then Smokey's glove comes up out of the dirt and the dust and there's the damn ball, stickin' out of the very top of his glove's webbing, and after a split second we all see the first base ump give him the thumb and we all realize that's it, he's out, and holy shit we won, and holy shit Rube just threw a no-hitter, a fuckin' no-hitter in his second game, and suddenly the bench just explodes and we was all sprintin' across the field and dog pilin' on Smokey and Rube and throwin' all kinds of shit and smackin' each other on the back and rollin' around on the infield grass there and all of the pressure of those last couple of innings just comes pourin' out of everyone, especially Rube.

As we was walkin' back to the dugout, a bunch of kids were lyin' on the roof above us and leanin' over askin' Rube for his autograph. He said "sure" and started signin' just like a big leaguer, except he signed his name real careful for each of 'em, not just a scrawl and a big long line like you do when you do this a hundred times a day. And as he's signin' for the last kid, Speedy comes over and says hey, he's still got the ball

64

from that last out and you want it, Rube? And Rube looks at him and says "sure, give it to me" and Speedy does and then Rube just looks at the kid and steps down toward the dugout and flips the kid the ball. The kid says "holy shit, thanks, Mr. Tyler!" and Rube just beams and shuffles down the steps into the dugout.

"Hell, Rube, that ball might have ended up in the Hall of Fame someday, why'd you just give it to the kid?"

"Cuz' he wanted it. I ain't got no use for it. And I doubt I'd ever see it in the Hall, anyways."

I just patted him on the head and it didn't even occur to me that that was kind of a strange thing to say. We got into the clubhouse and everyone's yellin' like hell and beatin' up on Rube and chantin "NO-NO, NO-NO" over and over again. Someone had run out and got some cheap champagne, and they handed Rube and Speedy a couple of bottles and they got to work sprayin' everyone down and screamin', too. Then someone yelled "SPEECH!" and Rube got pushed up on top of one of the benches. He looked around, pretty uncomfortable, and everyone quieted down.

"Boys," he said, "Thanks for backin' me up. And thanks for lettin' me be part of your team. I know most of you wondered what this old guy was doin' workin' out with you, and I hope I can earn my spot here. And I hope I can pitch like that again."

He choked up a little bit, and then said "And I just want to say, I've been sittin' on my ass for twenty-two years hopin' for a chance to play ball. I don't know if you all realize how lucky all of us are to take home a paycheck for playin' this game, but I love it, and I'm just glad as hell to be playin' it. Especially with all of you. Thanks again, and let's do it one more time in a couple of days."

I pushed my way over to him and gave him a big hug and told him how damned proud I was of him and how I was sure he was gonna pitch like that again real soon, and I wanted to take everyone out for a couple of beers after dinner. And we all went out, to the Tip Top Tap, and got pretty smashed, the whole team, and I didn't give a damn that we had a game the next morning, I bought a couple of rounds and we toasted Rube and the Westerns and the River League and A-League Baseball until they kicked our sorry asses out at two o'clock. As we rolled out of the bar I noticed that Rube was standin' a bit straighter than anyone and I gave him hell about his tolerance level and he allowed as to how he probably had drunk more Old Style in his life than everyone on the team put together, and then as we was walkin' down the highway back to the motel he slapped me on the back and said how he was really grateful for me checkin' out his pitch, that he was havin' the time of his life and the past couple of weeks had meant the world to him.

"Hell, Rube," I said, "Any hurler can shut down Dubuque like that? I'm just glad as hell to have you."

Practice the next mornin' was supposed to start at 10:00, but Hobie and I didn't show up until 11:00, and Brickyard showed up after lunch.

5th Inning

There were copies of the Dubuque *Telegraph Herald* all over the locker room that afternoon, with the headline "Western's Pitcher Shuts Down Browns, Throws No Hitter." The article summed things up real nice:

"Rookie Westerns Pitcher Rube Tyler, pitching for his hometown team for only the second time, displayed an unhittable knuckleball that stifled the Browns' batters for nine complete, hitless innings. Under gathering storm clouds, Tyler's pitches danced, bounced, and curved their way toward home plate, and a handful of walks were as close as Dubuque came to finding the plate themselves all afternoon."

Rube seemed almost embarrassed by the attention, but he took it well, joshin' with his teammates and sayin' he hoped it wasn't a fluke, that he wanted to get out there again and mow some more River Leaguers down. Brickyard said he didn't seem sore at all, they threw a bit during the afternoon and Rube said his arm could go all day, any day, but he just wasn't used to standin' up so long at a time.

Anyway, the Browns got their revenge that afternoon. Without Rube out there we had Hot Rod Barber throwin', and Brickyard allowed as to how he might still be drunk. Again. After two innings Bricky had seen enough and he put Moose out there to mop up as many innings as he could. When we was up at bat Rube sat himself next to Moose and asked all kinds of questions about defense and pitchin' strategy, and in return Moose was askin' him about the knuckleball and how the hell did he throw it and what the hell was his secret, anyway, and Rube showed him a bit but he wasn't givin' everything away and I myself wondered what the hell was up and even though we'd been through his mechanics and everything what he did with his fingers on that ball wasn't something any of us could talk to him about, seein' as how none of us could throw the damned thing.

I did know that he used a two-fingered grip, he held it with his index finger and pinky and as the ball came over his shoulder he started flickin' it out with his two middle fingers. If you timed that just right, you got the velocity from the arm and the flat out lack of spin from the fingers, but coordinatin' those right was damned near impossible. It was too easy to flick it just a split second too early and actually shoot it up out of your fingers, meanin' the ball would arc up and fall down. Or you could flick it *down* by accident and bounce it off the dirt. *And* then there was flickin' it just right so that it didn't spin. That was real easy to screw up, too. Getting all this right, getting the motions and the timin' right, could take a lifetime. Could take, say, twenty years. No one in their right mind had that much patience, and then even once you threw it once, how long would it take you to throw it again? And then how long would it take you to throw it consistently, so that you weren't givin' up a home run every fifth pitch? That's why there ain't more than one or two knucklers who get to the bigs at a time. No one has that much time on their hands. No one but Rube, anyway.

Brickyard and I looked over at Moose and Rube talkin', and Brickyard said somethin' about two guys bein' past their prime but one of 'em pickin up one last moment of glory, and I reckoned that maybe Moose still had time to learn some new tricks, but Brickyard didn't think so and thought Moose had better be lookin' for work at the hardware store the way things were headin' with him. We ended up on the very short end of an11-3 ballgame, though Hack hit his sixth home run of the season which tied him for seventh in the league, which for us wasn't too bad.

So that was the road trip. We finished it 1-5, which put us at 6-12 and at the bottom of the league only a couple of weeks into the damn season. It was a pretty quiet bus ride back to Keokuk, and though Rube had ample reason to celebrate, the other boys on the bus knew they was playin' for a pretty suck-ass team. Rube knew that too, but Rube didn't give a shit. Rube just knew he was playin', that's all. When we got back to the ballpark and was unpackin', Harry Hulbert himself was standin' there, and I said "Hey, Harry, come to see your team back from their big road trip," like it was a normal thing, but he hadn't come out to meet the team back ever and I was wonderin' whether maybe I was gonna get fired or not, and I got real worried when he said "I need to talk with you," nothin' more, just turned around and marched to his office up next to the press box, and I followed with my tail between my legs, since I knew this team stunk to high heaven and I was sure as hell gonna to get blamed for it.

When we got up there Harry sat down behind his desk and I sat in one of the two metal foldin' chairs. He looked at me and said "Who in the hell is Rube Tyler, and how is he pitchin' no hitters for our team?" I explained to him that we'd done everything by the book and that I'd gone through player relations like I was supposed to, and he himself had signed the contract for the three week evaluation, and just as I was startin' to get my back up he looked at me and said that he'd had sixteen calls that day from sportswriters who'd heard that a forty-year old knuckleballer had done somethin' up in Dubuque and did he know

68

anything about it. Sixteen, he said. That was more than he'd had all last season. What was goin' on with this guy?

"He's got himself a hell of a knuckleball," I said. "I reckon he's been workin' on it most of his life."

"Batters can't hit it?" Harry asked.

"Oh, sure, they can hit it. If they can find it, they can hit it a country mile. But it usually ain't where they left it, if you get me," I said.

"You think this is a fluke?" Harry said.

"I don't know. His arm could probably fall off at any minute and it wouldn't surprise me," I said. "He ain't in any kind of shape, and other than throwin' the ball in his backyard I don't think he's taken care of himself real well. I don't know if he'll last the season or not."

"I don't give a sweet Goddamn about the season," Harry said. "Just tell me when his next start is. It was front page news in the *Daily Gate* yesterday and I want to announce his next start so that folks'll buy tickets. He just might be the best hope this team's got of a sellout this season and I want to ride his ass before it gives out, if you get my drift."

"We got a day off tomorrow, then I got Fresh Freddie pitchin' Friday night and I reckon Rube goes Saturday afternoon. That work for your little marketing plan?"

"Hell yes," said Harry. "And you need to be here at eleven tomorrow morning for a real honest-to-God press conference. I got sports writers as far away as Kansas City want to know who the hell this guy is and whether he's the real deal or not."

"I ain't gonna tell them that, but you want me here, I'll be here. What about Rube?"

"You think he's got the presence of mind to speak to the press yet?"

"Nope."

"Then let's keep him a man of mystery. Introduce him after his home debut."

"Alright, then. I'll be here tomorrow."

"In uniform. And shave, Orval."

I did, too, seein' as how I hadn't talked to more than two reporters at a time since the last run the Westerns made at the League championship. I showed up in the freshest uniform I had, all dolled up, and found the clubhouse rearranged into a press room and sure as hell there were eight reporters there, and yes, one of them had driven all the way from KC, and Harry introduced me and said that I was here to talk about the whole team, but he knew they was interested in one player in particular and that I'd tell 'em what I thought of him and then answer any questions.

I cleared my throat. "Well, you all are here because of Rube Tyler's no-hitter the other day. Rube's a local boy, and we're givin' him a three week evaluation on orders from the organization. Rube throws a heckuva good knuckle ball, and I think we're findin' that it's not only competitive, it's a winnin' thing in this League, for sure. Whether that serves him further up the ladder I don't know, but we're gonna see what he does in this couple of weeks and then let the big club's scouts figure out where he fits in the organization best. That's all I have to say, but Harry wants me to answer your questions, so I'll do it."

Harry kinda glared at me, then pointed at a local reporter with his hand up.

"Orval, is it true Rube Tyler's forty years old?

"Yep. Forty's pretty old for a player, especially in A-ball, but everything I've heard says that a knuckleballer can almost throw forever since there ain't as much strain on his joints. Age don't make no difference to me or to the organization if he can strike guys out."

"Where'd you find him?"

"He tried out for us. The organization had heard about him through a local source" which was true but not entirely honest "and asked us to take a look. He tried out for us and we thought his knuckler was somethin' else."

"Can he throw any other pitches?"

"He don't have to."

"Can you explain a knuckleball for our readers?"

Aw, shit. Of course I *can*, but who the hell wants to read that if they don't already know what one is? I gave 'em the basic physics and aerodynamics, and then this idiot asked a follow up question.

"How do you throw one?"

"*You* don't. Rube's been workin' on it his whole life. There are about twelve people alive right now who can throw a decent one."

Then the guy from Kansas City raised his hand.

"What do you think—is he a major league pitcher, or is this just a fluky single-A thing?"

I thought about that one for a minute.

"Son," I said, "I don't know. I ain't seen enough knuckleballers in my day to be able to classify them. But he's the best one I've seen. Ever. Better than Niekro, Wood, even Hoyt Wilhelm. I'll tell you that."

"But given his age, do you think he can pitch at a higher level?"

Higher level than what, where my career had ended up? I wanted to tell him to screw himself, but instead I said "I don't have any idea. But why don't you come to the park Saturday and see for yourself."

"Alright," said Harry. "I think that's answered everyone? Orval's right, don't take his word for it, don't take mine. Anyone who wants to see the River League's best knuckleball pitcher ought to come out to Veterans Stadium this Saturday, game time two o'clock, and see for themselves. Reserved seats $5.00, grandstand $3.00. Everyone got that? This Saturday, two o'clock. Make sure your readers know about that. Plenty of parking. Ice cold beer, too."

So for the first time in a long time, thanks to Harry's ace marketing strategy of goin' along with a good player who'd landed in our lap, the Westerns was a media sensation. The *Daily Gate* published a real nice story on the man of mystery, and they went and dug up his old yearbook photo and ran it on the front of the sports page on Saturday morning, along with the headline "Keokuk Native in Dream Start Today for Westerns."

Now I'd love to say that all this attention led to a mob scene Saturday, but the truth was that it stirred up some mild interest, enough for a sellout but not the clamorin' fans Harry had dreamed of. Most of the folks there were long time fans but there were a few curiosity seekers and some that I reckoned had just seen the paper and had forgotten that the Westerns played ball and it was the season and there were worse ways to spend a Saturday afternoon and hey, let's go get some cheap seats and make up the rest on overpriced beer? Anyway, it was more people than we'd played in front of for a long time and when Rube got to the park he looked pretty well chuffed. Harry had asked whether maybe he oughta get a special introduction or somethin' and I said I thought that was maybe goin' too far, let's see how this game went and then decide whether we oughta hook our marketing wagons to him or not.

It was good to be back in Veterans Memorial Stadium, that's for sure, and the ass-kicking we'd taken on the road, Rube's gem and that one other win excepted, faded as we settled back into our old digs and into the dents on the benches that our asses had worn into the seats. It was a crisp May day, a bit cool still but perfectly clear, and by game time things had warmed up and it was a hell of a day for baseball. The boys enjoyed puttin' on a show during beepee and seein' the seats fill up. I looked over at Brickyard watchin' Rube warm up and I thought he looked just a bit sour, so I jogged on out to see what was up.

"Rube's overthrowin' it," Brickyard said. "He's got great motion, but he's chuckin' it too hard and he can't find the Goddamned plate."

I looked over at him and watched him throw one that sailed over Speedy's head.

"Shit, Rube, what was that, anyway?"

"I dunno, Coach. I can't seem to get 'em where they need to go. I'll get it worked out though."

I stood there for a while watchin', but he wasn't gettin' it worked out. A couple of 'em bounced, one went wide, and another Speedy didn't even get up for.

"Fuck this," I told Brickyard. Tell him to get his act together or he ain't pitchin' for us. I'll scratch him before I let that out on the mound."

I jogged back to the dugout and found Moose.

"You alright to pitch today if Rube seizes up?" I asked him.

"Sure, Coach. Whatever you need."

"Alright. Get out to right field and start throwin' with Solly."

Now I knew that I'd be in deep if Rube Tyler didn't start that afternoon. I knew that Harry would be all up in my face and that folks in the stands would be pissed as hell that they'd paid good money, maybe even five dollars plus four for a cup of warm beer, to see some new sensation, somethin' that would bring them out of their crummy little lives in Keokuk, Iowa, and that all they'd seen was Moose Mays givin' up 13 hits and a couple of three-run homers again. But I had my standards. If a guy couldn't find the plate, there was no Goddamned sense in sending him out there, I reckoned. Screw you, Harry.

The one thing we had goin' for us was that Hannibal was second to last in the league, ahead of us by two games and not lookin' rock solid through their lineup. At least, I thought, we could count on the meat of their order to swing at a lot of pretty bad stuff, and judgin' from what I'd seen there would be plenty of that to swing at. I asked Brickyard what he thought and he said it wasn't goin' to be pretty but Tyler seemed to be getting it together, anyway.

Some four-year-old sang the anthem and forgot most of the words but at least she sang the damn thing straight, and then it was *play ball* and Rube took the mound and threw a few to Speedy before the Giants' leadoff hitter stepped in. Rube reared back, grooved the straightest damned ball I'd ever seen right at 'im, and that ball went flyin' off the bat like it had been fired out of a Goddamned cannon, clear over the right field fence and about halfway across the Mississsippi before it splashed down next to some pontoon boat and a pretty surprised family enjoyin' a Saturday of sunshine and fallin' baseballs. 1-0, Giants.

The crowd looked out at the mound with their jaws agape, wonderin' what the hell had just happened and was *this* the guy, *this* guy out there on the mound with the beer gut and the bad mustache and the coke bottle glasses? *This* guy who'd just thrown the fattest Goddamned cheese ball that'd ever been thrown in Veterans Stadium, a pitch that most of them, even the fat grandmas with control panty hose and a walker, might have thrown in their own backyard? What the hell was goin' on?

"Aw, shit," said Brickyard.

"Shit nothin'," I said. "You said he was gettin' it together, what was that?"

Brickyard jumped up and ran out to the mound. Speedy joined him there and they had a prolonged discussion on the merits of Rube's first pitch. The umpire went out there real quick, wonderin' what the hell they were doin' carryin' on like that one pitch into a long afternoon game.

"You boys ever play this game before?" he asked. "Come on, let's play ball, not just talk about it."

Brickyard came back, grim-faced.

"What's up with him, anyway?" I asked.

"He don't know. Said he just needed a couple of pitches to warm up. Said he was nervous pitchin' here at home. Hell, I don't know."

"Well he'd better get over it," I said. "I'm gonna send Moose out to the pen."

"Mmmm, don't do that just yet," said Brickyard. "I think he might get it together, and if he sees you sendin' Moose out there he's gonna panic."

"What, so now I gotta worry about his self-esteem? Screw that, I ain't gonna sit around too long."

"Just wait," said Brickyard. "I'm getting to recognize good Rube and bad Rube. That's bad Rube out there right now, but if you can live through another couple of pitches, I think good Rube is tryin' like hell to get out."

"Jesus," I said. "I gotta tell you, I fuckin' hate bad Rube."

"Just wait," said Brickyard. "Just wait."

And he was right that the next six pitches were pretty tough to watch. His next pitch sailed behind their second batter, then he finally just gave up and hit him on the ass. Their third batter hooked up with a slightly fadin' straight ball and lined it down the first base line and into foul territory where it took Stuffy Flack just a beat too long to get to it

73

and by the time he did and got the ball back there was runners on second and third, no outs.

Their cleanup hitter whiffed on one pitch, and that got the crowd cheerin' a bit, but then he just crushed the next one clean over the scoreboard in center field, and all three of those Hannibal Giants came trottin' home. 4-0, no outs.

Now the crowd was pretty mad. They couldn't figure out what we had up our sleeves, and I looked up and I could see Harry getting up from his seat in the press box and headin' our way. I looked over at Brickyard and I said "seriously, you gotta tell me right now what the hell is goin' on," and Brickyard said he thought things would be alright but now he was sweatin' just a bit.

"Aw, hell," I said and sauntered out myself. Speedy caught up too and he looked at me all worried.

"Boy, what the hell is wrong with you today?"

Rube looked down at his shoes and scuffed the mound with his foot.

"Have you lost your Goddamned mind? Or can you just not throw the damn knuckler anymore?"

Now Rube looked up, like he was hopin' for some kind of divine intervention.

"I can get it back, Coach. I'm just settlin' in. I was pretty pepped up comin' in here in front of the home crowd and all. Just like that first game. Give me another hitter or two and I'll start layin' 'em out, I swear to God I will."

I crossed my arms and looked at Speedy, who give me a look like he don't know what the hell to do, but he'd be real glad to not have to chase anymore junk in the dirt, that's for sure. I squinted at Rube for a second, then I noticed the ump was walkin' up to us.

"Damn, boys, break it up. Coach, your boy here ain't pitchin' so well, you gonna make a move or stick with him? Because either way you gotta get off my Goddamned field so we can play this game."

I shook my head. "I'm stickin' with him, blue. But Rube, pull your shit together. Now."

I ambled back to the dugout, long enough to give him time to take a big, deep breath and focus his mind. By the time I got to the dugout he was windin' up on the mound, and now he let one fly with some giddyup to it, and the Giants hitter went chasin' after it like he was swattin' at a hummingbird or something.

"STRIKE ONE!"

74

"Now THAT"S more like it, son!" I shouted, and I looked around and saw a few folks in the stand take notice. "Throw another one like that!"

But he didn't. He threw one low and in the dirt. 1-1. Then he threw another one high, but this time it wasn't high 'til it was almost to the plate, and the batter took the bait pretty hard.

"STRIKE TWO!"

Some polite applause in the grandstand. Rube shook himself out, and Brickyard moved forward to the edge of the bench, his jaw workin' a sunflower seed real good. He watched as Rube reared back and nursed the ball into the air, flutterin' and dancin', and the batter just closed his eyes and took a big ol' swing.

"STRIKE THREE!"

"ATTABOY!" shouted Brickyard, and the bench broke out in a nice round of applause. Out in the grandstand folks cheered, though you could tell they was still pissed about the whole 4-0 score with one out in the first. Brickyard started chewin' a hole through his lip, and I figured he was more anticipatin' what was to come at this point than bein' nervous about whether Rube was gonna have a nervous breakdown out there on the mound, so I relaxed just a little bit.

He got out of that inning on two long fly balls and I was startin' to think maybe that was his out pitch. But in between he settled down a little bit. He threw a couple of wild ones but it didn't matter cause there wasn't nobody on, and then sprinkled in between them wild ones were some pretty damn fine pitches that tied those boys up pretty good. He came joggin' back to the dugout with his head hangin' a little bit and I told him to not worry about it, that we'd get 'em back, and all he had to do from here on out was to just throw that crazy shit he threw and not look back.

"I know, coach. Somethin' might be gainin' on me." This boy had him an appreciation for the game's history, I'll tell you that. He flopped down on the bench and everyone went over and bucked him up and told him they was gonna get a whole mess of runs for him to work with. Rube looked tired, but as he pulled on his lucky glove over his right hand he looked focused, too.

"You ended strong, son," I told him.

And I'll be damned if the boys didn't go out there and get him at least a couple of runs, anyway. Hollocher led off with a clean single, and then after Smokey and Hoops struck out, Hack hit himself a beauty of a double, bringin' Hollocher in. Then Gunner popped one down the right field line, only the wind caught it and pushed it around the pole for a homer, so that after Pantyhose struck out we was only down by two.

Now when Rube took the mound he looked like a comedian getting ready to kill the room. He started flippin' them pitches by batters and a few times by Speedy like he was throwin' up butterflies, and those batters just sat there and whiffed away at pitches like they hadn't ever seen before. A couple of his throws got grazed in the second, but they either flew back into the crowd harmlessly or else they drizzled up over the infield where they was easy pickin's for Gunner and Hack. But for the most part he hit a rhythm, and you could hear the ball whizzin' through the air, hear the bat aim for it, and then hear the ball hit Speedy's glove, or the ground, or the ump, or some other part of Speedy, and then usually a soft "sum*bitch*" from the batter as he trudged back to the dugout. And in the background, I am here to tell you, there started to be dead, freakin' silence. Oh, sure, the fans cheered like hell for a strikeout, or a good play in the infield, but once Rube got all settled down he had that crowd in the palm of his knuckleballin' hand. They sat there in awe as they watched their pitcher, their Keokuk Westerns' pitcher, mow down them Giants one after the other.

As I may have mentioned, this was not normal for our fans to see. We had a reputation for wild pitchin', for gopherball pitchin', for the kind of pitchin' where you see the score and go well hell, that wasn't so bad, we only lost by two touchdowns, and then you realize you're lookin' at a Goddamned baseball score, not a football score. Hell, there was one or two seasons I wasn't sure I wasn't seein' a *basketball* score the next mornin' in the sports pages. The Westerns had occasionally lost a game by more than 13 runs, and one season Brickyard and I had a bet on how many teams were gonna bat around on us in a single inning (eleven). The problem was that pitchin' up and down the ladder, even at the big club, had been pretty suck-ass, too, so anytime there was a prospect out there they didn't even bother pitchin' him at Keokuk, they just sent him straight to Peoria, or Carolina. Meanwhile what we *did* get was the chaff that the organization just wanted to park for a season and see how many miracles we could get out of the Iowa cornfields. And the answer was pretty Goddamned few.

We had one pitcher, fellow by the name of Honcho Dinkins, who I swear I knew when he showed up that we should never have even given the boy a second look. He had a lazy eye, and he good as admitted that he saw double, so he was just most of the time guessin' which plate he was throwin' too. But he at least had velocity—he threw damn near 90 miles an hour, which in the River League is all star material, he just threw it to the wrong plate about half the time. We had other guys who didn't have no velocity at all, they might find the plate all the time, every single pitch, but the problem was that they was chuckin' it *right over the plate* at about 72 miles per hour, and it was leavin' the ballpark a whole lot faster than that. Pancake McGrath lasted a whole Goddamned season with us, and I remember callin' the head of player development and sayin' I'd rather have Hobie go out there and chuck gopherballs, since Hobie at least I could count on to have his fly zipped. And then of course we'd picked up Hot Rod, and Moose, and those guys were our rock solid starters the last season even though Hot Rod was drunk half the games and hung over the other half.

So yes, boy howdy, our fans had suffered through some ferociously bad pitchin', and they'd seen all kinds of crap, but what they hadn't seen, what they'd never witnessed in Veterans Memorial stadium, was a knuckleballer, at least not one like this. They had seen wild pitches, and they had seen slow pitches, but they had never seen those together, and they had never seen those together makin' the kind of poetry and art that Rube Tyler was out there makin' right now. They had never seen much good pitchin' *period* at Veterans, and they had certainly never seen someone scare the piss out of River League hitters like Rube was startin' to. He set 'em up and laid 'em out again in the third, strikin' out all three, the last two lookin' when they just gave up and stood there hopin' for a ball, and those pitches just magically broke over the plate at the last second. Suddenly, Rube had his shit together, friends, and he was throwin' like a physics wizard out there. His pitches were clockin' a good 65 miles per hour, but just like in practice they were doin' that lazy speed goin' in all kinds of directions, and by the fifth inning the score was still 4-2 and the Giants hadn't had a baserunner since the first. Four more perfect innings, and now the crowd was goin' nuts, but only when someone got out. In between there was hushed silence, like they was in a church instead of a ballpark, and they just sat there and tried to figure out how they was supposed to respond to a Keokuk Westerns pitcher that could play the Goddamned game.

"Hey, Rube," said Hack, "nice of you to give up all them runs so's we can talk to you this game."

Rube just smiled. "Yup," he said, "I got kinda lonely that last game. You gotta do your job now, though, Hack, get me some of them runs."

"I ain't gonna waste no good hits if you're just gonna give up another couple of taters in the ninth."

"Don't worry about that. I got 'em baffled now." Rube coughed a little and hacked up a big looger. Hack just leaned back and laughed.

"I reckon you do, Rube, I reckon you do."

Hack didn't hit no home runs that day, but Hoops did, with a man on, to tie things up in the sixth. Rube had given up two lucky hits in the top, but neither of them boys came home. In the seventh, he got a little sloppy, and after he walked two I went out there with Brickyard to talk him down. Brickyard told him to just breathe, Goddamnit, and he slowed down a bit and then mowed down three in a row. The crowd went completely fuckin' nuts at that point, 'cuz what they liked most wasn't just perfect pitchin', they liked a guy who could work out of them jams that our boys always seemed to be gettin' into. They maybe thought Rube was getting off too easy when he was on fire, but when he could let it out a bit, and then pull it back in with that magic, that's what that crowd liked best.

Rube was breathin' pretty heavy when he came in after the seventh and I wondered should I take him out, after all this was gonna be his third complete game in eight days otherwise, but Brickyard reckoned he'd be fine. That's the beauty of the knuckler, is that you don't stress your arm none and hell, you could probably go two days in a row. But if you were getting that good action and didn't have to go to any relievers, then your whole bullpen got a day off, and that was just fine with me 'cuz Moose wasn't exactly the guy I wanted to see out there.

In the eighth Rube just set 'em up and mowed 'em down, one-two-three, on just thirteen pitches. I don't know why the Giants were swingin' so hard at him, but they were, and they were just cold. None of them bats even touched the ball until the third batter got a piece of it before it ended up in Speedy's glove on the third strike. We all gave him a standin' ovation as he came off the field after that, and Buddy up in the announcer's booth broke all sense of decorum and neutrality and shouted "WESTERN'S PITCHER RUBE TYLER STRIKES OUT THE SIDE! LADIES AND GENTLEMEN, RUBE TYLER!" The crowd gave him a pretty good cheer too, and he bounded off the field with a big ol' smile on his face and a spring in his step. There was no way I was takin' him out after that, believe me.

We put together a hell of a rally in the bottom of the eighth against their bullpen. Somethin' in Rube's confidence, and in the big damn rest our boys was gettin' in the field, had relaxed our hitters, and we had the heart of our order up and damned if they didn't pepper those Giants hurlers with everything they could muster. Smokey started off with a double, followed by a clean single by Hack that brought him in after a close play at the plate. Then Pantyhose hit his first tater of the season, bringin' in Hack. Speedy popped out, and Ee-Yah walked and stole a base, then Stuffy bounced one off the River Motors sign out in right field scorin' him and we was up 6-4. By this point the whole crowd was on its feet, the boys on the bench was goin' crazy poundin' the roof of the dugout, and Hobie and I were sittin' back enjoyin' the show, givin' boys the green light to swing away, to steal, to do whatever the hell they felt like doin', cuz we felt like we had this in the bag with Rube finishin' up in the ninth. Gunner finally struck out and Smokey grounded out to finish the inning, but up four runs felt pretty good.

Now Rube was all riled up and ready to just go out and win this game on one pitch, though, and Brickyard tried to settle him down but it didn't work, and sure enough he just grooved that first pitch in the ninth and *pow* out it went straight as hell over the centerfield scoreboard and I reckon it was still goin' up when it cleared the wall. Our boys out in the field watched it go and you could hear the crowd suck in their breath and wonder whether maybe we was gonna blow this after all. I sent Brickyard out to see what the hell that was all about and he came back chucklin', sayin' that Rube said he was just goofin' around and Brickyard told him don't you do that again, but really he said he'd just gotten too hepped up and he'd settle down.

"You're like a Goddamned horse whisperer with that boy," I said.

"Well, mostly a pitchin' coach has gotta be a psychiatrist, I reckon," Brickyard said.

And Brickyard was right. I didn't understand pitchers one bit. Of course, I didn't understand any of these Goddamned snowflakes, sayin' they couldn't hit for shit because their feelings had been hurt by somethin' or other, I never knew what the hell to say to 'em. But Brickyard he took the time and had the patience to talk these boys out of whatever was buggin' them, even while my eyes were poppin' out of their sockets gettin' all pissed off. And I had to admit, I sure as hell didn't understand Rube. I mean, I felt for him, and I wanted him to do well, and I wanted to be supportive and mostly I wanted him to win twenty games for us. But he sure as hell was fragile, and these bedwettin' moments out there on the mound were startin' to piss me off just a bit.

"What was really botherin' him?" I asked.

"You don't wanna know," said Brickyard.

"Bullshit I don't," I said. I gotta make a report on this guy at the end of this game, I thought. I damn well better know what's up with him.

Brickyard chuckled. "He said he had to pee. He forgot to take a piss while he was watchin' our boys rally."

"Get the fuck out," I said.

"No, seriously, I think he might piss his pants out there."

I looked out and Rube was sure enough holdin' his legs together just a little.

"Well what in hell did you tell him?"

"I told him it sure would be funny if he couldn't hold it, but I didn't reckon we could stop the game so he could take a leak."

I shook my head. "We gotta tell this guy when to go to the bathroom?" I said.

"I don't know," said Brickyard.

Rube reared back and hurled the next pitch. The batter swung and fouled it off.

"Get Moose up," I said. "If Rube's gotta come out of the game to take a leak, we're gonna need him in."

Rube got another strike. He wasn't sufferin' just yet, but boy he was distracted. I couldn't decide whether that was good or bad.

Brickyard let me know what he thought. "I think if he ain't concentratin' too hard it might help him," he said. "I think his problem is that he's thinkin' too much sometimes."

Alright, I said, but these people didn't pay five bucks a seat to watch a grown man piss his pants. We gotta find some other way to take care of that.

Rube got himself a strikeout and looked pleadingly over in our direction. I started off the bench but Brickyard held me back.

Rube looked up at the heavens and then I swear he took just a bit off the next one, makin' it break just enough so that the batter tipped it, but not enough that he'd miss. The ball shot straight up, a real cloud buster, and then plummeted down right on top of the base, droppin' right into Speedy's glove.

"TWO AWAY!" Buddy shouted over the P.A. Now the crowd stood up, cheerin' slowly but buildin' up in enthusiasm. Rube didn't take much time between pitches, and now he just stood back and chucked it, and the Giants hitter took a huge cut and drove it right into the ground. It bounced over Rube's head and Ee-Yah picked it up and tossed it over to Hack for the third out.

"WESTERNS WIN!" yelled Buddy, "RUBE TYLER PITCHES A GEM IN HIS VETERANS STADIUM DEB-YOOOOO! WESTERNS WIN!"

The team all headed for Rube but he just sprinted off the field, past me and Brickyard, who was doubled over laughin', and he ran into the clubhouse and took that whiz that had been buildin' up for a couple of innings. Meanwhile the crowd was going apeshit, wonderin' what the hell he was doin', and demandin' a curtain call.

"Better hurry up back there," yelled Brickyard. The team was standin' at the top of the dugout now waitin' for him, and I joined 'em, and after what seemed like ten minutes of the crowd chantin' "WE WANT RUBE" over and over he finally came out, pullin' up his pants

80

as he came out, a big ol' dribble down his left leg, and then he put Brickyard in a headlock and the two of them ran up through the assembled Westerns and out onto the field and there was the loudest cheer I've ever heard from our fans and he tipped his cap and gave Brickyard a playful punch in the nose and then the two of them came down and we all went into the clubhouse and celebrated another patented Rube Tyler come from behind victory.

While we're sittin' around in our jock straps, Harry comes in and tells us that there's a reporter there from the Quad Cities and he's got a TV news crew with him. I tell him he's full of it, but he says no, he's serious, and can Tyler and I come out and talk. I tell him "not like this, not in our jocks we cain't," and he says "well get dressed then and get out to the field. Tell Rube to put his warmup jersey on instead of that…suit."

So Cal and I go out and there's the guy, a young guy with a shirt and tie and everything, and sure as hell he's got a camera crew there. Now, even when we won the River League six years ago we didn't get no TV coverage, so this is a new thing for me, first time probably since I was coachin' third base up at Des Moines that I've even been on TV. Rube and I walk out, and he says "This is crazy. This is absolutely crazy. Two weeks ago I was sittin' on my ass at the plastics factory…"

"And you're still sittin' on your ass, just for a crappy single-A team. Remember that. You don't want this to be your peak, son."

Then the reporter was all over us.

"Hi, Rube, Zed Bechamel, Channel 7 News, Rock Island. Can you tell us a bit about this pitch that seems to have your league's hitter so confused?"

"It's just a knuckleball. Just something I've been workin' on for a few years and it finally seemed to come right.""Can you tell me how you throw it?"

"No."

Zed pauses. He looks at his cameraman, and then he breaks character for a second.

"Uh, Rube, it'd be real nice if you'd play along here."

"Sorry. I spent more than half my life figurin' it out. Got my secrets."

Another pause. I can't help but chuckle a bit.

"Uh. OK." Zed gets his face back on. "So we're here with rookie pitcher Rube Tyler, who's off to an historic start in the River League with his mysterious knuckleball. Rube, what's goin' through your mind when you're out on the mound facing hitters half your age?"

"I'm mostly tryin' not to puke."

Zed lets the microphone drop down to his waist. He stares at Rube, pleadin' with his eyes, sayin' *I am twenty-one years old, and I'm workin' for a crappy TV news station, and I've driven 90 minutes to Keokuk to try to get one Goddamned quote from you for the feel-good story on our sports minute. Will you please play ball and act like a professional athlete who's actually interested in media attention...*

"Naw, Zed. What I'm thinkin' is tryin' to align the energy fields out around the mound, tryin' to get them workin' on the ball in just the right way so that sucker goes dancin' over the plate. I'm communing with native American spirits, and with an old Zen master of mine, and with whatever else I can find out there that might help the ball in its psychic journey toward the plate."

Zed is squeezin' his eyes shut now, shakin' his head, ready to just up and quit.

"OK, and what's it like havin' so much success in the first week or two of your professional career?"

"It doesn't suck too much, I'll tell you that."

Now I'm tryin' like hell not to bust a gut, and then Zed asks me a question.

"Now, Mr. Sheckard, you've had a long career coachin' and managin' in the minor leagues. Have you ever seen anything quite like this?"

I decide to cut the kid a break and give him the full on slab of coachin' quotes:

"No, Zed, I have not. Rube here is throwin' some unhittable stuff, and he's got some work to do, but this is what effort and concentration can do for a player. What I've been seein' out here is one of the best knuckleballs I think the game's ever seen, and I reckon folks oughta get out to Veterans Stadium to see Rube Tyler throw before he gets moved up in the organization, which I reckon's gonna happen if he gets another game or two like this in."

There. That oughta make Harry happy, too.

"OK, thanks Orval Sheckard, manager of the Keokuk Westerns, and Rube Tyler, rookie knuckleball pitcher and part time comedian. Folks, the Westerns are just starting an eight game homestand, and we understand Tyler should be pitchin' again against their big rivals the Burlington Bees this coming Wednesday night, game time is 6:30 and tickets are just $5.00. Zed Bechamel, Channel 7 Sports."

I held out my hand to thank him, and Zed said "Right. Good luck to you both," and glared at Rube as he packed his stuff up. That night I took Rube out to the Frog in the Hole and we knocked back quite a few. He asked me if I meant what I said about movin' up, and I said I had, and he said he hadn't ever lived outside Keokuk before.

"Well, son, I wouldn't pack my bags just yet. But my guess is you'll be in Peoria in another couple of weeks."

"I ain't ever even been to Peoria," he said."Well pitch good there," I said, "cause it's a shithole and you'll want to move along pretty quick."

Rube laughed. I asked him why he'd given that TV guy such a hard time and he said "Aw, I was just playing. It was just me havin' fun."

"Well, Rube, you get up another level or two, you're going to have to put on a TV face every now and then. You gotta think about how the public sees you once you start movin' up."

"I don't care about that, Coach," he said. "I just want to get out there and throw that sweet-assed knuckler again."

6th Inning

SCOUTING REPORT

Player:	Tyler, Rube
Age:	40 (this is not a typo)
Height:	6'-1"
Weight:	230
Position:	Pitcher
B/T:	None/Right
Acquired:	Evaluation contract, Keokuk Westerns.
Comments:	Rube Tyler has pitched three games and has shown a very fine knuckleball in each. He has shown some control problems early, but when he is on top of his game his knuckleball is almost unhittable. Speed is in the mid-60s at its best, but the motion is better than any knuckler I've ever seen. No hitting ability, no fielding ability, but these may not be important compared to his ability to confuse and strike out batters. Needs to work out more, watch diet to avoid fatigue.
Recommend:	2-3 more games at this level then promotion to regular Single A.

I faxed Rube's scouting report to the big club in Chicago, and I reckon I had to look up the number on account of not having had anyone near good enough to tell them about in a few years. About two hours after I sent it through I had the assistant general manager for player development, Freddy Birdsfoot, on the phone yellin' at me like I'd shot his dog.

"The hell you sendin' us a report on a 40 year old lunk of fat like this guy," he said. "The fuck we want with this?"

"Well, Freddy, I gotta tell you. Age, build, and reputation aside, what we're seein' out of Rube is, in my opinion, a major league knuckler.

I don't pretend that he's a Cy Young winner, but I also don't think anyone in the show can hit his shit."

"Where the hell did we find him, anyway? And how the hell did he get an evaluation contract with us?"

I politely explained that he himself had signed the damn thing, and that maybe, just maybe, Rube's age had been transposed—say someone had maybe turned "40" into "20" by mistake—these things can happen, Freddy, my typin' ain't shit. He's a local boy, I told him, workin' in the plant down here and I just saw him throw and thought maybe he could help us out with beepee, and then the scout who came to look at Moose and Hot Rod, he…

"Bullshit. I don't know what the hell you got up your sleeve, but we ain't spendin' any money on this prick. I got a scout in the area and I want him to see what we got down there in Keokuk this week. Can you throw…uh…who's this…Barber and Bush sometime mid-week?"

"Sure I can," I said, "but let me throw Tyler, too. Just for fun. Let's see what your overpaid scout thinks of his knuckleball and my judgment."

"Throw whatever you want," Freddy said, "Just let him see whatever sorry-assed pitchin' you got down there too, in addition to this hobo knuckler."

I didn't tell Rube about that call, or my scouting report, and in fact I didn't tell Brickyard or Hobie, neither. I just said I'd been cautious, measured my words and didn't try to get the big club's hopes up and didn't want to get Rube in over his head too soon. Besides, it was early May, and if things didn't work out, I sure as hell wanted this knuckleball on my team later in the season when our relievers' arms started crappin' out.

We had one more game against the Giants, and we won that one, too. But then the Bees came into town, and their lineup had some serious hitters to deal with. Their leadoff hitter, Flamethrower McGee, was hittin' .415 and had stolen 12 bases already. They didn't have much in the two and three spots, but then they had a new outfielder, Mugs Standish, who had clobbered 10 home runs in the cleanup spot in addition to hittin' in the high .380s. He looked like he wasn't long for the River League, but the Bees were the bottom rung on St. Louis' roster, and they looked pretty solid all the way up in the field. So we reckoned we was probably stuck with this guy long term. Burlington is right up the river from us, so there was what passed for a rivalry, but their manager, Tug Johnson, and I were good friends and we'd coached together up in the Dakota League years ago and I always looked forward to getting together with him and sharin' old stories and drinkin' a few.

They got into town Monday mornin', and I saw ol' Tug right before they started noon practice on our field. He came over to our dugout and asked how the hell I was and how was our season goin', and then he said he meant beside the team's record.

"Screw you, Tug," I said. "We're better than our record looks."

"Shoot, everyone's better than their record," Tug said.

I shook his hand and we chewed the fat for a while standing outside our dugout watchin' his boys go to work.

"Your boy McGee looks pretty sharp."

"Yup, he's runnin' like hell. Good to have some speed up front."

"I reckon. Wish we had some of that."

"Who you got leadin' off?"

"Goin' back and forth between Hollocher and Flack."

"Flack...that douchebag? The hell is he still doin' on your team?"

"Piddlin' down the line to first is what he's usually doin'."

"Ha! Well, I hear you've got yourself a hell of a knuckleballer. Where in hell did you find him?"

"Out on route 212. He's somethin' to watch, I can tell you that."

"I don't remember this league havin' a queerball pitcher ever before. I see nobody's been hittin' him."

"Nobody's been hittin' him real good, anyway," I says. "He's got some good motion, but he sometimes has some control issues. Fragile, too."

"That's the way them boys are. Alright, Orval, I gotta go get these boys goin'. We goin' out for beers tonight?"

"Hell, yes. Me and Hobie are lookin' forward to it. I want to know some things about that McGee boy of yours...like what kind of pitches he can't hit."

"Well, you'll have to buy me more than a few rounds before I tell you that, Orval, but I look forward to it."

Sure enough, Flamethrower McGee went 4 for 4 that afternoon, and their boy Mugs brought him in three times, twice on towering home runs that made the considerably smaller Veterans crowd gasp in amazement. They also scored a couple on some pepper ball they hit off of Freddie Fresh, and a solo shot in the eighth by their shortstop. So that was eight for them. Now, we got ourselves a couple of runs in the second, on account of Hack got hit by a pitch in the ass and Smokey bunted him over and managed to beat the throw out anyway. Pantyhose hit a lucky single that brought 'em both home. But those were the only two runs we scored all afternoon, despite Hobie pitchin' a hissy fit after we went one-two-three in the fifth and yellin' at them boys that if we went three and out again we was gonna have a 7 A.M. practice and we'd hit beepee till game time if we had to, Goddamnit.

Brickyard had a date that night so it was just me and Hobie meetin' Tug at the Frog in the Hole, Keokuk's finest. The Frog's been there since long before my tenure in the River League, and it's a bit of a rough place unless you know the management and are willing to occasionally give out some free seats to the patrons. Me and Tug had been catchin' up there since my first season with the Westerns, and that night we sat at the old wood table and took in the smells and sounds of a mostly empty bar. Now, neither of us exactly fit in—I didn't have no leather jacket and I showed up in my Plymouth, not on a Harley. But the bar gals there know me, and they're willin' to flirt with me in exchange for a few extra bucks tip at the end of the evening. And they're real good about keepin' your glass full and besides, they're young and they wear real tight t-shirts and shorts in the summer and I like that. A lot. So the Frog is my evenin' office, and it's where I take visitin' dignitaries and VIPs like Tug. I buy the first pitcher and we both thank the waitress when she drops it off.

"Thanks, honey, I've been lookin' forward to this since the second inning tonight."

"You're welcome, Orval. Your boys win?"

"Hell, no. Sweetie, this here's Tug, he's the manager of the Bees and his team just kicked our asses tonight."

They exchange hellos and Tug tries but fails to maintain eye contact.

"Alright, boys," she says. "Y'all enjoy your beers and you let me know when you need another pitcher of suds."

"Yes, ma'am," I say as she saunters back to the bar. Tug and I don't say anything until she's all the way back.

"Well, Goddamn, Tug," I break the silence, "that was a hell of a shitstorm your boys hit off us today."

"It's startin' to look like a good year for us, I guess. You shoulda pulled your pitcher sooner, I reckon."

"Hell, you ain't seen much of our relief this year," I said.

Tug just smiled, starin' into his beer. He waited a couple of minutes and then cut to the chase.

"How long you gonna keep doin' this, Orval," he asked.

"Hell, I don't know. Till they pull the cleats off my cold, dead body, I hope."

Tug smirked.

"Why, how long you gonna do this?"

"Not much more, Orval, not much more."

"What? You got your team right where you want 'em...you're lookin' good for the championship this year. And hell, I hear they might open up that job in Palm Beach. That'd be pretty damn sweet, you ask me. Good place to finish up your career there if you could get promoted."

Tug put his beer down on the table. "I'm sick, Orval. Cancer."

"Oh, damn, I'm sorry, Tug. Damn." I didn't know what to say. Tug and me had been tight for so long and we'd raised hell for so long this was somethin' completely out of the blue.

"How bad?"

"Not bad at all. Not now, anyway. But when I found out I started thinkin' about what time I got left and how I want to spend it. I got grandkids now, Orval, and I don't see 'em at all during the summer."

I reckoned I understood that. I'd been married to the game for so long that kids and grandkids never figured into my old age plans. And neither did the weak-assed pension I was gonna get when I finally hung 'em up.

"I found some land up in Wisconsin, Orval, and I reckon after this season I'm done. I'm gonna go build me a cabin and Doris and I are gonna move up there and we're gonna just set and get to know each other again and then the grandkids are gonna come up all summer and we're gonna teach 'em how to fish, pitch, and bunt and all that shit grandfathers are supposed to do. All that assumin' I ain't dyin' anytime soon. You oughta come up and help us build it. Give you a chance to build something real."

I told him I'd come see him and we'd fish some in the offseason.

"You ain't thought of retirin' Orval? Ever?"

"Well I guess when I start pissin' my pants in the dugout I'll probably call it quits, Tug," I said. "But I ain't got the savings you do, and I ain't got family. I got ball, and I reckon once someone takes this away from me I'll just curl up and kick up my heels."

Tug smiled and reckoned for all we had in common there was a lot that we had different, too.

"You want to end your career here?" he said.

"No, but I probably will. This team ain't gettin' no better anytime soon and the teams up the ladder all have good managers. Besides, I don't think the big club sees me as a big league manager in trainin'."

It was a long story, but I'd had my chance. I'd been bench coachin' down in Daytona and got the call to AAA back in my late 30s. They were groomin' me, and if I'd played my cards right I probably woulda spent a year or two there and then maybe managed West

Tennessee or somethin', and maybe just maybe woulda made it back to AAA as a manager. The club saw potential in what I was doin' with the players and I could see my way clear to gettin' that managers job, or maybe even coachin' up in Chicago. I flew up there to talk with them twice and they was real friendly and said they were gonna save a place for me.

But that was before that bench clearin' brawl in Des Moines against Nashville. Their pitcher had beaned our guy, right in the head, and we'd all run out lookin' for payback. Our guy was out like a light, so he didn't have the wherewithal to charge the mound, but our first baseman blindsided their pitcher with a good left hook and I'd been the first one out there, and instead of pullin' our guy off I whaled away at that asshole, too, and got a few good shots in.

Now, the reality of baseball fights is that punches almost never get thrown. Everyone goes out and stands around and looks at their team sayin' "Hold me back, don't let me get 'em," and nothin'—*nothin'*—never happens. And if it does, most of the players and coaches are out there to pull people apart, 'cuz it doesn't take much to break a finger in your glove hand, and then you're out for a few weeks. Baseball fights are like strip clubs: all show, no action. Except this time, I was pissed. That series had been full of beanballs, but if you're gonna hit a guy, hit him on the ass, or if you really want it to hurt, hit him on the wrists, or the elbow. You do not throw at a player's head. You. Do. Not. So I was out of my mind by that point. I'll be honest, I wanted to hurt the guy. I wanted to teach him a lesson. I wanted to fuck him up and teach him some respect for the unwritten rules of the game. Unfortunately for me, I did. I did fuck him up. I busted his jaw, and while that might have got me laid if it had been a bar fight, what it really got me, since it was in a professional baseball stadium, was suspended. And then busted down to A ball.

So, did I want to spend the rest of my career at Keokuk? No, but I'd spent the last twenty years in Danville, and Huntington, and Santo Domingo. I'd lived in Ogden, Utah for two months, in San Jose, California, for three. I didn't stay hired by Eugene long enough to do a single load of laundry, and then I spent a whole season living in a Motel 6 in Burlington, Vermont. In other words, I paid for my crime. But by the time the Cubs hired me back to manage the lowest team on their farm, in greater metropolitan Keokuk, Iowa, I was well over the age limit for promising managerial material. I was lucky to have picked up this job, and probably only got it because most of the big names in the organization hadn't been around long enough to remember the photo of Orval Sheckard cold cockin' that young pitcher—a pitcher who went on,

89

by the way, to throw a season and a half in the show while I was doin' time shaggin' flies and carryin' bats for the Myrtle Beach Pelicans.

"I don't know what other option I got, Tug," I said. "Short of a life changin' experience like you're describin', I guess I'll probably stay here as long as they'll pay me, and by then I'll have paid off the mobile home and I'll probably just stick around where the beers are cold and the welcome's warm." I nodded over to our bar girl.

Tug said he reckoned he understood. Baseball was all I had, all I wanted, and once it was gone I would be, too.

"How old's that queerball pitcher of yours?" he asked.

"Forty." I said, and I didn't have to add that I knew full well Rube Tyler was exactly the age I'd been when I'd thrown my career away with that punch. And here he was just startin'.

"Shit," said Tug. "I hear he's got a better knuckler than Niekro. That true?"

I was past the point of puttin' Tug on, so I gave him my honest assessment.

"Hell, yes."

"Hm," he smirked. "I guess there's some surprises down here in River League ball after all. I don't want to watch my hitters face him, but I damn sure want to see him pitch."

"Day after tomorrow, Tug, I promise you'll see somethin' you'll remember."

That next night we threw Preacher Bush against them Burlington boys and he did alright. He shut down Mugs pretty good, walked him once but painted the corners on him and didn't let him put any good wood on the ball. Chicago had that scout down and I reckon they liked what they saw, seein' as how they stuck around the whole game and had the radar gun on him the whole damn time. The Bees still managed to score two playin' small ball, but our boys kept playin' large ball, and Smokey hit two home runs, one of 'em with a man on, and that was all we needed, though Hack also hit a dinger and we got a couple of garbage runs in the ninth. I warmed up Rube before the game and asked him how he was doin', and was he nervous like he was the last game and he told me no, he was pretty level-headed and he was a bit worried about that Standish kid but not enough to lose his cool.

Still, when practice time came around before Wednesday night's game, there was ol' Rube in the men's room with the squirts somethin' fierce, and I asked him was he alright and he said sure, fine, just somethin' he ate. I told him I didn't want him crappin' his uniform on the mound, especially with them scouts out there, and he sorta groaned and I just got the hell outta there. Anyway, he was fine through

90

afternoon practice and he didn't eat much for dinner and then when he got out to throw to warm up before the game he seemed alright to me.

Before the game the scout came down to say howdy. "Who the hell is this you're throwin' tonight?" he said.

"Aw, this is the man of mystery your boss was so het up about. I want you to see this guy," I said. "He may not even register on your gun his pitches are so damned slow, but I reckon you'll be pretty damned impressed."

"Sez you," he shot back at me. "If I take off after the first inning I can be back in Chicago by midnight."

"Tell you what," I said. "You stick around as long as Rube's winnin' this game, and at the end I'll buy you a pitcher of cold beer and take you out to that white trash strip club across the river."

"Aw, hell. You're on, Orval," he said.

It was a warm night that night, with a slow breeze blowin' out toward the river and the smell of fresh dirt blowin' in from the fields west of town. Things was startin' to grow in them fields, whether farmers was ready or not, and everything had a fresh green fuzz on it like it all knew what was comin'. Brickyard warmed Rube up and then as the anthem was playin' I looked over at him and I saw a man focused on the next two and a half hours, and his destiny, all at the same time. That scout in the stands held on to his immediate future, and he knew it, and he knew that his whole life revolved around what he did in the next couple of hours. Hell, maybe in the next few minutes. When the ump called 'em out onto the field, he didn't run, he walked, nice and slow, out to the mound, took the throw from Speedy, and set to work.

Now, I'd like to tell you that Rube threw another no-hitter, maybe even a perfect game, or at least a shutout. He didn't, but he came damned close. What he threw was an outstanding game, where he was in command the entire time, where the batters was back on their heels for every pitch not knowin' where to swing, or whether to swing, and by the end of it forgettin' how to swing. Rube's pitches danced in that warm, fertile air that night like some kind of natural phenomena, like the northern lights, or like storm clouds, or jumpin' beans. They moved with an order that exceeded all of our abilities to understand it, but with an order nonetheless, one that Rube was in touch with, and no one else on that field that night could have been. He laid 'em out in the first, the second, and the third, got through the whole damn lineup on 32 pitches, striking out five of 'em. The crowd cheered him on, willin' him to throw that stuff that no one could hit and that precious few could follow. For most of 'em, Rube might as well have been throwin' paper airplanes, for all they understood about aerodynamics and physics and the laws of

91

Brownian motion. But they loved watchin' them Bees swing and miss, and they loved watchin' 'em strike out even more, and by the end of the third they was on their feet screamin' at Rube to strike that last man out, and sure as hell he did, a big giant upward *whoomph* of a pitch that the batter came all the way around on before he realized he'd missed it in all three dimensions plus he'd been way early, makin' it all four.

I looked across at Tug as Rube came out to start the fourth, and he looked back at me and mouthed "*ho-lee shit,*" and I just laughed and crossed my arms and spat on the dugout floor. Goddamn this game could be fun sometimes, especially if you was winnin', which we were by that point on account of a double by Stuffy Flack that turned into a run when Speedy singled him home in the third. As Rube was warmin' up I took a few steps out onto the field to see if I could find that scout, and there he was in the front row right behind home plate, he looked like he was smackin' his radar gun on the side not believin' what it was sayin' and his jaw was about an inch off the rail in front of him, disbelievin' but also droolin' with the prospect of Rube's unhittable knuckler against big league hitters.

To the extent that they did, things fell apart for Rube a bit in the fourth. Flamethrower bunted his way on, a total fluke and I swear he just closed his damned eyes and threw the bat through the strike zone. The ball came right back at Rube and he muffed the pickup but threw to first anyway. Hack barely grabbed it out of the air but it was too late and his foot came off the damned bag anyway. The Scout picked his jaw back up after that play, for sure. Rube got flustered by that just a bit, and their second batter just laid off everything he threw, ran the count full and then he just laid back, closed his eyes and thought of Kansas, and took his chances that Rube's next pitch would be in the dirt, or behind him, or over his head, and he just happened to be right. Two on, no outs. Brickyard jogged out there and gave him a swat on the ass and told him to just pull himself together, and he got the next guy out on three pitches, all of 'em swingin' strikes and none of 'em anywhere near the strike zone, one of 'em in the dirt four feet in front of home plate even as the batter was followin' through.

Now you can fool some of the people all of the time, and all of the people some of the time, but you cannot fool Mugs Standish all of the time, and as he stood in Rube stared him down and growled a little bit. I got you once, sucker, he seemed to be sayin', and I'm gonna get you again. But he didn't. Mugs laid back an extra half second, took a wild guess where the ball was gonna be at that exact moment, and went for broke. As I said, with that knuckleball, a guess is as good as thinkin' you know, and one time out of maybe a hundred you're gonna be right enough, and this, folks, was one time out of a thousand, because Mugs hit the crap out of that ball, caught every single last ounce of it, and sent it so damned far over the right field wall that I reckon it might have hit Indiana. *BAM!* Poor Stuffy didn't even run after it, he just watched it go up and up and up, over his head and I swear it was still climbin', just tracin' out a laser shot line up into the sky and maybe just maybe into the great beyond.

"Holy fuckin' shit," said Brickyard as Mugs started around the bases.

"3-1," I said. "And with the Chicago scout here, too."

I looked across the way at Tug, who was leanin' over the rail laughin' his ass off.

So technically I didn't owe that scout a night at the titty bar anymore, and he coulda got up and left and probably Freddy Birdsfoot woulda been totally happy, probably happier, even, than what ended up happenin'. Because what ended up happenin' was that Brickyard went out again, asked Rube was he OK and Rube said "hell, yes, that was the luckiest damn swing in League history," and Rube went on to strike the next two Bees out. On six pitches. And the scout might have been packin' up, but maybe just caught one or two of those pitches out of the corner of his eye, and decided aw, shit, maybe one more inning. And then, when Rube took those three out in a row, this time on a strikeout, a pop fly, and an easy ground ball to short, maybe that scout thought that titty bar sounded pretty good after a tough week on the road, and other than that one inning Rube's shit had been pretty sweet anyhow.

And then, after we tied it up on a home run in the eighth by Hack, and a walk, a stolen base, a pop fly and a single, that scout decided that maybe he'd stick out a close game and see who won, and he'd be home sometime tomorrow anyway. And finally, when we went to the top of the tenth and I left Rube in, seein' as how he told me he wasn't anything close to tired, and he proceeded to shut them Bees down in the tenth and in the eleventh, when we finally feasted on their weak-assed relief pitchin' and won it 4-3 on a down-the-line pole shot by Smokey, that scout's faith was richly rewarded, because Rube's final box score looked somethin' like this:

	IP	R	ER	H	SO	BB
Tyler	11.0	3	3	2	19	4

Now, for those of you who ain't adept at readin' into a box score like that, nineteen strikeouts is a completely obscene amount of batter-borne frustration, and eleven innings is more than any big leaguer's pitched in one game in thirty years. Rube Tyler fuckin' *two-hit* the Burlington Bees for what most pitchers would call two games, and he threw almost *five times* the number of strikeouts that he did walks. You can look at that box score and tell me that ain't a perfect game, but brother, that was the most perfect game I ever seen in my whole life. The fans, they let Rube know it, too, because they gave him a standin' ovation at the end of every single inning after that fourth, and when he came out to throw the tenth they would not sit down, they stood and they stamped their feet and they yelled like hell every single pitch of those last two innings. They loved the guy. He was one of them, but he was also throwin' somethin' they had never seen before. They *loved this guy*. He was out there workin' overtime, just like he had been at the plastics plant, just like them poor suckers in those seats did, and they wouldn't let him go quietly, either. They stood up and cheered and went absolutely apeshit after Smokey's walkoff homer, and everyone knew what they was after. Rube had just gone back into the clubhouse with everyone else after Smokey came across the plate, but now his teammates had to drag him back into the dugout and push him out onto the field, and there, at 11:15 on a Wednesday night, a stadium full of Westerns fans sang his praises for a good thirteen minutes. Not a soul left until he had tipped his cap for the hundredth time, the noise had finally died down just a fraction, and he had slowly made his way back down into the dugout. Even then, I reckon some fans, the real baseball connoisseurs, just stood there and drank in the last few minutes of what I reckon was, after that one inning, the single finest pitching performance in the history of the River League. I sure as hell did, and before I ran back into the clubhouse I scanned the crowd and saw that that Chicago boy did, too.

"Helluva game, Rube," I said when I got back down there. "I reckon you showed that scout a thing or two. Get your civvies on, and then I'm takin' you and that scout to the Lusty Lady. Hell, I'm takin' everyone! Titties and beer are on me tonight, boys," and that made 'em yell even louder, all except Preacher, who looked at me all disappointed.

That scout caught up with us and I insisted that he was comin' with all of us, and we did, we drove across the river to Hamilton and we just walked right in like we owned that place, and that night we did. Someone had called them up and when we walked in the DJ announced us and told everyone about the win and about Rube's ace pitchin', and that he wasn't payin' for nothin' that night, and I told the girl behind the bar that none of my boys were payin' for anything anyways, and it was all goin' on my tab, thanks. She winked at me and blew me a kiss and that made it all worth it, I guess, 'cuz those boys put back quite a few

94

pitchers and more than a couple of lap dances. "Tips are on your own boys," I told 'em.

Rube drank quite a few but he was still conversational when I pulled him over to our table and introduced him to Charlie Snodkiss, the scout, who I had gotten to know just a bit over cold beers and under warm dancers. Charlie had been askin' me everything about Rube and I'd told him what I knew, told him that this was the best damn pitchin' prospect I'd ever seen and that I'd stake my career, or what was left of it, on that knuckleball of his, because I'd never seen anything like that before. Yes, he was a bit fragile, and a bit wild, but I reckoned with the proper coachin' he'd be fine at a couple levels up, and maybe, just maybe, he could be a major leaguer someday.

"Either of you boys want a dance?"

"Aw, no thank you, honey, we're talkin' business here."

"OK, just let me know. Good to see you again, Orval!"

Charlie looked at her, and looked at me, and shook his head. "Damn, Orval, I don't reckon I've seen a single-A pitcher ever that could throw like that. He's a prospect, alright. I'd want to see him against hitters a level or two up before I said much more, but goddamnit that was just about perfect," he said, looking at his beer.

"So's that," I said, looking at the stage.

"I just can't believe this kid...this guy, fell into your lap. You musta pissed your pants when you saw him."

I had to admit that I had, and I hadn't at first thought about Rube movin' up. I'd seen him and I'd thought about what he could do for the Westerns all season. But now I knew it was only a matter of time before he wasn't with us anymore, and he was headin' up the ladder. That made me kinda sad, even though I couldn't wait to see him get bumped up, and to see what kind of effect it had on him.

When Rube came over, he had a stripper on each arm. The boys had kept him busy, tippin' the girls to pay attention to his big ass, and he was havin' quite the night. I introduced him to Charlie and sat back knowin' I might be watchin' something mildly historic, and it was. Rube kept both women on his knees the whole time as he told Charlie about his pitchin', how he'd been practicin' for somethin' like twenty years and how over the last couple of months it had finally come together, to the point where he felt like he needed to show someone.

"And where was you workin', again?"

"Iowa Plastics, out by the airport. I ran the injection molder for, oh, I don't know, maybe ten years."

"Well, son, those days are done. You call them boys up and tell 'em you quit, because I'm gonna tell the club to sign you. You may be

95

the oldest player we ever signed to a rookie contract, but Goddamnit, we're gonna sign your ass."

Rube just beamed. He looked at the girls, one after the other, and said "you hear that, ladies? I'm gonna be a pro-fesh-unnal ball player. Gonna pitch for the Chicago Cubs."

Charlie smiled back, pattin' one of the girls on the thigh, just a bit too high. "Well, we'll see about that. But you're gonna be playin' somewhere other than Keokuk soon, that's for damn sure."

Rube looked over at me, kinda apologetically, and bless his heart, he said "I kinda like it here, though. Got all my stuff here, got Coach here, I don't know…"

"Hell, Rube," I shot back. "You think they got pretty girls here, wait till you get to Peoria, or Carolina." The girls didn't like that much, but it was true. Rube was sittin' in a two-bit club on the wrong side of the river with two redneck strippers, neither of 'em had a full mouth of teeth and between 'em enough tattoos and scars to cover an infantry platoon. He was makin' $300 a week with us, livin' in a trailer and buyin' his own shoes. And his pitch maybe, just maybe, was gonna land him in a lakefront condo with the finest girls and shoes the big city had to offer. Damn. What a game.

Rube went home with them two girls and I didn't want to know anything more about his evening. Hobie had to drive me home, and Charlie, he reckoned he'd better sleep in his car in the parking lot before getting back to Chicago. "Hell," he said. "I can shower at that truck stop in Galesburg. Helluva pitcher you got, Orval. Helluva team. Helluvan evening."

The next morrnin' I just felt bad for myself, on account of I never made it out of my uniform and apparently decided that the floor was just as good as the bed. The phone rang at 8:30, and I rolled over and drug myself over to it.

"Hello?" I rasped, tryin' to cough the strip club taste out of my mouth.

"This Orval Sheckard?"

"I reckon so," I said, though I had to think about it for a minute.

"This is Randy, over at the Lusty Lady. You know you left your card here last night?"

"I reckon I did."

"Well, you got a tab here to sign for, too. Pretty considerable, so if you don't mind comin' over sometime this mornin' and settlin' up we'd be real grateful."

"How big's 'pretty considerable?'" I asked.

"$1,356. And seventy-two cents."

I did the math in my head real quick and figured that was about right.

I hung up, stood in the shower for about half an hour, and then put on my spare uniform and called Hobie for a ride to the ballpark.

That day's game, as you can probably imagine, did not go so well. Preacher was pitchin', and he was pitchin' pissed on account of he knew all about the revelry the night before and he felt left out and mad that we'd all gone and done all that shit that he was railin' about, drinkin' and cussin', and whorin', and he'd had to go home to his church-lady wife and since it wasn't Sunday night he wasn't getting any of what we got. Course probably only Rube got any anyways, and even then maybe we shoulda stopped him, saved him from himself, but you know what I mean. Our defense fell apart early, and they batted around in the third and then again in the fifth. I finally put in Moose in the sixth, and told him he was it, I was leavin' him in no matter how bad it got, and boy, it did get bad, and even though Hack and Smokey both hit taters we ended up on the wrong end of a 14-3 score. Honestly I didn't give a rat's ass. I found that I had more or less put the rest of the team out of my mind after seein' Rube's game last night and I had to pull myself back into the game and remember that these other boys was tryin' to get to where he was goin', too. But I felt too much like hell to yell at 'em, and if they were as sore as I was from all that carryin' on that was as much my fault as anyone else's, and so I just pulled 'em all together in the clubhouse and told 'em never mind, we had one more game against the Bees and we'd even the series and say the hell with it. Go out and get some rest, boys.

That night it was Tug's turn out at the Lusty Lady. I signed for my tab, I picked up my card, and I let Tug pay. I also got home by about midnight, to find a message on my answerin' machine.

"Orval, this is Freddy Birdsfoot. Give me a call in Chicago when you get this. Whenever you get this. Thanks."

I called him up.

"What's up, Freddy, you want to give me shit about my scoutin' report again?"

"Nope. I want you to get your boy ready."

"He goin' up to Peoria?"

"Nope. I read Rube's report, I read your report. I looked at our team, and our startin' pitchin', and the fact that we're neck and neck with St. Louis, and I reckon Rube's goin' straight to AAA. I just talked to the manager there. I want you to start him on Saturday, and then he's goin' to start up there Wednesday. Your job is to get his ass ready, get him prepared, and get him to Des Moines so he can sign his professional contract on Monday."

"Des Moines? Man, I don't disagree with you, but that's a hell of a leap. You sure?"

"I'm sure. From what Charlie said I don't think Rube Tyler's gonna be in Des Moines that long, either."

"Sweet Jesus. Alright, Freddy. Consider it done."

Well alright. Rube Tyler was goin' to Triple-A. I paused to contemplate that for a minute. He'd already risen farther than he'd ever really imagined. And now he was gonna leave Keokuk, gonna leave the River League, gonna leave me and the team behind and go on to somethin' even bigger and better. Holy shit.

7th Inning

Tug, Brickyard and I went out for Shirley Temples that night after I talked to Freddy. I figured I'd let Rube get a good night's sleep before I broke the news to him, and I wanted to have an evening alone with the idea of him leavin' so soon, anyway. I'd gotten pretty fond of his presence in the dugout, like there was another grownup hangin' around the playground, you know? Anyways, I hardly had time alone with it anyway, seein' as how I couldn't resist spillin' the beans to those guys about ten seconds after we sat down.

"Guess what, Brickyard," I said, puttin' my arm around his shouldes like you'd do with a kid who'd lost his dog. "Rube's goin' to Des Moines."

"No kiddin'," he said. "Seriously?"

"Yup. Just talked with Freddy up at the big club. He's pitchin' for us Saturday, and for Des Moines on Wednesday. Skippin' Peoria, skippin' Carolina. Straight to Triple-A."

Brickyard's eyes got wide. I could tell he wasn't entirely comfortable with this.

"This is a good thing, Bricky," I said. "Imagine what Rube's gonna get to do. Hell, he might be throwin' for Chicago soon, he starts mowin' them Pacific Coast League boys down."

Tug looked at both of us. "Shit," he said. "I'm just glad we ain't gonna see him again."

Brickyard got a slightly pained look on his face. "Orval," he said to me, "I'm real happy for him, but I don't think that boy's ready."

"Ready? What the hell you mean, 'ready?' That boy's about to break every pitchin' record in the River League, and he ain't even warmed up yet! Ask Tug here does he think he's ready."

"If it gets him out of my league," Tug said, "I'll say he's ready."

"Naw, Orval, I know he's got a pitch that cain't be hit. I just don't think he's mentally ready. You saw how fragile he was with men on, or even startin' in an unfamiliar situation. I don't think that coach up at Iowa's gonna be as careful with him. They give a damn about winnin' up there, you know."

I squinted at Brickyard. "Hell, I care about winnin', too. So he'll give up the five-run inning his first game and then he'll get used to it."

"I don't know, Orval. He ain't ever been away from home for that long. I worry about him."

"Well, shit, he can come back down here in between games, it's what, a three hour drive?"

Brickyard didn't say nothin', he just looked at the non-alcoholic beverage clutched in his mitt hand and sighed.

"Anyways, look, it ain't our decision. Let the big club make those and let's just get on with things. To Rube Tyler, newest player for the Iowa Cubs."

"To Rube!"

Friday we had a night game, but I couldn't wait that long. I drove over to Rube's trailer about 10:00 and knocked on the thin metal door.

"Rube!"

Long pause. "Who is it?"

"It's me, Orval. You up?"

I peered in to the wreckage that was Rube's living room. Old burrito wrappers competed for space with unwashed plates of food, an old TV sat in the corner looking at a couch that had a big ol' Rube-shaped dent in it and an empty 2-liter bottle of pop sittin' next to it. There was more beer cans layin' around than I cared to count, and on the wall a poster of Tom Candiotti, the Pirates knuckler from back in the day. Where the hell did he get that, I wondered? And when?

Rube shuffled up to the door. As he opened it, a stale cloud of cheese puffs, sweat socks, and stale Old Style wafted around me.

"Goddamn, Rube. You need a woman."

Rube just chuckled. "Maybe I got one. In the back."

"Well, maybe you do. But you better tell her to pack her damn bags."

Rube looked at me and gave me that blink I hadn't seen in a couple of weeks. "Huh? I'm gettin' cut?"

"Nope. Promoted. Straight to Triple-A. You pitch for us Saturday, and up in Des Moines on Wednesday. Congratulations, you monkey-fucker of a pitcher. You're goin' straight to the last rung on the ladder and you ain't even stoppin' in Peoria or Carolina."

Rube blinked again. Slowly it dawned on him what I was sayin'. He gripped the side of the door to steady himself, shook his head, and breathed out real slow.

"No shit?" he said.

"No shit."

"You ain't screwin' with me, this is for real."

"I would screw around with you about a lot of things, son, but not this. The club got your report. They think you're major league material. They don't want to waste time."

Rube shook his head, and then slowly it sank in. He let go of the door, grabbed me around the shoulders, and held on to me like I was the last life ring on a sinkin' ship. It occurred to me that his mustache had cheese in it, and then he hollered in my ear as loud as anyone I'd ever heard.

"AAAOOWWWWWWWWWW! AAAOOWWWWWWWW! AAAOOWWWWWW! I'm goin' to Des Moines, baby, I am goin' to Des Moines!"

"Congratulations, son," I said, tryin' to wrench myself free. It also occurred to me that he hadn't showered since last night's game. At least.

"Coach," he said, lettin' me go, "I just want to say how grateful I am to you for lettin' me show you my pitch that one night. I can't believe this. It's all happened so damned fast. Anyway, I just wanna thank you. Thank you for givin' me a chance, and lettin' me work with Brickyard and lettin' me play with the boys."

"Just go up there and haul ass, like you've been doin'," I said. "Just make the most of it."

"I will, Coach, I will. God. Damn. Triple A. Who would have guessed?" He coughed a bit, then really hacked up good. "Sorry, I think I broke somethin' yellin'."

"It's alright, son. Enjoy this. See you at the park at noon for practice. And don't forget, you still got one more game to pitch for me, so don't go all apeshit tonight."

"Don't worry, Coach, I'll throw you a gem Saturday."

From the back of the trailer I heard a gravelly but definitely feminine voice. "Everything OK, Rube?"

Rube just looked at me. I shook my head. It was one of those chicks from the Lusty Lady from the other night.

"Boy, I wouldn't a thought you had it in you."

"Lemme tell you somethin', Coach, the only break we took was for the game last night."

"Damn. Well, save somethin' for the big leagues, alright?"

Rube winked at me and shut the door. More than I needed to know right there, I tell you what.

Well, Tug and the Bees kicked our asses again that night. He was headed back up to Burlington right after the game, he said somethin' about their bars bein' classier than ours, and I am here to tell you that's complete bullshit, but anyway I said bye to him as he was gettin' on their bus and see you back up there in a couple of weeks, and he said yep, we'll kick your asses then, too.

That night I drove up the river to the old State Park and parked on the bluff, lookin' over at Illinois and at the brightest night of stars Keokuk had seen in quite a while. Hobie had wanted to go out to the Frog, and Brickyard he wanted to go back across the river, but I was tired, and I felt like I hadn't had a minute to myself since the season had started, and especially since Rube Tyler had shown up. I was sad about ol' Tug, sad that he'd gotten sick and sad that he was leavin' the game, but I was also bothered. He and I were the same age, and I wondered why it was that I didn't have any kind of mind to quit, that I just wanted to keep on goin', preferably dyin' with my boots on, in an argument over a blown call at home if I could. I was also a little pissed that I'd ended up at this point in my life still livin' month to month, still livin' in a Single-A town, still drivin' a 1988 Plymouth Valiant, no wife, no kids. Tug was lookin' forward to spendin' time with his family, and I was just lookin' forward to the next game. Anyway, I sat on the hood of my car and looked out at the sky, and saw a couple of shootin' stars. Now, I ain't suspicious, which sets me apart from most baseball guys. I think somethin' happens or it don't, and there ain't nothin' out there can influence whether it does. But I saw them shootin' stars and just for a minute I thought somethin' was gonna work out alright. Somethin' big. Maybe Rube. Maybe Rube was gonna be my swan song. Maybe he was the reason I'd been stuck in Keokuk for so long. Maybe. Or maybe not. Maybe it wasn't gonna work out. Maybe Brickyard was right and this was gonna be a massive flame job. Or, even if it worked, maybe I just happened to be there, happened to be at the right place at the right time to pick up the greatest knuckleballer I'd ever seen. I popped open a cold beer and decided not to think about it that deep. What was gonna happen was gonna happen, and I was just along for the ride.

Clinton got into town Friday afternoon and they got ready for the evenin' game while we was finishin' up afternoon practice. I had Rube and Moose throw around to keep loose and to give them a chance to talk. Rube was kinda takin' the ride that Moose had figured was his this season, and I knew Moose was kinda pissed about it, but I think he also knew that the writin' was on the wall. With Rube goin' up, though, Moose was maybe gonna be back in our startin' rotation, and so he was gonna at least get some more pitchin' in before he had to hang 'em up.

Anyways, we beat the crap out of Clinton Friday night, in front of a pretty big crowd. It was half-price beer night, and they was nice and rowdy for us. We hit three homers—Smokey, Hack, and Hoops all tatered, and we ended up winnin' 6-2. At the end of the game I asked Buddy if I could grab the mike for just a minute.

"Ladies and Gentlemen," I said, as folks was wanderin' out of the ballpark, "I jes' wanna tell you that Rube Tyler, our promisin' not-so-young rookie, has been called up by the organization."

There were a few cheers, and I could see a few people lookin' down at me like they was disappointed, and a few others who hadn't even heard his name yet, and then some who had just had way too many half-price beers.

"He's pitched some of the best games I've seen in my career with the Westerns, and he'll be pitchin' his last game tomorrow for us. So if you got time, and you want one last chance to see the best knuckleball ever to mow down the River League, come on out and see us here at Keokuk Veterans' Stadium. Game time, 2:00 o'clock."

Now, word of Rube's promotion had hit the local paper, and the radio, so when Saturday rolled around there was plenty of cars in the lot even before we started mornin' practice. Folks was tailgatin', drinkin' in one of the first really hot days we'd had that year, and you could tell some of 'em knew what they were gonna see that afternoon. I even saw me a Rube Tyler number 56 jersey on one guy, and I wondered was he gonna come up to me and tell me he had a pitch or not. He didn't, but he did offer me a cold one on the way in.

Rube showed up on time, and he had a good size cloud of kids and even a few grownups followin' him, tryin' to get his autograph on one piece of memorabilia or another. Rube was still signin' slow, takin' care to make every letter just as neat as he could, and I reckoned someone up at Des Moines was gonna have to teach him how to sign his name a bit quicker.

"How you doin', Rube," I asked. "Gonna go out with a bang today?"

"I hope it's a lot quieter than that," he said.

"Nervous?"

"About today? Naw. I'm feelin' pretty good about today. About Monday, and Wednesday? Hell, yes."

I smiled. "Just take it one day at a time. Try to enjoy your time out there on the mound today, and don't think about what's comin' up."

"Sure, coach. Sure."

Before the game in the clubhouse the boys had got Rube a big ol' cake, and Speedy had made a speech about how he was glad as hell to see Rube go, on account of he was getting tired of chasin' those pitches all over the backstop. Brickyard had bought him a nice watch, nothin' too fancy, but engraved on the back with the team logo and the scores from

103

the games he'd pitched for us, all four of 'em. There was a blank spot at the bottom for that day's game, and Rube got a little choked up when he was thankin' Bricky. Then they asked me to say a few words, and I choked up, too, but I told the boys how privileged they had been to see a performance like what Rube had put on since he got here.

"What you all seen these last couple of weeks has been miraculous. It oughta show you what folks can do when they get focused and disciplined and decide they want somethin' more than anything else. Ol' Rube here earned his trip up the ladder, earned it every evenin' he went out and threw that ball behind his trailer. It's been a long, long road for him, but it's payin' off, and son, I just couldn't be happier for you. Let's all get behind him today and give him some good defense, and some runs."

Then the boys all cheered and pushed Rube up to the front of the room.

"I don't even know what to say," he said. "I just wish I could bring all of you with me up to Des Moines. I ain't ever gonna forget that you guys were behind me. Aw, forget it. Let's just go win this one. Let's not win it for me, or anyone else, let's just win it."

The place went nuts, and I reckoned this game was gonna be somethin' special. Mind you, my idea of what was a special game had changed, had changed a lot, in the last three weeks. But what with my moment of peace the night before and the way that room seemed charged up, I knew.

From Rube's first pitch, I knew he was dialed in even sharper than he'd ever been before. He didn't have any of that nervous Nellie look about him, didn't throw up before the game, didn't even breathe hard joggin' out to the mound. During his warm-ups he even lobbed a couple of eephus pitches to Speedy, maybe 15 feet up in the air and damned if they didn't land right on home plate.

"Boy, you better not pull that shit in the game!" I shouted, and I could see Rube laughin' that he'd pissed me off a little.

When the ump said "Play Ball!" there was a full house—a genuine, standin' room only, wall-to-wall full house at Keokuk Veterans. Every one of the 1,900 seats had been sold, and they'd sold another 500 tickets to folks who lined up along the fences down the foul lines to see a pretty historic moment, maybe. It was a beautiful damned day, the baseball Gods had smiled on us once, and we all reckoned they might smile on us again if we prayed to 'em hard enough.

Now, that full house watched as Rube put three straight pitches by that first Colts batter, absolutely killed him with dancin' knuckleballs that went every single direction at once. Three pitches, three swings, three total whiffs, and that first out went down in a grand total of 43 seconds. The batter just stood there after strike three, starin' out at Rube and tryin' like hell to figure out what had just happened. Then he looked up at the sky, tossed his bat toward the dugout, and walked back real slow, askin' himself how was anyone supposed to bat against that.

The crowd was out of their minds. This was what they'd come to see. They'd come to see them Clinton boys swing for the fences and end up on their asses, with the end of the bat bouncin' off the dirt and their ankles all twisted up and them mouthin' cuss words left and right as Rube Tyler's amazin' dancin' knuckleball made droolin' idiots of them all. The second batter went down on four pitches, one of 'em was such a crazy knuckler that it bounced about two-thirds of the way to the plate and even he wasn't gonna swing at that. But he swung like hell at the next one and he shouldn't have, and that was out number two. Now the crowd started standin' up, standin' up in the first inning like it was the last, and Rube didn't let 'em down. This batter laid off the first pitch, and got rewarded for his relaxed attitude with a ball, but then he laid off the next one and it whistled down through the strike zone after first headin' up for the clouds. Then he swung at the next one and missed, laid off the next one and the count went 2-2, and then finally Rube gave him a whirling dervish of a throw, one that corkscrewed out of space from the batter's ear to his nuts, and he coulda swung three times and missed it each one, but he only swung once, and missed it anyway. Three outs, twelve pitches, and every one of them worth the price of admission alone. The fans cheered as loud as I'd ever heard, and that last batter just broke his bat over his knee and sauntered back to the safety of the dugout to pick up his glove.

Now, I reckon the Colts' manager, Buckwheat Cooney, told their pitcher that he was gonna have to have the game of his life if he wanted a win out of this, since it didn't appear likely they was gonna get many runs. And their pitcher came prepared, knowin' I guess that there's be folks watchin', and probably some scouts from Triple A on account of them wantin' to see what the hell Rube Tyler was up to. So he threw like hell, he had a pretty blisterin' fastball, and our guys had some trouble with it. Rube got through the first with stuff movin' all over the place, and this guy, fella by the name of Del Scott, he got by with stuff movin' like a laser, straight at the catcher and just tryin' to be faster than the batters. Hollocher led off and he rode the count full before swingin' way late on an almost big league 88 mph fastball, and then Gunner and Smokey both made contact but popped out. We was done with inning one and ten minutes hadn't gone by.

"Keep this up," I said to Bricky, "and we can have Rube out at the Lusty Lady before sunset."

"The hell we can," he said, "since it looks like we'd be here for an extra eight innings without any hits."

"Well, I like our odds of Rube outlastin' this Scott guy. He's got heat, but our boy can go all night."

"So I hear," said Brickyard and I snorted.

The fans gave Rube a standin' ovation when he came out in the second and he tipped his cap and got to work. He faced down their big left-handed slugger, Chuck Henshaw, like a man on a mission. Henshaw dug in and snarled at Rube, and Rube snarled right back and threw him a hell of a pitch, spiralin', movin' up and down, slowin' down and speedin' up, the whole nine yards. Henshaw spun himself around tryin' to get at it and cussed loud enough for the whole grandstand to hear when he missed. Then on the next pitch Rube got one off that sunk just a little bit more than Henshaw thought it was gonna, and he topped that ball so hard it bounced off the plate and into Speedy's glove.

Now, the last pitch Rube threw at him that bat was the scary one, the one that slipped off his fingers just wrong and rolled just a bit too much. Rube knew it when it left his hand that he'd screwed the pooch, but ol' Chuck Henshaw was so pissed off and so keen to beat the hell out of anything that he swung just a little early and pulled that thing down the right field line. The crowd sucked in its breath and you could hear them do it, it all happened at once and real fast. The ball had the angle, that's for damn sure, but not quite the momentum, and Stuffy, he chased that thing down and snared it with a divin' catch right out there on the warnin' track, bumpin' up into the wall with his glove after he plucked that thing off the dirt. Once he held it up that stadium let that breath out all at once in a huge cheer that was as much for Rube as it was for Stuffy.

Brickyard couldn't watch when that ball went off Henshaw's bat, and when he heard the cheer he cracked one eye and looked up at me.

"The hell happened?" he said.

"Divine intervention," I said.

"Well, then, thank Jesus."

"Mm-hmm."

Henshaw was the only threat that inning, though their number 5 guy took the count full before he whiffed on a dyin' duck. I'd started namin' Rube's pitches and I reckoned he had about five of 'em. There was the Corkscrew, which spiraled around a couple of times before it zeroed in on the strike zone. There was that Dyin' Duck, which seemed to hit a brick wall about two-thirds of the way to the plate and just drop out of the sky. There was the Roller Coaster, which seemed to go up and down three or four times, and there was the Drunken Hooker, which wobbled it's way toward home and screwed the batter at the last minute. And finally, there was the Ski Jump. Somehow this one looked low until the last minute, when that air piled up on the underside of the ball and shot it upwards through the strike zone, or took it out of the strike zone and toward the batter's head. Either way, Brickyard and I reckoned there wasn't a hitter alive who could hit that one, who could either lay off it when it was lookin' good, or who could change his mind and swing when it was lookin' low. It was a pretty fearsome repertoire of pitches, and the fact that all of 'em were goin' less than changeup speed, somewhere south of 65 miles an hour at their best, made 'em all the harder to hit. Tug had reckoned, too, that after that game his hitters were gonna have to go back into the cages for hours to re-time their swings, on account of they'd been waitin' so long by the end of the game that it had thrown off years of their timin'.

Clinton's next hitter, Woody Root, stepped in like he'd already given up, and Rube just tossed a couple of minor league roller coasters at 'im. Root swung at all three of 'em, but he was swingin' like he just wanted to sit the hell down and I reckoned Rube coulda just chucked his fastball, or really, just his straightball, down the pike and it would have been just as hard to hit. Root slunk off to the dugout as the crowd stood up again, and our boys came in to take their hacks.

Scott still had his act together, but Paskert got him a bloop single and that seemed to unnerve him just a bit. He took the count full on Stuffy before getting him to pop out to second, and then Speedy came up and tagged his next fastball way the hell out in center. I thought this one was a goner, too, but their centerfielder made a catch just as good as Stuffy's in that last inning and that was it. The crowd applauded that play almost as much as they'd cheered for Stuffy's dive, and that made me pretty proud of our fans, who loved their team but also knew the game and knew when they'd seen it played right.

Rube cruised through the third and the fourth. The Colts' ninth hitter, Pinky Urbanski, stroked a grounder right between Smokey and Hack in the third. Both of 'em went for it, and for a second it looked like Pinky was gonna get a cheap-assed hit. But Smokey got to it, smothered it, and before I knew what was happenin' Rube was over on first and catchin' Smokey's toss.

"Damn," I heard Hobie say. "Did we teach that boy to play defense?"

"He's pickin' somethin' up," I said. "That wasn't major league speed, but hell if he didn't get the job done."

"ALRIGHT RUBE!" the boys on the bench cheered. "Way to get to that bag, old man!"

Rube was smiling, but he was also winded, and when he jogged in he flopped down on the bench like a big ol' sea cow gaspin' for air.

"Nice play, son," I said. "We teach you to do that?"

"I'm getting my legs back," he said. "And my instincts. I was off the mound headin' for the bag before I was done hearin' the crack of the bat."

"Keep that up," I tell him, "and your scoutin' report's gonna be a lie, sayin' you cain't play defense."

Meanwhile our hitters was startin' to find their pitcher's weak spot. Hoops told me and the boys that he was timin' Scott's throws pretty good, liftin' his foot off the ground when Scott started comin' forward and cockin' the bat, and then waitin' the amount of time it took to put his foot down before decidin' whether to go after it or not. "He ain't got but one pitch, coach," Hoops said. "Work out how to hit that and we're home free." He and the other boys started hittin' a groove, and pretty soon we started pepperin' the Colts' defense with grounders and fly balls. That was music to my ears, 'cuz there's three stages to hittin' a pitcher. The first is just flailin' away, not hittin' shit. Then, once you get his location down, you can hit the ball every time, but not where you want it. That's when you start poppin' them balls off down the lines, or into the ground. Finally, once you figure out where your bat needs to start movin', and when exactly to try to make contact, you can put that ball wherever you want, provided you can get around fast enough. In the majors, a really quick fastball ain't hittable once it's over about 96 miles an hour, you're just guessin', really. But down here you don't ever see that 96 mile an hour fastball, cause once someone throws it they end up in Peoria. No, what you get is your bread and butter 85 mile and hour, entirely hittable gopher ball, and even though Scott was throwin' a bit faster than that, our boys figured out pretty quick where to pick up the extra tenth of a second they needed to stroke that ball perfect.

In the fourth, Hack figured it out and smacked a beauty of a line drive straight out into center. Once I saw that I knew it was pretty much our game. Speedy brought him home a couple of hitters later with another line drive, this one in the gap in right. 1-0. That was all we got that inning, but after Rube set 'em down again in the fifth, the top of our lineup came up and went to work. Hollocher led off with a tasty blooper over first base. Gunner moved him along with a single down the line in left. Scott was flustered now, and I made his life worse by givin' the sign for Hollocher to steal. It was a close thing, but he made it, and then Smokey hit a high fly ball to the deepest part of Veterans Stadium, just to the right of straightaway center, and their guy caught it but Hollocher bounced home and Gunner got to second. Now, with Hack up, Buckwheat came out to discuss the matter with his hurler. I don't know what they discussed, they might have told him to pitch Hack low, or they might have been discussing the price of lite beer in Tibet, but it didn't matter because Hack picked his pitch and golfed one that wasn't low enough way over the wall in right field, to the lasting delight of the Veterans faithful. 4-0, there, fastball guy on the mound, and what do you think of that?

Del told us all what he thought of that by cussin' on the mound and throwin' his glove, but he managed to finish up that inning respectably, which brought out Rube for the sixth, without lettin' a man on base. Now the boys had started movin' away from him again, just like that game up in Dubuque, and he had just sat there like Buddha, smilin' to himself and takin' it all in that he had another Goddamned perfect game goin', he had a stripper waitin' for him somewheres up in the stands, and he had a game to pitch in Des Moines in a couple of days. Life was pretty good for Rube Tyler right then, let me tell you. Life was pretty damn good. But now he coughed a bit and hauled his sorry ass out to the mound and warmed up, ready to hand the bottom third of the Clinton lineup their butts to 'em on a silver platter, with a side order of baseball that they couldn't hit if they'd prayed a million years straight.

Their leadoff guy just swung away, missin' everything but just wantin' to get it over with, and their second guy popped out just in front of the plate, but then their third guy figured he'd just take his chances, and he sat back like he was waitin' for a bus, lettin' Rube throw whatever the hell he wanted. And even though he got a couple down the pike, he also let a couple get out of the zone, and pretty soon we's at 3-2, a full count, and the crowd now is standin', knowin' that Rube's got perfection on the line here in the seventh. Rube took a big breath, like he was enjoyin' the fact that he'd just been through eighteen straight batters, and then he hacked a couple of big ol' coughs up and looked down at the mound and got to work.

"TIME!" yelled Buckwheat and he came runnin' out to the ump and started yellin' like hell. So I got up off my ass and ran out there too, and all I caught was "...just look at his hands, then."

"The hell you talkin', about, Cooney?" I said.

The ump looked at me. "He reckons your boy out there just coughed up a loogie to grease up the ball."

"Aw, bullshit. B-ull-shi-t. He's just got some upper respiratory thing, that's all, he ain't greasin' up the ball with lung butter, come on, now."

The ump looked at me. "Still, let's take a look."

We marched out to Rube. "Show 'em your hand, son," I said. "Buckwheat here wants to make sure you ain't been greasin' your fingers with snot."

Rube stared at me. His jaw dropped a bit.

"What?" he asked. "You wanna see my hand?"

"Yeah, just show 'em your goddamned hand, show 'em there ain't any snot, or spit, or K-Y jelly or nothin' on there."

Buckwheat snorted. "And your cap, too. I ain't ever seen no one throw a knuckler like that didn't have spit or some junk on it."

Rube looked at me nervously. "It's alright, son. Just show 'em your hand. Show 'em your fingertips and your cap. Your belt buckle, too, while you're at it. Hell, Buckwheat, just 'cuz your boys cain't hit it, don't mean our boy's cheatin'."

Rube cleared his throat. "Sure," he said. "Just the ump, right?"

"Yeah, just show the ump your fingertips. Come on, let's get on with it."

Rube extended his right hand toward the ump, who took a look and snorted.

"Well, them's some ugly fingertips, but there ain't nothin' on 'em," the ump said. Rube pulled his hand back kinda quick. "Let's see your cap, too."

Rube quickly took off his cap and the ump looked at the brim. "Nope. Nothin' there, either. Come on, Bucky, let's just play the game."

"Check his belt, while you're at it," I said, crossing my arms in front of my chest. "You gonna accuse my boy of cheatin', I want to make sure we cover every possibility, here."

Rube took his belt off, right there in front of God, country, and Veterans Stadium. The crowd cheered. "Nope," the ump said, disgusted now with the whole thing. "Nothin' there either." He jabbed Buckwheat in the ribs. "Play. Ball."

I hung out for a bit while Rube put his belt on. He was shaking. "Come on, now, Rube," I said. "Ain't anthing to worry about. His hitters couldn't touch you, so he's got to stand up for his boys call you out like that. Cheap-assed shit, but that's his job. Just put it behind you."

"Sorry, Coach," he said. "I just got this thing about people touchin' my pitching hand."

"Yeah, I know. The glove." I said.

"Yeah," he said. "That."

"Well, it's over. Just git your belt back on and get the magic back. Full count here, so you gotta throw this sumbitch a strike."

110

"Gotcha, coach," he said, but he was still rattled. I put my hand on his shoulder.

"Just pitch. Don't think about it."

He nodded. I went back to the dugout, but I almost sprinted back out when I saw him tryin' to cool down. Something about that encounter really pissed him off, and now he wasn't focused. I looked over at Bricky. Bricky frowned.

Rube reared back, threw, and the pitch sailed over the batter's head, Speedy's glove, and the first three rows of Westerns' fans. Just like that, the perfect game was gone. The hitter jogged out to first base, and Chuck Henshaw stepped in, smellin' blood. Rube danced around him at first, but got behind 2-0. Speedy went out to talk with him, and I sent Brickyard out, too. "Talk him off the ledge," I said. "Again."

He talked him off the ledge, alright. The next pitch was a groove job, and Henshaw came around on it and sent it screamin' out over the left field fence with a mighty blow. No-hitter and shutout, all gone at once. Their boys trotted around the bases and Brickyard and I jogged out to the mound.

"That's alright, Rube," I said. "We still got 'em 4-2. And we're gonna beat 'em, too. Hack just told me he's gonna hit at least one more off their relief corps. So just relax, Whatever's gettin' to you, just let it go,   OK?"
"Yeah," said Brickyard. "Come on, son. Get this out and it's all downhill."

Rube nodded. He seemed to relax a little, the crush of Henshaw's home run maybe took a little bit of the tension out of him. Me and Brickyard went back, and Rube went on to mow down their fifth batter for the third out on three pitches.

"That's what we're talkin' about!" I yelled at him as he came in. When he sat down on the bench all the boys realized they could talk to him now, and no matter what this was the last time they was gonna have Rube Tyler in the dugout, probably ever, so they all started razzin' him and mussin' up his hair and jokin' around with him. I looked over at him and thought about what a wild couple of weeks he'd been through, and how I sure had enjoyed watchin' him pitch and earn a spot on the team, and then tear through the league in only what, five games? Speedy pulled the ol' gum bubble on the cap on his way out of the dugout and it took the ump to point it out to him about halfway through his warmup pitches.

Anyway, he faced down the Colts in the eighth like a man possessed. Struck the first two out, and then faced down Urbanski for the final out. Pinky just stood in there and pretty much closed his eyes, but

111

he swung at everything and managed to tap the ball down the line to third. Gunner picked it up and hurled it over to Hack at first, just barely missin' Rube, who'd just popped up from his follow through to see where the hell the ball had gone.

We picked up one more in the eighth. Smokey doubled and Hack brought him home with a warnin' track flyout to make it 5-2. I told all the boys to go out to the field, but I held Rube back for just a minute.

"What, Coach?"

"I want you to take this in. Remember that this is your first pro ball home, and we'll always be here for you. Take that walk out to the mound slow, and tip your cap, so's you can thank all those fans that came out today to see you pitch."

"Right. Gotcha, Coach."

I held him up for just a few more seconds, till all our fielders was in place, and then nudged him up the dugout steps. The crowd cheered like crazy, every one of 'em stood up, and Buddy up in the press box made a point of sayin' Rube's name and remindin' everyone that he was goin' up the road to Des Moines on Monday, and how proud we all was to have had him here for the short time we did. Rube tipped his cap, and all our boys put down their gloves and cheered for him, too. I have to say, I teared up just a bit seein' all this, and I reckon Rube did, too. This was his last day in his new home, and as scared as he'd been a few days before, he had got so comfortable bein' here that I knew he was gonna miss it. He took his warmup pitches, but the crowd still stood, and when the umpire told everyone to play ball, the crowd wouldn't stop. They kept cheerin' like crazy, and Rube didn't dissapoint. He threw crazy stuff to their first batter, almost like he'd gotten his second wind and had gone from bein' a starter to a fireballin' reliever. Those pitches danced so nice in that mid-afternoon sun it was almost like listenin' to music. Their hitter touched two of 'em, both of them foul balls, but he didn't have a chance, and Rube finished him off with a dyin' duck, fallin' away right when it looked like the batter might get a tasty slice of fenceball.

Same story with their second batter. Rube painted around him, hittin' all the corners with crazy-assed shit, scarin' him and his whole team showin' what he could do even after he'd been out all day throwin' that stuff. Sat him down on four pitches, too, the last one a called strike that had started headin' for the Colts' dugout and ended up headin' for ours, runnin' across the plate left to right and just kissin' the batter's elbow as it did. Poor kid just dropped his bat, put his hands on his hips, and shook his head, and he probably went home and had nightmares about that pitch for the rest of the season.

Now. One batter left. Rube gets this guy out and he has a 4-1 professional record, all five of 'em complete games, and he heads up to the big city with a clear conscience and a nearly spotless record. He doesn't, and he has to face Hanshaw again, and he don't want that, I don't want that, and Brickyard don't want that. Bricky and I look at each other, but we decide to let things go. We've got a three run lead, Rube's been throwin' serious shit all afternoon, so what the hell. Let's let it ride and see what happens.

And what happens is this. The batter steps in. The crowd, already on their feet, start stompin' on the bleachers, shoutin' out real loud, and hittin' anything they can find together. Speedy crouches down, the ump zeroes in, and Rube stares down their piece of crap third hitter. I look over at Buckwheat, and he's just lookin' down at the floor of the visitor's dugout. Rube winds up, and lets go, and it's the last pitch he'll ever throw as a Western, all over the place and with a nice big scoop of whiff at the end. For a split second, no one says a word—the Stadium is, for the tiniest moment, silent—but then everyone erupts, the crowd starts throwin' stuff in the air, the Westerns all charge the mound, from the field and from the bench, Speedy jumps into Rube's arms in a great big bear hug, and behind 'em all I just amble out, lookin' out at the crowd, who'll stay standin' on their feet and cheerin' for a good ten minutes while Rube endures the growin' dog pile. Buddy's down on the field with a microphone all of a sudden, but he never makes it to Rube. He finds me, and asks me what do I think, is Rube Tyler gonna pitch for Chicago ever? And I say hell yes he is, too, maybe just in a few weeks, and then Buddy asks is he the best knuckleballer I've ever seen and I say sure, he's the best anyone's ever seen and if you don't believe it why don't you go ask them Colts hitters over there. Even those boys over in the visiting dugout are clappin', seein' as how they've just seen the greatest pitchin' performance they'll probably ever get to see.

There's cheap booze in the clubhouse again thanks to Harry, and Rube makes another little speech, sayin' how grateful he is again and hey, come see him up in Des Moines seein' as how he ain't ever been up there and it would be nice to see a friendly face or two. And I tell him Des Moines, hell, they'll be seein' you in Chicago by the end of the season and he just shakes his head and says he don't know about that, and then pretty soon we's all piled in to my Plymouth and sure as hell we're headin' across the river for one last night of debauchery. Sunday we got a noon game, but I don't give a damn about it, and then Monday we got an off day and me and the Valiant are gonna drive Rube on to meet his destiny. Rube coughed up half a lung in the car on the way over there, and Moose, sittin' in the back, tells him not to get any of that shit on a baseball or that Buckwheat Cooney'll have a conniption and try to throw you out again, and we all laugh like hell at that and don't stop till we've got mouths full of beer and eyes full of titties over at the Lady.

8th Inning

We won the game Sunday, but not due to any real brilliance on the field. Clinton hitters had their timin' all messed up, and Preacher, he went to work on 'em, pitchin' a pretty decent seven innings and only givin' up three runs. Meanwhile we'd put five on the board playin' small ball, a stolen base here, a bloop single there, and a rally like we wasn't really used to puttin' together, and we'd managed five. Moose came in in the eighth, and we all held our breath but he came through, pitched two fine innings and only gave up three hits and a run, and we squeaked by.

Now, the big club was puttin' Rube up in an apartment in Des Moines, so I told Brickyard to spend Sunday evening kinda coachin' him through what he'd need out of his trailer to get by up in the city. Coffee maker? Yes. Fryin' pan? Yes. Suit? Yes. Case of beer? No. Porn? No. Rube started to get that he'd be able to get what he needed up there, and also that at that next level he had to watch himself a little bit, and some of the habits he'd let slide had better get knocked off if he wanted to compete at the next level.

Monday mornin' I drove out to pick him up, and he was ready, suitcase ready, lucky glove on the pitchin' hand savin' the magic, shaved, even, wearin' his new suit.

"You ready?"

"Ready as I'll ever be, I suppose."

"Nervous?"

"About Triple-A? A little. About leavin' this place? A lot."

"Well, don't worry, you can come back here on your days off. Ain't that far up the road, you know. Always be a home for you out at the Stadium."

Rube nodded and threw his suitcase in the trunk. He coughed vigorously from the effort, and he didn't stop once he'd gotten in.

"Boy, you need a Halls or something? That's a nasty cough you got."

"Just the allergies, I reckon, plus I've had a little cold the last couple of days." He hacked again, coverin' up with his sleeve.

We drove on up, through Mount Pleasant and Fairfield, getting coffee from the hippy Hare Krishna place there, and then amblin' up through Oskaloosa. We talked the whole way, about baseball mostly, but also about what was happenin' to him, how strange it was to be plucked from your normal, daily life and have somethin' that might just make your craziest dreams actually happen.

"I reckon you might be the luckiest forty-year old on the face of the planet," I told him. "Most guys would give their nuts for doin' what you're doin' today, ridin' up to pitch Triple-A."

"I cain't quite believe it," Rube said, lookin' out the window at the corn growin', now almost up to a grown man's knees. "I mean, I always wanted this to happen, but I'd pretty much given up hope."

I asked him a question I'd been thinkin' about for a long time. "How did you come to catch me and Brickyard on that one night," I asked him. "Not the first night, the night I told you to get lost. The second night. I never heard how you came to be talkin' to Bricky."

Rube sighed. "Well, first off, I was pretty drunk. I'd been to the first few games, and I finally told myself that this was it, that if I didn't do it now I'd die without ever knowin' whether I coulda done it or not. I was nervous as hell, but it was also just killin' me. I figured that when I could throw a hundred knuckleballs just about perfect, I oughta let someone know. I did it the week before, and then I went to each game thinkin' I'd bust up my courage and find you or him, but it took me a couple of tries. Then after you said you didn't want to see it that first night, I came back and had a couple of extra beers for courage and waited for Brickyard instead. Took every bit of nerve I had to say hello."

"What'd you tell him?"

"I told him that all I wanted him to do was just stop, right where he was, comin' out of the stadium. Just stop, and I wanted five seconds of his time, and then he could go if he wanted to. So he did, he stopped, and he crossed his arms, and then I threw my pitch."

"And he must have dropped like a fish when he saw it."

"Not the first time. The first time he didn't really pick up on what he was seein'. He asked me what the hell that was, and it looked awful slow and my mechanics was a mess, and then I told him to watch where the ball went and I did it again, and that's when he dropped his arms to his side and asked me could I do it again. I threw it a few more times and then he went to get you."

We drove on until we were just outside of Des Moines, and then I told him this was probably the last calm moment of his season, and did he have any questions.

"Just one."

"What's that."

"You think I can make it to Chicago?"

I thought about it for a minute. I mean, I knew he could. I knew that pitch could strike out any major leaguer that dared try to hit it. But I

116

didn't know what I should tell him. I didn't know if sayin' yes was gonna put that extra pressure on him and crack that fragile mind of his wide open, or if sayin' I didn't know mighta done the same thing. So I smiled, looked over at him, then back out at the road stretchin' ahead to the city, and I told him.

"Rube,' I said, "I do think you can make it. I think you got some work to do up here, and I think you gotta be patient and learn the fielding position at this level, and you gotta work to get your mind under its own control. But son, you got a hell of a pitch, and yes, it'll do fine up in the big league."

He nodded. "Thanks," he said. "I think so, too."

"This is the last chance I got to give you advice," I said. "I ain't got nothin' to say about your pitchin'. That's all fine. But I do feel like tellin' you that your life up here's gonna be different. People are gonna expect things from you, and want to ride your career with you, and hold you up as all kinds of examples. None of that's more important than pitchin', OK? Nothin' anyone says or asks of you or talks about is as important as what goes on between the lines. I want to tell you to keep your eyes on the prize, keep your focus. Listen to the coaches up here, they're some of the best, and don't forget who you are and where you come from, alright?"

Rube was lookin' out the window at the growin' corn and at Des Moines, comin' up on the horizon. "I hear you, Coach," he said. "I gotta not get distracted."

"Exactly," I told him.

So I got him to the Iowa Cubs ballpark and we walked in to their offices and I told the receptionist there that hey, I got your new pitcher and she kinda looked at me and went through some files and said that yes, she guessed we did. We waited for a bit until their manager, Sam DuFrene came out, and I said hi and introduced myself and Rube.

"We heard a lot about you, Rube," Sam said. "All good. Let me get you set up with our staff, we got some stuff for you to sign and your apartment up here to sort out, and then we gotta get you set up with your equipment and a uniform." He looked right at Rube's gut. "That may take a bit."

"Alright, Rube, you're in good hands up here, son. Thanks for everything you've done, and remember you're always welcome down in Keokuk."

Rube shook my hand. "Thanks for everything, Coach," he said. "I won't forget you."

"Make us proud," I said to him. "Make us proud."

117

And in some ways that was that. I'd done my job, I'd spotted talent and moved it on up the path. Only you know the rest of the story and know that wasn't nearly the end, and somehow I knew that too. I got back in my car and got lost headin' for the highway, finally said the hell with it and stopped for a loose meat sandwich and directions, and then I found my way and drove back to Keokuk, all on back roads this time, took me the better part of the afternoon. I was sad to see Rube go. Happy, of course, for him, and for the organization, and for the sport in general. But I was gonna miss his pitchin', that was for sure, and I'd grown kinda fond of the guy, too, over the couple of weeks I'd gotten to know him. He was somethin' else, a self-made pitcher, hadn't come up through the system or played by the rules or anything. Just had an idea that if he worked at it for twenty years he'd maybe get one shot, one shot between the time he got really good and the time his body just gave out, and he'd timed it pretty well. I hoped he was gonna be alright.

Hobie ran practice that afternoon so we could get ready for the Red Wings the next day. I showed up at the end and cussed and yelled a little bit just for show, and then the three of us went out to the Frog in the Hole and toasted Rube Taylor, knuckleballers and middle aged guys everywhere, and the game of baseball. I thought about him that night, his first night up in the city, and wondered what he was thinkin' about, and whether he was nervous or not. And then I just started thinkin' about our game Tuesday night.

Freddie Fresh pitched that game for us, and I have to say we looked like we'd picked it up a notch against the Red Wings. Freddie pitched a pretty damn good game and I left him in until the seventh and then Moose was able to finish it up alright. He got in trouble some in the ninth but pitched out of it and we won it 3-1. After the game I was givin' Moose shit about puttin' guys on and he looks at me and sez "It's gonna be OK, Coach. I've been workin' on a knuckler," and I just laughed and told him not to screw around with that stuff, he couldn't afford to mess up what little timing he had.

Rube called me Wednesday after lunch and told me he was shittin' bricks and he was worried about how it was gonna go. He sounded pretty rough and I asked him if he was OK. He was still feelin' punk, he said, and he hadn't slept most of the last two nights on account of the city bein' such a loud place and his bein' sick and all worked up about movin' up.

"But son, you seemed fine on the ride up. What's gotten at you now?"

"I don't know, Coach. I like it here, I like the coaches, but I sure felt a lot more comfortable down there in Keokuk with you all."

"Well, hell, son, of course you did. That's because we're nothin' more than babysitters down here. You got some serious coaches up there and they're gonna work you a little bit harder than we've been. That's their job, they gotta be a little harder on you."

"I know that, and the pitchin' coach up here, uh…"

"Hick," I said, "Hick Cooper."

"Yeah, Hick. He's been good about workin' with me, we spent most of yesterday goin' over my motion, which it turns out could be a lot more efficient, anyway, I like him fine, I just don't know if I'm supposed to be up here."

"Fuck that," I told him. "That's the organization's decision, not yours. Don't start second guessin' them."

"I reckon I'll be better once I get one game behind me."

"Just relax, Rube. Enjoy this if you can. Remember, you got nothin' to lose."

"I just don't want to let anyone down," he said, and coughed away from the phone.

"Only person you got to worry about with that is yourself, Rube," I told him, "and you've already done yourself proud. Just don't forget to breathe, and remember what it feels like to mow them hitters down, OK?"

"OK, Coach. I'll do my best."

I went and told Brickyard about that, and he reckoned Rube was gonna be in trouble that night. I told him to give Hick a call and fill him in on Rube Tyler's psychological profile, and see what they could work out.

That night's game in Keokuk was like bein' shot full of bees for three hours straight. Rube's replacement, an eighteen year old clusterfuck of a kid named Duffy Pinch, got the start, but I reckon he was so high when he took the ball that he had to pick which of the two, or three, or four hitters he was seein' to throw to. But the Red Wings was throwin' a junk baller at us, too, so the first couple of innings were a real exhibition of Single-A ball at its worst. By the end of the third the score was 8-7, with a total of six wild pitches, eight walks, an inside-the-park home run, the infield fly rule called twice, and three hit batsmen. I just put my head between my knees and told Hobie to punch me in the nuts when it was over.

Things settled down a little bit after that, but by the end I'd put in half our relievers, sent young Duffy Pinch home to a rehab counselor, and we ended up winnin' 12-8. I threw a fit in the locker room afterwards, yellin' at those boys that it wasn't all that pothead pitcher's fault and they played like shit out there and then I went into my office and slammed the door and just sat there for a few minutes. When I heard the knock I lost it.

"The hell you want out there?" I yelled.

Brickyard mumbled back. "Never mind," he said. "You don't want to see this anyway."

I got up and opened the door. "See what?"

Brickyard handed me the fax. Circled on it was Rube Tyler's line for that night from up in Des Moines.

"Sweet Jesus," I said. "Sweet merciful Jesus."

The line read like a funeral:

	IP	R	ER	H	SO	BB
Tyler	2.1	7	6	3	2	8

"What," I said, "what the hell happened?"

"I haven't had the full report," Brickyard said. "Just a quick WTF phone message from Hick, and this fax."

"Well they didn't hit him all that much," I said.

"Two home runs." Brickyard said. "Two home runs, a couple of wild pitches, an error on an easy grounder back to him. I think he just completely lost it up there."

"Damn. I reckon he did. You think he's gonna be alright?"

"Not without some help."

"What kind of help do you think he..." I stopped and thought about it. I could see where Brickyard was goin' with this.

"I think he needs a familiar face up there."

"He might. But meanwhile what the hell do we do down here?"

Brickyard handed me the other fax. The one that was right under Rube's line score. The one that said the organization was givin' up on Moose Mays and that he'd pitched his last game for the Westerns.

"Aw, Jesus Christ," I said. "I gotta let him go tonight, too?"

"Listen to me," Brickyard said. "Call up Hick, tell him I'm comin' up. Tell him all they got to do is find me a trailer up in Des Moines, somethin' out in the flood plain, or behind the scoreboard, whatever. Just tell him that I can set Rube right. Meantime, you tell Moose he's been promoted to pitchin' coach, maybe just for a couple of weeks. He's smart, he knows everything I know, and I hear he's lookin' for work."

"Ain't my decision," I said. "But I'll put in a word. Anyway, you call Hick. I'm sure whatever it takes to keep Tyler on track will be worth it. We'll figure somethin' out down here."

Birckyard just nodded and went out to the phone in the clubhouse to call up to Des Moines. I called up to Chicago, to the director of coachin', and explained to him the situation.

"So this is about this knuckleballer," he said.

"Yep. My pitchin' coach reckons he's just fragile and needs a friendly face up in the dugout."

"You think it'll work?"

"I reckon it might. Bricky had a way with talkin' to him the few games he had with us."

"And what do you want to do about coverin' his position?"

"I want to hire this pitcher we're lettin' go. I know you got a couple of folks you want to try out, but this guy's got some rapport with our boys and I'd be happy workin' with him."

"Day to day. We'll draw up an interim deal. You got him for a couple of weeks, anyway, and then either Brickyard comes back or we'll move someone in. Or, if your boy works miracles, maybe you keep him for the rest of the season."

"I appreciate it, sir."

"Gotta be honest with you, it doesn't much matter to me. Right now we're half a game back of St. Louis for the division title, the season's getting to be half over, and we need all the help we can get. Do what you gotta do, we'll send you the contract, but just get that knuckleballer healthy so's he can throw at Houston and Milwaukee and St. Louis, alright?"

"Alright, sir. I'll take care of it. Thanks."

I told Brickyard and he high tailed it outta there to his pickup truck. "I reckon this is kind of an emergency," he told me. "I probably oughta have a damn siren on my truck."

I opened my door. "Moose," I said, "I need a word." Moose knew what was up. He ambled in and sat down. "So this is it," he asked. "Time for me to get that job application from the hardware store?"

"Not yet, son," I said. I asked him did he want to take Brickyard's job for a couple of weeks. Moose said where the hell was he goin? And I said Des Moines, to babysit Rube, and Moose thought about that and reckoned that made a lot of sense.

"Circle of life," I said. "Rube moves on, Brickyard gets to go to Triple A for a while, and you get a chance to coach for a bit, if you want it."

"Beats hell outta sellin' hammers."

"Means you get to work outdoors for at least a couple more weeks," I said.

Moose agreed, and I told him we'd keep him on board at least until Brickyard got back, which might be tomorrow, depending on what ol' Hick decided to do about Rube. Moose was pretty happy about that, about endin' his career with some coachin' time, and he thought maybe he'd like to make a second career out of that. I told him this was a good chance for him, then, and we shook hands on it.

"Come on out to the Frog with me and Hobie tonight," I told Moose. "We gotta have us a coachin' meeting."

"I reckon we do," said Moose, and we went out and got pretty drunk and filled him in on all the team gossip he'd missed out on. What Pantyhose really got charged with (indecent exposure and misdemeanor theft), whether Preacher was really as uptight as he seemed (we'd seen him take off from the motel one night in Winona with two girls that wasn't his girlfriend, and maybe wasn't even girls), and whether Hack was drunk or not the night last year that he hit four home runs in four at bats (yep). We told him how we wanted him to run pitchin' practice, and he knew the routine that Brickyard had but there was a couple things we thought he oughta cover more, and he thought so too, and he sat there and made a list on the back of an Old Style coaster, a list that he'd have on his desk the next morning with some translations on it. After about the fourth round the conversation came around to Rube, and Moose asked me what the deal was with that glove of his.

"You know, sometimes with pitchers especially you gotta just coddle 'em. Let 'em have whatever superstition works for 'em. I know it's a little queer, but hey, if the magic ever got out, none of us would forgive ourselves, now would we?"

Moose allowed as to how that was probably right, and I gave him my two bits on pitchin' psychology.

"As long as you let 'em think you're gonna strike 'em out, that you're the alpha male in that particular relationship, you've got the upper hand. I reckon a good part of what Rube's got is batters seein' that first pitch and freakin' the hell out. He could probably lob a sucker pitch every so often and those batters, since they're on the short end of the stick psychologically, they still wouldn't know what hit 'em."

"Don't let 'em smell fear, basically," Hobie chimed in.

"That's right," I said. "Make the pitcher think he's invulnerable, and then send him out with his nostril's flarin'."

"We never showed Rube the other team's scoutin' reports," Hobie said. "Didn't want him worryin' could he get this or that guy out. Just throw your damn pitch, Rube, and make sure you think you can do it. That's about all that really matters."

It was kind of a long night by the time we was through. I got home and there was three messages on my machine, all from Rube about how bad the night had gone, how he was still sick, how he missed Keokuk and thought it had been a mistake to ship up to Des Moines so quick. Even though it was two in the mornin', I called him back and for the first time in his brief career, I chewed his ass out good. I told him that there was a Goddamn reason he was up in Des Moines, and he knew just like I knew that he could pitch at that level and beyond, that hell, all he had to do was focus on what he was doin' and anything was possible. Shit, boy, I told him, I don't wanna hear none of this self-pityin' bullshit. You're getting paid to throw the ball, just forget about what you think, or what you think you should be doin', and do your job. Do. Your. Fuckin'. Job.

Rube was pretty quiet on the other end of the phone. He heard what I had to say, but he was clearly still miserable.

"Brickyard's on his way," I told him. "He's gonna help out with you for a couple of weeks, so there'll be a friendly face up there."

Rube didn't say anything.

"Just hang in there, buddy," I told him. "Remember your first game with us didn't go all that well, neither. You'll get back on that bike, just you wait."

"Alright, Coach. I'll pull it together."

"You damn well better."

We hung up and I got me an idea. I left a message on Freddy's answerin' machine up at the big club sayin' that I was gonna need about five hundred bucks and a couple of tickets to Rube's next start, which I reckoned was Sunday afternoon, and then I drove across the river to the Lusty Lady and told the manager there I needed to talk to that girl who went home with Rube the other night. He knew which one, her name was Tammy, and it had pissed him off that she'd done it and had been braggin' to the other girls about it, and she was givin' him such a hard time back that he saw the wisdom of my plan. She came out and saw me and said hello, and I said did she want to make $500 real quick. Her eyes shot open at me and she said that wasn't the way to do it, and if I wanted to get laid I had to be a little more subtle than that, but hell, $500, what the hell did I want her to do, anyway?

I told her I wanted her and one of her girlfriends to go shoppin' in Des Moines for the weekend. I even had a place for her to stay, and a familiar face to show her around the big city. What happened between them was gonna be their business, I told her, but you'd be doin' me and the organization a solid. She took the money and Rube's new phone number, kissed me on the cheek, and told me thanks for getting her out of Keokuk for a couple of days.

Now, Moose fit in pretty well, he had a few leadership issues but those were understandable on account of his suddenly bein' management instead of a player. But the boys took to him pretty well and he seemed to turn the corner from pitchin' to teachin' pretty well. We had a good week, that week, too, splittin' a couple of games against Galesburg and then poundin' the shit out of Hannibal all weekend. That Saturday night game we hit two grand slams and turned a couple of sweet double plays that made me think there was hope, if we weren't 14-25 by that point. Still, it was fun to watch our boys get it right for a change, and to see them come into the clubhouse smilin', even without Rube there to lead 'em on, made the weekend worth it.

I didn't hear much from Rube those few days Tammy was up there. In fact, no one heard much from him. Brickyard covered for him at practice, sayin' he'd been even sicker than he'd seemed, and he managed to show up on Saturday. I called up there to see how things were goin' finally, and Brickyard told me that Rube was as mellow as he'd ever seen him, and that was a stroke of genius and probably the only way that boy was gonna get through these last couple of days. Finally I talked to Rube on the phone and he sounded pretty happy, alright, and I asked him how his last couple of days had been and he said he wasn't really at liberty to say, but he was feelin' a whole lot better about himself and his situation. Still feelin' like hell, he said, but he reckoned he could get through it now.

Sunday was our last game against Hannibal, but I was havin' trouble concentratin'. Them boys up in Des Moines was playin' at the same time we were, and it was all I could do to not run up to the scorer's booth and see did they have any news in from up there. Meanwhile Preacher pitched a pretty good four innings but then he crapped out and I had yet another young guy to put in, Elmer Zabel, and he actually got through the rest of the game OK—gave up a couple of runs and made two really dumbass plays in the field, but managed to stem most of the damage and we pulled that one out, 8-6, meanin' we had a four game winning streak goin'. A four game Goddamned wining streak and now we was 20-34. The playoffs were probably not in our cards, I thought, but at least we might pull it together and finish near .500.

After the game I hustled back into my office and picked up the phone and called Bricky. "How's it goin' up there," I said, out of breath, "how's our boy doin'?"

"Why don't you listen for yourself," he said, and he held the phone up to the crowd. They was all goin' absolutely crazy, and I

124

figured it had to be near the end of the game by now, and he would have told me if Rube had come out earlier, so this was likely pretty good news.

"He's doin' alright," I said, "sounds like he's done alright?"

"One-hitter. Top of the ninth. He's shut these guys down completely. As good a game as I've seen him pitch yet."

"Any walks?"

"Three, but he scattered 'em all. Otherwise it's been set 'em up, mow 'em down. He's workin' on his nineteenth strikeout."

"Nineteen...holy shit," I said. "Nineteen strikeouts? What's the League record, anyway?"

"I think they was sayin' Merv Rettenmund might have mowed down twenty-one back in the day. Anyway, he's on his last out, maybe. Listen up."

I did, and I heard the crowd suddenly light up, and the announcer in the background say "how about that! In his second game for Triple-A Iowa, Rube Tyler shuts down the Zephyrs, allowing just one hit, and the Cubs win it 3-0! How about a big hand for Iowa's new pitching sensation, Rube Tyler!"

"Well, Brickyard, I reckon you talked some sense into that boy this week."

"Sense, nothin'. I didn't see him until yesterday."

"Well, clearly you gotta tell ol' Hick that he needs your coachin' and that stripper's lovin' to be at his most effective."

"I think you're right, Orval," Bricky said. "I think you're right."

"Hell," I said, "The organization better put her on the payroll."

"I reckon we'll work somethin' out. How'd our boys do today?"

"Big win. Four in a row, Bricky. All since you left. Not that I'm makin' a connection or anything."

"Moose doin' OK?"

"He learned from the best. We could use you back, but we're gonna be OK for a while. Say, when things calm down up there tell Rube to give me a call and tell me how he's doin'."

"Alright, Orval, alright. Take it easy down there."

"Alright. Take care of our boy."

Well, goddamn. Rube was back on track, and all it took was getting laid. I sat back in my chair and felt a quiet surge of competence in having figured this one out, and I felt great for Rube getting a win like that up in Triple-A. Hell, Freddy was probably salivating, probably couldn't wait to put this boy in Wrigley and see if his magic worked up there, too. The big club was still neck-and-neck with St. Louis for the Division title, and they looked like they'd be tryin' to get one or two more pitchers to help 'em out. Better for Rube, their relief crew was battered up pretty good, so anyone who could go nine innings, even if they gave up a few hits and a couple of runs, was gonna help them save their firemen. Me? I'd have wanted to be in Rube's shoes given those odds. I told Hobie if he kept firin' away like that at those Triple-A boys I thought Rube'd be up there in three weeks, tops, makin' just six weeks from runnin' the injection molder to a nice apartment on the Lake Shore and all them Chicago girls and cold Oldies he could stand. Boy, I remember thinkin', that boy's got life by the tail right now, don't he?

All through July I was watchin' three teams. I was watchin' our boys, of course, and watchin' Moose work with them pitchers and do some good. I was watchin' Iowa, 'cuz of course I wanted to keep track of Rube. And, also because I wanted to keep track of Rube, I was watchin' Chicago, kinda hopin' one of their pitchers might get hurt—nothin' bad, mind you, maybe a bad hangnail, or a bruised wrist, kind of thing that might keep a guy out for two starts and let some new blood up from Triple-A. So that kept me just a bit busy. Our pitchers pulled out some nice games, thanks to Moose's patient coachin' and I think spurred on a bit by seein' one of their own do so well. We slugged it out with Rochester at home, takin' 'em two out of three, and then we went on a road trip through the League's southern division, sweepin' Hannibal in three games and splittin' two with Galesburg before takin' two out of three from Quincy. Hack put on a pretty good show, hittin' a couple of home runs and battin' about .420 for the trip, and watchin' him swing with some confidence made me feel like maybe he was gonna end up in Peoria by season's end.

Chicago kept winnin', but so did St. Louis, and the pitchin' staff up there kept lookin' tired but healthy. While we was in Galesburg I got a call from Freddy askin' me what I thought of Rube, and did I reckon he'd add somethin' to the club, and I told him hell yes, ain't no hitter alive can catch up with them dancin' knuckleballs, and I figured he'd written that down and probably taken it to some general manager's meeting or something right after that. Still, I knew they'd give him some time at Triple-A before doin' anything rash.

Meanwhile, Rube was tearin' shit up. He pitched a two-hitter at Colorado Springs, strikin' out fifteen of their hitters, and then he came real close to no-hittin' Albuquerque out on a road trip, finally givin' up a hit and a home run in the bottom of the eighth. Still, he won that game, and he pitched all the way through both of those. Right after the Colorado game the paper up in Des Moines did an article on him, talkin' about his unhittable knuckler and how he'd come out of nowheres and had run through the River League like it was standin' still. Rube said some real nice things about Keokuk, and about us, but most of all they

126

was askin' him whether he thought he was goin' to Chicago or not, and he was real modest about it and said he was happy enough in Triple-A, and Des Moines was as big a city as he ever cared to live in, but he'd go wherever that queer-assed pitch of his took him, that's for sure. They put in a nice picture of him, showin' his gut but also that fear-inducin' look he got in his eyes facin' down them hitters.

When we got back from Quincy we had two off days in a row before Red Wing showed up in town, and that just happened to coincide with Rube's first game back from Albuquerque so Hobie and me drove up to Des Moines to see him play. Brickyard met us at the park before practice started and we got in to help pitch some beepee and watch the crowd fill up. Word had gotten around the city about this new knuckleballer, whose pitch was worth the price of admission alone, never mind whether the I-Cubs got any hits or not, and sure enough, those five thousand seats up there filled up by game time. The *Chicago Tribune* had its lead sportswriter there to see if there was any substance to this phenom, and the press from around the region had also figured out there was a good story in a forty-year old plastics worker livin' out every middle-aged guy's dream. So while Rube was warmin' up, the P.R. folks up in Des Moines found me and hooked me up with some reporters from Minneapolis and St. Louis and they asked me about Rube and could I tell them the story of how he'd tried out and those first couple of games in Keokuk. Now, I ain't used to talkin' to the press much, except if it's the Keokuk paper, so this was quite a change of pace for me. I told 'em the truth, mostly, but I also backpedaled a little on just how good Rube was. I told 'em he'd been fine down in the River League, and he was pretty hot right now, but let's just give him a little time and see what he does. All them reporters wanted me to say he was the second coming, of course, that he was gonna be the guy to push the big team over the top and get them to the Series, but I didn't encourage that kind of speculation. I just kept that part real quiet.

Rube came over after the Cubs was done warmin' up and he gave me a big bear hug and asked how I was and how Moose was doin' and all that, and I told him and then told him he looked like he'd lost some weight and how was things up here in the big city. He talked to me all about his apartment and livin' downtown near all the bars and nightclubs and stuff, and how he'd made some good friends on the team and how much he'd gotten used to big city life and how the I-Cubs was treatin' him real good. Then he mentioned how much Tammy liked it up here, too, and it took me a minute to realize he was talkin' about the stripper I'd sent up here and I said you two are still a thing, then and he said yeah, she'd even flown out to Albuquerque with him. So things was good for

Rube. Things was real good. He and I threw around for a bit and then he went back in to the clubhouse, leavin' me and Hobie out on the field to soak in the Triple-A atmosphere. This is where it all happened, of course, this is where my career came crashing down, and I could point right to the place where I'd slugged the guy, and I even walked over by there before the Round Rock boys came out to warm up. I was the only person in the park that story mattered to now, I realized, though this was the first time since then that I'd even set foot in the stadium.

Hick came out and said hi to us both and thanked us for comin' and seein' them on our day off, and then he asked me did I want to coach first that day and I said hell yes, so they got me a spare uniform and I got to sit on the bench while Rube was pitchin' and hang out on the field while the I-Cubs was battin'. I didn't do too bad considerin' I had no idea what the signs were, but Hick didn't lay anything tough on me or his hitters. And he didn't have to. One of them Des Moines boys hit a two-run homer in the second, and Rube pitched about what we'd all come to expect by now. He hit a rough patch in the fourth, puttin' two men on, but neither one of them scored, and aside from the one other walk and two bloop singles he was damn near perfect. Struck out fourteen, to the cheers of the entire grandstand, and made a nice play coverin' first after the ball got by him and out almost to the outfield. He introduced me to all the team and told 'em how I'd gotten him started, how much it meant to him to start out in Keokuk, and what a great coach I was. I shucked all that talk, but damn I had fun watchin' him confuse the livin' shit out of them hitters that day. Hick finally took him out in the eighth, just to get his reliever some work, and the whole stadium stood up and chanted his name, and he came out and took a curtain call, and right then I knew that he was destined for the big leagues. He suddenly had the presence, that authority that said he belonged on that field. When the game was over me and Hobie and Brickyard waited back in the locker room until the crush of reporters was done, and Hobie said it was like we'd seen his big comin' out party, that he reckoned everything was gonna change for him once this story was on the front page of the *Tribune*'s sports section. Finally everyone cleared out, and I told Rube we wanted to take him out for a beer, and he said that would be great, there was a place right up the street from the ballpark, and he'd meet us there in an hour.

We had a hell of a night. Rube bought rounds for us, we bought rounds for him, and we got pretty drunk. Rube's new girlfriend joined us for a couple of drinks, but then she left us boys alone and finally we closed the place down and settled one of the biggest bar tabs for four people I'd seen in quite a while. When we got outside, Rube started coughin', hacked up a lung and a half, and Brickyard looked over at me with concern in his eyes. Rube said he was still tryin' to kick this cold of his, and Bricky told him he better quit smokin' so much or he'd never kick anything. After we got the big guy back to his apartment, the three of us walked around till we found an all-night diner that would serve us some good food to sponge up all them drinks, and I asked Brickyard was Rube okay, and he said he didn't know, but that cough of his was getting worse every day. He reckoned Hick oughta give him a couple of starts off and let him kick it, but Rube was spendin' his nights drinkin' cheap beer and smokin' cheap cigarettes goin' at it with his new girlfriend and he wasn't sure he was getting any sleep at all. He was worried, I knew.

As we paid our check, Brickyard's cell phone rang. It was Hick, relayin' a message from Freddy. One of Chicago's pitchers had just pulled a muscle while he was puttin' some groceries into his SUV. He was gonna be on the fifteen day D.L. and Freddy wanted to come out and see Rube's next start. If it went well, there was gonna be a slot up in Chicago.

9th Inning

I had to get back to Keokuk, but damn, I wanted to stick around to see Rube's face when Brickyard told him. Bricky was worried about whether Rube was gonna be excited or whether he was gonna freak, and I worried more about whether he was gonna do both. Anyway, Hobie and I poured ourselves back into my car and we drove slow and straight back to Keokuk, and we was at least sober by the time we stopped for breakfast just outside Mt. Pleasant. I had just enough time to shower, get a couple of hours sleep and put on another pot of coffee before practice that mornin'.

Neither Hobie nor I could concentrate those next couple of days. I called Rube and congratulated him and asked him how he was doin', and he told me he was fine, that Brickyard was workin' with him to make sure he was in top form but also to keep his mind in the right place.

"How you feelin'?" I asked him.

"I feel like hell, coach," he said. "I can't kick whatever this thing is."

"You oughta see the Doc about that," I told him. He reminded me that he had a thing about doctors, and about needles, and I gave up and told him to just get as much rest as he could and to listen to his trainers up there.

Red Wing showed up around lunch time and I went over and said hi to Lefty. He asked me about Rube and I told him it looked like he was getting a tryout, probably Friday the way the schedule was lookin', and he shook his head and said he'd never heard of anyone move up so fast, and I told him hell, if you'd been payin' attention to his knuckleball you wouldn't have been the least bit surprised , and I reckon he'd have been glad to see him go up so fast. "Hell of a story," he said, and I agreed with him.

Now I was still hungover by the time the game started that evening, and I was tired and felt like shit, and things just went to hell. Freddie McInnis was startin', and in the first inning I thought about takin' him out, but then after he blew off a couple of my signs I thought hell with it, I'm gonna leave that boy in as long as I can, to punish him if nothin' else, because he was givin' 'em up left and right. We was down 6-2 in the third before I finally said the hell with it and started chuckin' relievers at 'em, and by the time we got to the eighth we was down 10-2 and I told Hobie the hell with it, I might as well just go home and sleep

130

things off the way things was goin'. Smokey helped us out with a two run shot in the bottom of the ninth, but no one got excited and most of the crowd had headed home by then, and rightly so.

We split the next two with Red Wing, makin' us 25-31. With just over five weeks to go in our season, we could still make .500 if we won a shitload of games and it was all I could do to not make a big deal of this fact after getting our asses kicked. Rochester was comin' in to town and they was leadin' the league at 37-21 and I knew we had our work cut out for us. But all that afternoon all I could think of was what was goin' on up in Des Moines. Brickyard had called to tell me that Freddy Birdsfoot himself was going to come out and see Rube's knuckler first hand, along with a couple of scouts from all over the organization. That worried the hell out of me, since I figured Rube would be tighter than a spring knowin' all those folks was gonna be there, but I couldn't blame Freddy for wantin' some backup. He had a big decision to make. Iowa had a couple other decent pitchers who could have been on the block, and it wasn't no small thing to say to the GM up in Chicago that they oughta go with some forty-year old with a trick pitch, it wasn't no small thing at all.

But the funny part, Brickyard said, was that Rube was a picture of calm that whole day. I phoned him twice, and Rube once, and I swear to God I was more nervous than either of them was. Bricky said later it was like Rube was goin' out to fulfill some kind of destiny, that he acted like it was completely out of his hands and so he was just relaxed as hell, loose as a goose jokin' around with his teammates and with Brickyard and Hick during warm-ups. Brickyard even told me he'd been kiddin' around with Freddy and the scouts when they introduced themselves. He said there were reporters everywhere, from Chicago, from St. Louis, from every TV station and newspaper in Iowa, and even from the *Sporting News* and some paper in Japan. It was a circus, Brickyard said, a goddamned circus for our boy.

When I called Rube he was sittin' in the clubhouse and I told him good luck, just concentrate on throwin' them pitches and don't think about those scouts, and he said actually he reckoned he'd be thinkin' about 'em the whole time.

"How do you figure that?" I asked him. "Don't you think you oughta focus on your pitchin' and kinda put them out of your mind?"

"Nope," he said. "They're there to see me throw that knuckler, and I want to put a show on for 'em. Make 'em know that I belong up with them big boys."

131

Well, alright, Rube, I thought. Alright. The guy had grown himself a pair in the last couple of weeks. A big, brass pair by the sound of it.

"Good for you, son," I told him. "Give 'em hell out there tonight."

"I reckon I will, Coach," he said. "I reckon I will."

And boy, did he. Rube went out and rewrote the record books for the Iowa Cubs and the Pacific Coast League that night against Nashville. He finally got his perfect game, couldn't have done it at a better time or in front of a better crowd. He set twenty-seven of 'em up, and knocked twenty-seven of 'em down. Struck out nineteen again, and the other seven were just harmless ground balls. Brickyard said it was the most awesome God-damned thing he'd ever seen, that the Nashville hitters were just breakin' their bats walkin' back to the dugouts. Brickyard told me, too, that the hitters were just swingin' blind, swingin' at everything especially after he struck out three straight lookin'. It was like there was some kind of hypnotic spell them batters was under, he told me, and it was like the ball was defying gravity and the hitters were tryin' to adjust ten times every pitch and there was just no way any human mind could keep up with the freaky weirdness of his pitches. He told me that as queer as Rube's pitches were with us, they had an extra kick to 'em now, now that Hick and the coaches up there had looked a little at his mechanics. "It's like they took that unhittable pitcher we had and gave him two or three extra little tools to work with," Brickyard said, and at the end he said that the crowd—full house, plus every standing room seat the city fire marshal would let 'em sell—was on its feet the whole top of the ninth and then they gave Rube a standing ovation that lasted a full ten minutes. Even them Nashville boys got up on the top step and gave him a big round of applause for kickin' their asses so bad.

I had sat the whole evening in the dugout runnin' back and forth to the clubhouse to check my phone and see how things was goin', and I almost lost the game for us givin' a steal sign with two outs when I thought there was only one in the sixth. We managed to win, anyway, and when I got back into the clubhouse I listened to that last phone message and went out into the locker room and announced to the boys that Rube had pitched him a perfect game up in Des Moines and in front of those Cubs scouts, and everyone gave a big cheer. While I was gettin' out of my uniform and into my street clothes the phone rang, and I picked it up and it was Rube, wantin' to tell me all about the evenin', and I sat there in my jock listenin' to him give me the play-by-play and tellin' me how just awesome it felt to be out there, but now he was just tired as hell and still feelin' like shit, but he didn't care because this, this feelin' right

132

here, of winnin' and winnin' big and at the right time, was just about the first time he'd ever felt this good about things.

"Well, Rube, that's just awesome. Couldn't be prouder of you, and the boys here all send their best, too. I want to come see you up in Chicago in a couple of weeks," I told him, and he said that was getting ahead of things, but sure, he'd like to bring the whole team up if he could, if he did really get up there.

I was still sittin' there in my jock when the phone rang again. I knew who it was. "Hi, Freddie," I said. "Still think my pitcher's a piece of shit?"

"Nope," he said. "I think he's a major league knuckler. He's comin' up to the big club next week."

"Goddamn," I said. "I think that's the right call. I ain't never seen anything like his pitchin', and from what I hear he was even better tonight than I'd ever seen him."

"You oughta see that video," Freddy said. "Those were some of the scariest damn pitches I've ever seen. It may be that major league batters won't get so fooled, or frustrated, but damn, even it he's half as effective up there he'll be the biggest thing that's happened to our club in years."

"Glad you liked him," I told Freddy, "and I'm glad you gave him a chance. I think he's the real deal, the best knuckler ever, and I think he'll win some games for you."

"Hell, yes," Freddy said. "He'll win some games alright."

Now I was on the phone all that next week, talkin' to reporters, talkin' to the big club about how to handle Rube, talkin' to Brickyard about how to handle Rube, and talkin' to Rube about dealin' with the pressure he was under all of a sudden. Freddie agreed to bring Brickyard along up to Chicago, sort of as a chaperone and personal coach, and I told Rube I'd help him out any way I could. He asked if I'd sit in on his contract negotiations, and I told him he oughta get a good lawyer, but he said he didn't care, it didn't matter to him how much he made and he trusted me to make sure he wasn't getting screwed over. So I drove up to Chicago that Saturday, leavin' the club with Hobie and Moose to run for the day, and we met with Freddy and with the Cubs' general manager, Weldon Leonard and about a dozen other suits and hashed out what Rube was gonna make and for how long. Weldon, of course, didn't want to sign Rube for any longer than he had to on account of his age and his lack of trainin', and Rube said that was fine with him, he was happy to have a job through September.

"We're hopin' to keep you busy through October, son," Weldon said.

Rube said he understood that. Said he didn't want any commitment past the end of the season, just wanted to do what he could for now and worry about what happened next later. He started shittin' bricks, though, when it came to the medical clause. Said he didn't want any needles, didn't want any doctors stickin' their fingers up his ass or nothin' like that.

"Son,"said Weldon, "We're about to spend an assload of money on you. You buy a car, you kick the tires."

"Come on, Rube,' I said, "this chance, and this money, it's gotta be worth some doc checking you out. Besides, you need to see someone about that cough anyway."

So we argued about that for a while, and finally Weldon said he didn't give a damn, really, that if he was just hirin' Rube through the end of the season it didn't matter, but if there was any talk of a contract after that he needed a full physical. "Finger up the ass and everything."

So that was that. Rube signed the paper just like he signed baseballs, slow and careful. He'd make the league minimum, pro rated for the remainder of the season, which came to about $45,000, or more than he'd made in a year at the plastics plant. We all shook hands in the owner's box at Wrigley Field, and Rube asked could he see the mound and Weldon said sure. So we all walked down there, down on to the holy of holies, perfectly trimmed and waitin' for the team to come back on Monday and meet their new pitcher.

"Goddamn," Rube said. "This place is pretty big."

"60'-6" to the plate, Rube," Brickyard said.

Rube looked around, and Weldon looked at him lookin' around. "Think you can pitch here?" he said.

"I reckon so," Rube answered him. 'I reckon I better, seein' as how you're payin' me."

"Good," his new boss told him, "seein' as how you're startin' Tuesday."

The club had one of Weldon's assistants take us all out for dinner that night, in a real nice place up on top of one of the big skyscrapers over by the lake. From our table we could see the lights at Wrigley, and I have to say it was a real nice evening and it made me think about what it would have been like if my coaching career had stayed on track and I'd ended up here, drinkin' wine from some fancy South American country and eatin' steaks with fancy leaves and crap all over 'em and nice soft cloth napkins, instead of nukin' macaroni and cheese and washin' it down with a light beer or six. I had to admit that it was pretty nice, though it had been quite a long time since I'd worn a tie, that's for sure. Anyway, afterwards I left Bricky and Rube with their new minder and drove back to Keokuk, listenin' to one country and western station after the other and practically in tears over how things was workin' out for ol' Rube.

Sunday mornin' it was pissin' down rain. I stopped in at the local diner for some hash and eggs and then got to the ballpark before anyone else. Hobie showed up and I told him all about the Chicago trip, and he told me about losin' in the Goddamned fourteenth inning.

"Well, I reckon we're gonna get a day off today," I said.

"Supposed to clear," Hobie told me, "supposed to clear by mid-afternoon."

I leaned back on the bench, watchin' the rain bounce off our turf and watchin' it run off down the dugout steps.

"Maybe our boys need a rest after that," I said. "Call 'em up and tell 'em no practice. Show up at 1:00 and we'll see whether the game gets started or not. But don't make 'em come in this mornin', we can't practice on that field."

Hobie went in and started callin', and I sat there for a bit just takin' in the quiet mornin', and part of me was glad I was sittin' in Keokuk instead of up in Chicago. Not all of me, but part of me. The part that liked the quiet of my six minute drive from the trailer to the field, that liked bein' able to get hash and eggs instead of some fancy-assed coffee drink, that liked bein' able to blow off practice once or twice because I knew no one felt like it, and what the hell did it matter at this level, anyway, where one guy from every six or eight years ended up makin' that trip up the ladder to Chicago.

The game ended up getting called off, and Moose and Hobie and I broke out the cheap scotch after all the boys had gone back home and we sat there in the dugout, and then in the stands when it did clear up, just doin' shot after shot and toastin' Rube Tyler and the hell of a season we'd been havin'. Moose asked all kinds of questions about how they was gonna treat him, and when he was gonna start and all that.

Monday we had off, and so we was back Tuesday and once again I couldn't stand tryin' to keep our crap together while I was thinkin' about Rube up in Chicago. He'd called Monday and sounded sicker than ever but mentally pretty ready, and Brickyard said he was in as good a shape as he was gonna be, so it was all up to the baseball Gods anyways by that point.

I couldn't help myself, and I put a radio in the dugout Tuesday night, listenin' to the Cubs game on WGN. I told the boys that this was supposed to be motivatin', but of course it wasn't, it was just distractin'. Buddy was announcin' the Cubs score all night anyway, and it was a good thing, since that kept the crowd's mind off the 7-2 thrashing we was

135

takin' at the hands of Winona. Rube had started off a little rough, walked two guys in the first inning, but then he settled down and even though he gave up some hits, he baffled them major league boys just like we'd thought he might. The Reds scored a couple of runs off him, and once they had runners on he wasn't quite as smooth as we all might have liked. But he got through it, and Brickyard said later it was like he'd finally cottoned on to the idea that it was all just in his head, and that if he could convince himself of what he knew anyway, that he was the best damn knuckleball pitcher ever to grace a major league mound, he wouldn't get all choked up over himself and he'd be fine.

I still have the collection of newspaper clippings from the next morning. "Middle-Aged Knuckleballer Toasts the Reds," was the front page of the *Chicago Tribune*. "Age over Beauty," was the *Sun-Times'* version. I thought their beat writer got it just about right:

Wearing number 86, the only jersey the team had in his portly size, Rube Tyler came out of nowhere yesterday to completely redefine the North Siders' rotation. Chucking knuckleballs that registered only in the high 60s, Tyler's motion was unlike anything anyone in the majors has seen in a generation, if ever. The Reds, admittedly not the sharpest hitters in the league this year, couldn't find the ball, and Tyler picked up an easy 4-0 victory. It was his first, but it will likely not be his last.

The Chicago press mobbed the clubhouse afterwards, and the manager up there, Nixey Decker, had a hard time keepin' things in line. They wanted his opinion, wanted to know more about Rube, wanted to see Rube in person, and wanted to know was this it, was this the piece he needed to take the team to the promised land. The video of that postgame interview is amazing, even now, to see the frenzy. Nixey couldn's hardly stand up straight, so many reporters had mikes and cameras in his face.

"Nixey, where did this guy come from?"

"Hell, I'm not even sure. I know he wasn't at Des Moines more than a couple of weeks. Before that I don't even know—Peoria, I guess? Oh, no, sorry, Keokuk. Short Season Single-A."

"Ever had someone come up so fast before?"

"Nope, but then again I ain't ever had a knuckleballer like that drop out of the sky into my dugout, neither."

"How typical was his stuff today?"

"That's a stupid question. I ain't ever seen this kid before, so I don't know whether this was typical or not. If it is, we got us a helluva pitcher at just the right time."

"How old is he, exactly? The rumor is that he's about forty?"

136

"I think that's right. But that ain't necessarily old for a knuckler. Them Niekro boys threw well into their 40s, I think. Like forty-eight? Forty-eight. So I reckon Tyler might have another six or seven years in him."

"Would he be the oldest rookie ever in the majors?"

"Hell, no. Satchel Paige was 42. He's a kid relative to that. Look, age is relative. The knuckler don't put any strain on your joints, which is what's the first thing to go when you get old."

"Have you ever seen movement like that on a knuckleball before?"

Here the room went completely silent. Nixey paused for a moment, and the reporters all leaned in. He looked up at the camera.

"You asked me if I've ever seen a pitch dance like that? Son, I hit against Niekro. I hit against Charlie Hough. They used to say it was like tryin' to eat Jell-O with chopsticks, and I just never tried to hit those two, 'cuz I worried I'd never be able to swing normal again. Those two were hard enough to hit, but they didn't hold a candle to what I saw out there tonight. Rube Tyler…Rube Tyler's got a pitch that cannot be hit. Yep. He's got the best knuckleball maybe ever."

Then the video cuts to Rube. He's standin' there, scrapin' shaving cream off his face on account of getting hit with a cream pie just as the reporters was getting to him, like a real rookie. His hat's on crooked, and he's got shaving cream all in his mustache, and he's got the biggest shit-eatin' grin on his face you can imagine.

"Rube, that was one of the most impressive major league debuts we've seen in years. Can you tell us how it feels to pitch a complete game shutout in your first big league game?"

"Feels great. Feels really great. I can't tell you how happy I am to be up here."

"Describe your pitch for us a little. How exactly do you throw a knuckleball, or is it a secret?"

"Ain't no secret at all. You just flick that ball between your pinky and your index finger, don't throw too hard, and try not to spin it."

"That's it? That sounds like anyone could do it."

"Anyone could. That's the beautiful part. Anyone could."

Off screen the reporter says "but you did, right?" And Rube laughs and says "God-damned right I did."

He called me that night, at about 3:00 in the morning. He'd been out somewhere, and he was clearly pretty lit. but I was so proud to hear from him, and to hear his account of how the game had gone. I asked had he been nervous and he said only at the start, and that once he had a couple of throws down he felt like that was where he belonged. He said

137

the rough patches had unsettled him, but he just concentrated on breathin' slow, like Brickyard had told him, and he'd sailed through it.

"Strangest thing, though." he said to me.

"What's that, Rube?"

"You would not believe how loud that crowd was. I'd never heard anything like it. Even before I'd thrown much, they were so loud I couldn't hear my catcher or the coaches. Crazy shit, Coach, crazy shit."

I asked how he was feelin', and he said he still felt like puke, but it didn't matter now that he was where he needed to be.

"Take care of yourself up there, Rube," I said. "I want to come up and see you pitch once our season's done."

"Aw, Coach, come on. You're gonna need to stick around for the playoffs."

"Nope. That ain't gonna happen this year. I want to finish this crappy season up and then come up and see you throw that butterfly ball against them big boys."

"Anytime you want, Coach. They give me ten tickets every time I pitch."

It wasn't any easier coachin' after that. My mind was split, keepin' track of our boys in Keokuk while watchin' the calendar and seein' when Rube's next game was. Brickyard called me every day, sometimes lookin' for advice, and sometimes just lettin' me know what was goin' on. Nixey put him in the regular five-man rotation at first, but when he realized that Rube could have pitched day-in, day-out, he switched things around so that Rube could pitch every fourth day, splittin' the rotation around him so that his other boys could get an extra day of rest. His first two weeks he pitched four games including that first one against Cincinnati. He shut out the Mets and the Brewers, and then two-hit the Cardinals to give the Cubs a one game lead in the division. He stumbled in his next start against Houston, giving up three runs in one inning but otherwise pitchin' perfect—Brickyard said it was just like old times, but he settled down and got the job done.

By mid-August the Cubs were up two and a half games on St. Louis, thanks almost entirely to Rube. Whenever he pitched the press went apeshit, and I heard that tickets went for twice their face value those days. *Sports Illustrated* called me and said they was going to do an article on him and could they send their reporter down to Keokuk to talk to me and his former teammates, and I said that'd be real fine. The kid they sent hadn't been outside of a big city or college campus his whole life, I reckon, and when we took him out to the steak joint outside of town and he asked for a vegetarian menu I realized we wasn't gonna be able to get totally through to him. Anyway, he asked us a bunch of

138

questions and watched us practice for a while, then he said he was goin' out to the plastics factory to interview his old boss and co-workers. I asked if I could tag along, on account of I hadn't been out there before and I was curious myself to see just where he'd come from. It was a weird trip. His old boss barely remembered him, knew the name and knew where he had worked, but said he hadn't really ever talked with him about anything other than work. The other workers there said kinda the same thing, and after about twenty minutes the smell of all those plastic chemicals and crap started givin' me a headache and I had to go wait for the kid outside. When he came out I asked him was he gettin' what he needed, and he said yeah.

"The thing with these stories is that the big heroes are never the people who have really interesting lives otherwise," he said. "I'll make it sound like he's the salt of the earth, but this is usually the way this goes. No one ever knew him in high school or college or wherever, usually because he'd had been so damn focused on doin' one thing perfectly."

I drove him back up to the Quad Cities to catch his flight, and the next week there he was, Rube Tyler, on the front of *Sports Illustrated*, standin' on the mound and flickin' that pitch of his. The article was real nice, talkin' about his time with us and how we'd helped convince the club that he was worth a look. They found his old yearbook picture, and threw in the most depressing picture of that plastics plant they could find, and it all made a tidy story, that's for sure.

Rube finished up August with another win over St. Louis, and no one could have known it at the time, but that's where things started to go wrong. Rube looked like hell, but he was throwin' alright. In the sixth inning, the St. Louis manager called time and took the ump out to the mound, askin' him to look at the brim of Rube's cap. He reckoned Rube had been throwin' a spitball, and he had somethin' up under there that was helpin' him lube up the ball to make it slip out easier. The ump looked, said he didn't see anything, but that St. Louis asshole wasn't finished. He asked the ump to look behind Rube's ears, on the back of his glove, and on the inside of his jock strap. The ump wouldn't do that last one, but the manager yelled at Rube and grabbed his pitchin' hand and looked at it, and later told the press that he was sure somethin' was goin' on, because Rube's fingers looked all messed up and he was just convinced that there was some kind of foreign substance goin' on his hand. The ump told him to go to hell and play ball, and he was sorry about the fact that his hitters couldn't connect with Rube's pitches for shit, but that was the way the Goddamn game was played. Rube got real rattled and gave up two walks in a row, followed by a towerin' home run.

The Cubs put up a good show on offense, fortunately, and they won 7-5, but you could tell that Rube was real bothered by what had happened.

He called me up afterwards and he could barely speak between him bein' even sicker and him bein' pissed about getting called out on the mound. I tried to calm him down but he wouldn't stop, tellin' me about how the St. Louis manager was out to get him and his career was going to be for nothin' if that kept goin' on and how could they accuse him of cheatin'?

"Rube," I said, "that's his job. You gotta just ignore it, just forget about it. His hitters can't hit you, so he's gotta say somethin' to save face. Just relax. There're gonna be haters all over, especially on teams that are playin' against you. Get some rest, alright? Get some rest and let it go."

"Fucker grabbed my hand, too," he said.

"I know," I said, "I know you got a thing about that.

"Asshole," he said.

I called Brickyard right after that and told him what Rube had told me. Brickyard said that Rube had lost it after the game, and he didn't know how the hell to get past it. He was worried that every manager in the National League had watched that and was gonna do the same thing, callin' Rube out whenever things looked desperate and hopin' that Rube would lose his shit and give up a bunch of walks and a homer or two.

"Thing is, he looks so sick right now I don't know if he's gonna make it to the end of the season," Brickyard said. "I don't think he's had a good night's sleep since he got here."

"Damn. Well, take care of our boy as much as you can. Maybe Nixey oughta give him a week off, see the team doc about that."

"He won't see him. Won't set foot in the doc's office. Coughin' up a lung in the dugout once he comes in off the mound, throwin' up after every game—even the ones he ain't pitchin'—but don't want to do anything about it."

I didn't have nothin' to say to that. Rube had some issues, some big time issues. Maybe a psychiatrist was his first stop.

Anyway, by the first of September the guy had six wins, no losses, and an ERA of 0.85, leadin' the league by a mile. He was a genuine sensation in Chicago and the rest of the baseball world was pickin' up on him, too. Old Style hired him as a spokesman, and his face was smilin' down from posters hawkin' that weak-assed dishwater all over the Midwest. "Chicago's Oldest Rookie Drinks Old Style," the posters said, "and Maybe You Should, Too." Right around then he was on WGN, and I listened to him get interviewed by their big sports

140

personalities, and he held his own. They asked him about the knuckler, and he showed 'em how to do it, alright, but he also told them how long it had taken him to get it right, and so he didn't care who knew how to do it, so long as any competition didn't show up for another decade or two.

"And can anyone hit this thing?"

"If it's thrown right, nope. No hitter in the bigs or anywhere else has got the reflexes to adjust to a properly thrown knuckleball. It's a game of millimeters—hit the ball just a fraction too high or too low, and that line drive triple is an easy fly out, or an easy ground out. That's the laws of physics, and that's been my bread and butter on the mound."

Bricky told me later they had to put him on tape delay he was coughin' so bad. Sick as he was, though, he was still tearin' shit up on the mound. The sports pages was callin' him the second comin', sayin' this was it, Rube Tyler was the answer to the curse of the damn Billy Goat, this was gonna be the man that the team could ride to the Series. They made comparisons to all the knucklers, and to some of the best pitchers of all time, but they said this was different. This wasn't a tough pitch to hit, this was a damned sure thing every time Rube made it up to the mound. The one thing that wasn't goin' so well? Hittin'. Chicago bein' an N.L. club, Rube had to take a few swings each game, and that proved to be worth the attention of the entire press corps, too. It was hard to tell whether they was more interested in his pitchin', his beer gut, or his hittin' prowess. His first at bat he'd swung at everything. Every Goddamned pitch, and went out three straight. Now, realize that we had the DH back in Keokuk, a way of spotlightin' as many hitters as possible for the big club. But up there pitchers had to hit, or had to step up to the plate, anyways, and this proved to be quite the footnote to the whole Rube Tyler story, since in addition to maybe bein' the best monkeyballer in a hundred years to stand on the mound at Wrigley, he was easily the worst hitter ever to disgrace a major league plate. Finally Nixey told him to "just fuckin' *stand there*" on account of he was likely to hurt himself swingin', and he was pissin' the hell out of the coachin' staff by swingin' at all. Their hittin' coach tried his damndest, but by the end of August he garnered nineteen strikeouts in twenty at bats with one base on balls:

Much was made of his one walk, on account of the fact that the pitcher who did the deed was not only pulled from the game, but handed his outright release a couple of hours later. Not to mention that put Rube Tyler on base for the first time in his professional career, and while fans took bets on whether he was gonna attempt a steal or not, he ended up getting thrown out at second on a ball that would have been a triple for the runner if he hadn't had to sit there waitin' in line while Rube chuffed in to second, where the shortstop was waitin', ball in glove, for him to get

141

there. Nixey told the press that Rube's offense was a liability, to say the least, but he wasn't worried about producin' a lot of runs if Rube had his act together on the mound, anyways.

He had a couple of rougher starts around then, givin' up a run or two and then getting pulled quick before things got out of hand. He threw two in a row where he was gone in the sixth, and then in the fifth, but he'd been plenty solid up till then and the press seemed to forgive him gettin' tired and havin' to get bullpen help like a normal mortal. He laughed it off in the press, sayin' that his bad days were still gonna be enough to get them to the post season, and now up four games on the Cardinals it looked like that might be right.

By mid-September our season down in Keokuk was over and I'd done the job of sweepin' up the place, lockin' the clubhouse down, and givin' the team the good or bad news. Hack and Gunner got called up to Peoria, and Hack went on to finish the season over in Carolina, playin' Double-A ball. Gunner ended up back on our roster once Peoria was done playin', but I reckon the time up there did him good. Preacher Bush and Stuffy Flack got cut outright. Their careers was over, and I wished 'em luck but later I heard Preacher had gotten a job with some church in Oklahoma and I saw Stuffy at the hardware store downtown not two weeks after the season was over. We finished a rollickin' 29-36, just about our worst season yet, but five wins better than we woulda been if Rube hadn't shown up and worked his magic.

Now, here's where it gets tough to talk about, and where I start to choke up everytime I remember it. The way it happened was that Rube had phoned me up after our season was over and told me he had a whole block of tickets to his next start, and was me and whatever boys was still around interested in him comin' up. I told him hell, yes, and I called around and a bunch of 'em wanted to go. So we got a couple of rooms booked up in the city, and took Speedy's van and a couple of other cars and drove up there that Saturday for the afternoon game. Rube had told us he'd leave us passes for practice, and so when we got our tickets at will call they ushered us into the clubhouse and out onto the field. Seein' it fillin' up with people was a real thrill, and all the guys on the team were real quiet, lookin' around and takin' in the sights and sounds of the greatest major league park there is. The Braves were on the field when we got in, but pretty soon they came in and the Cubs started joggin' out.

I didn't recognize Rube at first, until I saw his number. He didn't just look bad. He looked broken. He'd lost about twenty pounds and his eyes were all sunken. He saw us and that huge, shit-eatin' grin spread across his face, but he couldn't even jog over to us—he just shuffled over and I was worried that all the back slappin' and huggin' he got from us was gonna crush him right in half. No one quite knew what to say. We was all glad to see him, and we was honored to be in his presence after all the times he'd been on TV and in the press. But all of us, the second we saw him, we were shocked into silence by what we saw. I told him how great it was to see him, and to see him here, and everyone else said yeah, that's right, we're all glad to see you here, and then after a couple of awkward moments, he said "Well, I better get warmed up," and off he went. Brickyard came over then and I asked him what the hell was goin' on, and he said he didn't know, but whatever was makin' Rube sick was runnin' a frightenin' course.

"Can he even pitch today?" I said. "Didn't look like he could walk, hardly."

Bricky just stood there for a minute. Then he said that Rube's last couple of starts had been more and more frightenin', that by the sixth inning or so some of his pitches had tailed off real bad, and it wasn't just movement, it was that Rube was getting to the point where he couldn't reach the plate. "He wasn't getting pulled because he was tired," Bricky told me. "He was getting pulled because he just literally couldn't throw the ball that far anymore." Rube had gone into the dugout after he got pulled in that last game and he'd passed out.

I was even more scared by what I saw warmin' up. Rube still had the motion, but if it was possible his velocity had dropped. His throws were low, all of 'em were low, and he couldn't follow through without almost fallin' off the mound. Something, I told Brickyard, was wrong. Something was seriously, seriously wrong, and I didn't give a damn what Rube thought, I was gonna personally take him to the doctor if I had to after the game. Anyway, we watched practice, and Nixey came over and said hi, and that he thought Rube was gonna be OK, just havin' trouble shakin' this bug. He shook hands with all the boys, told 'em he hoped he'd see 'em up here real soon, and then let us sit in the dugout while the team practiced.

Once the game started we had great seats, just behind home plate and close enough that we could watch the batters' expressions as they saw Rube's dancin' hummingbird pitches zero in on their mark. After Rube's first pitch I thought things would be fine, he had looked like hell in practice but he'd clearly picked it up for game time, and he set down the first three Braves hitters in order, strikin' all three of 'em out. He had to rest for a bit after each one, puttin' his hands on his knees and catchin' his breath, but he came back and fired up on the next hitter each time.

The Cubs put two on the board in the bottom of the first, so he had room to work. He wobbled a little bit, walkin' the second batter that inning on four low pitches. I told Hobie I thought almost everything had

143

ended up low, and that it was mostly his reputation by now that was keepin' them hitters from just layin' off of things. Hobie agreed, but then the next hitter popped out, and Rube got his third out on a weak ground ball to shortstop. His defense made the play, but Hobie and I looked at each other. The grounder had been close enough to the mound that any pitcher should have instinctively reached down for it. But Rube hadn't even seen it. He'd just gone straight to his restin' pose, hands on his knees gulpin' air. Not after runnin' or nothin'. Just after pitchin'.

He was late comin' out for the third. Brickyard told us later that he'd gone back into the clubhouse and thrown up again. When he did come out, he was slow goin' to the mound, just walkin', and not strollin' like he was overconfident, but walkin' like he couldn't move any faster. The ump looked out at him and Rube shook his head. No warm-ups.

"Savin' his energy," Hobie said.

Rube got the first guy to pop out, then he walked number two. That brought up the Braves' top of the order again, and you could see Rube reach back and try to pull whatever he could out of his achin', sick body. He managed to get two good pitches off, the first one of 'em tricked the hell out of the hitter and he swung and missed, the second one went in for a called strike. By this point Rube had sweated completely through his uniform and he was practically gaspin' on the mound. The catcher went out to see if he was OK and then jogged back to his spot and said somethin' to the ump. He flashed him some signs—still complete bullshit, just like we'd done down in Keokuk—and then Rube came set. He wound up, came over the top, and then his whole body came forward with the momentum of his arm. The ball ended up bouncin' off the infield grass about halfway to home plate, and Rube came crashin' down onto the mound in a cloud of dirt, face down, his feet and arms splayed out in a big "X". Nixey and the team trainers went sprintin' out as if they'd expected it, and the whole crowd stood up, gasped, and craned forward to see what the hell had happened. The catcher sprang up right in front of us and went runnin' out, too, and we all stood completely silent, watchin' Rube get tended to and hopin' to God he was alright.

They rolled him over on his back and raised his head up a bit. Someone went runnin' out with a cup of water or Gatorade, and one of the trainers came runnin' back into the dugout and went straight to the phone. Nixey came our way and said somethin' to the ump, who pulled out his lineup card and started scribblin', and then Hobie shouted out how was he and Nixey just looked up at us with a completely blank stare. After a couple of minutes with Rube just lyin' there prone on the grass they opened the gate in right field and backed an ambulance through it, and two paramedics took the stretcher out and headed for the mound, tryin' as hard as they could to be businesslike in front of a crowd like that.

"Oh, damn," said Hobie. "Damn, damn, damn. What the hell."

I patted his shoulder. "Well, Rube can't say nothin' about not seein' no doctor now," I said. "Now maybe he'll find out what the hell he's been sick with."

They strapped Rube to the stretcher and carried him off. He looked conscious, but barely so, and there was a round of quiet applause from the shocked crowd as the paramedics wheeled the stretcher toward the ambulance. After they loaded him up and shut the gate the driver gave one respectful wail of the siren. The Cubs' relief pitcher started takin' some warmup tosses and the crowd started collecting themselves after what they'd seen. Nixey came joggin' over to our seats and yelled up to me:

"He asked for you as they were getting him strapped in. They're goin' to Northwestern, downtown. You oughta go." I nodded and got up, pokin' Hobie and askin' him to come with us. The whole team, they wanted to come, too, but I told 'em to stay for the game, the whole game, and to call me before they went anywhere. "He'll be fine," I said, "and you oughta enjoy these seats."

Hobie and I caught a cab downtown. "Goddamn I hope he's alright," Hobie said, but I couldn't bring myself to wish that, because I knew the way things had gone for stuff I'd wished for the last couple of years and my track record wasn't that good. What the hell, I thought. One good thing in my season and now it's a Goddamned horror show and poor Rube is getting hauled off the field. Traffic was awful all the way down Lake Shore Drive and it took us half an hour before we got to the emergency room. I walked in and told the girl at reception who I was, and who I was here to see, and when I did the doctor standing behind her looked up, real sudden, and said "I need to talk to you."

Extra Innings

"You're Orval Sheckard?" the doc asked me.

"Yes, that's me."

"You were his manager earlier this summer?"

"Yes, just for a couple of weeks. What's wrong with him, anyway?"

"OK, look, before we talk I need you to sign this. And this. And I need to see some identification, can you leave your driver's license with the desk here? All we could get out of him was that he wanted you to be here, and that we should talk to you if we needed any information."

"Sure, whatever you need. I don't know nothin' about his medical history but he was one of my players and I'll help any way I can."

The doc took the forms and stuffed them onto a clipboard. He handed that off and asked me to follow him.

"He doesn't have any immediate family?"

"No, not that I know of. He's a ballplayer, so we might be all he's got." I thought about mentioning Tammy. Shit. Someone needed to call her. Brickyard and Freddy were on their way, they must have her number.

"OK. Well, I don't know how much I can tell you, but here's what would be helpful for us to know. Has he ever passed out before? Any seizures, is he diabetic, anything at all that you know about?"

"Not that I know of. He wasn't the fittest guy on the team, but he sure seemed plenty healthy when he was with us. I gotta tell you, though, he lost a hell of a lot of weight the last month or so."

"I know—big Cubs fan, here—so I was pretty shocked to see him when he came in. Any coronary problems?"

"Well, he ate like a truck driver, so it wouldn't surprise me, but I don't think so."

"Didn't the organization do a physical on him?"

"Not that I know of, it happened so damn fast, him comin' up here."

"Alright, now this one is going to seem a little strange, but it's important. Did he work around any toxic chemicals—emulsifiers, polymers, things like that?"

"With us? No, he just threw a baseball for us." Then my stomach turned a bit. "But, uh, before we picked him up he worked at a plastics factory out on the edge of town. Maybe he worked with that stuff out there."

The doc looked right at me when I said that. We'd come to another waiting room, with a couple of anxious and exhausted looking families sitting around on soulless sofas. A framed picture of a daisy sat on the wall, and it caught my eye and I thought I must be the first person ever to even notice it.

"That might be helpful. Thanks. You can have a seat. I don't know when we'll know anything, but we'll keep you informed."

"Can I see him?" I asked.

"We need to do some tests, and I can't let anyone see him anyway until a next of kin or an employer arrives," the doc said. "Sorry. He did ask about you, though, as they were loading him in to the ambulance. So as soon as we get the OK, you'll be on the list."

He turned and walked down the hall, stethoscope trailin' in the air as he walked. I sat myself down and Hobie did the same, and we just sat there, speechless. I felt like I was takin' the first deep breath I'd had since we arrived at the ballpark or maybe since that first day, the one with the flies. Just then Brickyard and Freddy showed up and saw us, and asked us what the hell was goin' on. Freddy was on his phone back to the ballpark right away, tellin' 'em what we'd told him, but basically we was all completely in the dark. Someone came out with a bunch of forms to sign and Freddy made his way through them. I asked Brickyard about Tammy, and he said he'd called and left a message, but who knows where she was and he hadn't seen her for a day or two, anyways.

We sat there for a couple of hours. Hobie went out and found some sandwiches and brought 'em back, but mostly we just sat there wonderin' how the hell had it happened like this, that we were sititn' around a hospital when just a couple of weeks ago this had been the best sports story for ages, guy realizes his childhood dream and goes from nobody to the cover of *Sports Illustrated* in a matter of weeks. We didn't talk much, just ate our sandwiches and looked at that damned picture of a daisy and every so often we'd look at each other and just shake our heads. Finally the boys called from the ballpark wonderin' where they should go and Hobie told 'em to drive his van down to the hospital and park it for him, and we didn't know nothin', but if they wanted to spend the night on their dime maybe we'd know somethin' in the mornin'. Freddy caught his eye and let him know that the club would pick up the hotel bill, and then he told Brickyard that they oughta come to the hospital and wait with us unless they needed to get home. So pretty soon a dozen of the Westerns come waltzin' in and they sat down silently with us and so we had more people to stare at.

147

Finally, about 7:30, the doc pokes his head in and says "Which one of you is Birdsfoot?" Freddy says it's him, and the doc motions him to come back. "Bransfield and Sheckard, you come back, too."

As we're walkin', the doc says that Rube is awake, but he's in bad shape. They don't know what's wrong yet, but he's given them permission to talk with the three of us, plus Tammy when she shows up. "You can see him, but keep it short. We've got a lot of work to do to figure out what's wrong." He goes on about the tests they did, and that it looks like he's got some serious liver damage, which ain't no surprise, but also his kidneys are havin' problems, too. Freddy asks him what the hell his prognosis is with problems like that, and the doc just doesn't say anything for a minute, and finally says that he don't have any idea and it depends on what the underlyin' issue is. But he reckons there's a hell of a lot of dialysis in Rube's future, and as to playin' ball he don't want to speculate at this point. Miracles happen, he says, but not in situations like this.

We get to Rube's room and everyone gets real quiet all of a sudden. I walk in first and he's lyin' on the hospital bed in one of them gowns, he's got an IV in him and all kinds of monitors around him, and he's gray, gray like a flannel gray that doesn't hardly look alive. He sees me and his eyes move, but no other part of his body does, and he just starts cryin', cryin' his eyes out.

"Coach," he says, "I'm sorry, I'm just so damn sorry it happened like this."

I'm completely taken aback, I can't figure out what he's talkin' about. I figure he's delirious, so I kinda play along.

"Hey, Rube, it's OK," I tell him, hopin' I'm sayin' the right thing. "You got nothin' to apologize for. I'm just glad you're alright, we was damn worried about you."

He's breathin' real hard and deep, suckin' in as much air as he can.

"I don't remember anything that happened. I pitched today?"

"Yes, you did. Just a couple of innings, but they was good innings."

"Then I collapsed," he muttered, "I collapsed and the next thing I knew I was getting put in the meat wagon. Then I was sittin' here."

"Take it easy," I told him. You're gonna be fine, the doc here says they're gonna take care of whatever it is that's got you down.

Rube sorta moved his head like he was shakin' off a sign. "It's done," he said. "It's all done. I did what I could, but I messed up, I messed up real bad."

148

"No, Rube, you did fine, you just passed out on the mound. You're gonna be OK."

Rube shook his head again. "No, Coach, I'm not. I fucked up."

I didn't know what to say, or what he was talkin' about. Freddy and Brickyard were standin' around, too, and they both put their hands on him and told him to hang tough, that they were sure they were gonna figure out how to fix whatever it was that had gone so wrong. Rube smiled weakly, gulped air, and then closed his eyes.

"OK, gents," the doc said, pattin' me on the shoulder. "I think that's all he's up for."

We filed out. I told Rube on my way out that I was gonna wait there at the hospital until they knew what was goin' on. Rube muttered Tammy's name, and Bricky told him she was comin', and we left his room.

"We're running some tests, but we won't know a thing until morning," the doctor said. 'You all oughta get some sleep tonight, we might have a very tough day tomorrow."

Freddy found hotel rooms for all of us. The team stayed down the street, but he found me a really nice place downtown, and he said someone would drop off some clothes in the morning. Hobie decided he'd head back to Keokuk with a couple of guys who had things to do or family to get back to, but Brickyard came downtown with me and got a room right next door. I got checked in and got into my room and just sat on the bed and I'm not ashamed to admit that I cried my Goddamn eyes out, tryin' to figure out what the hell had happened, why Rube was so sorry and what he was sorry for, and how the one Goddamned good thing that had happened this whole awful season had turned itself upside down. Why the hell had he gotten so sick? How does that make sense? Was he going to be OK? Was he going to pitch again? I turned on the TV. The Cubs had lost the game. There were two games left in the season and they were up by one. Like that mattered, but it did. It mattered to see that the Cubs were in first because of Rube's pitchin', and it mattered because he wasn't going to be there to save their asses if they self-destructed.

I didn't sleep well that night. Rube had messed up? How? Who blames themselves for passin' out on the mound? Was he talkin' about his drinkin? Seein' as how sure, he drank like a horse, but not as much as some kids I've seen. And not as much as me and Hobie. If he's in that bad shape, how bad are we gonna be?

Freddy showed up in the morning and he had some clothes for me and Brickyard. We got changed and then he said he could drive us over to the hospital. Tammy had shown up overnight and was by his

149

side, but the hospital was wonderin' if we knew of any actual family that Rube had. I said we sure didn't know of any in Keokuk but we could make some calls. We got over there and found Tammy in the waiting room, in tears. She said that Rube had basically passed out again right after we'd left and that he hadn't woken up. They'd started him on dialysis and a whole bunch of other shit but they still didn't know what the hell was wrong. We sat with her for a while and then I called Hobie and told him they was tryin' to find Rube's family and could he help by checkin' with people out there. He said sure and I started callin' around town, too. I called the high school, where I knew he'd gone, but all they knew was that he'd had a sister go to school with him at the same time, they thought his parents had moved but didn't know where. The folks at the plastics factory said they had a next of kin listed in the employment files, but they couldn't give it to me, and I asked them could they call them and give them my number and they said they'd try, and that was about it, that was as far as I could get.

By the middle of the day we'd gone in to see Rube but it was obvious he was out of it, so we just sat around the waiting room hopin' the docs would come out and tell us something. Around noon I went out and got another round of sandwiches, and by the time I got back the doc was just tellin' Freddy and Brickyard what he knew.

The doctor had pieced together as best he could what was wrong. The tests that they'd run overnight showed some kind of chemical imbalance, something about some damn polymerizer or something, but the symptoms Rube was showin' were so extreme that he didn't believe what he was seein' and asked for another round of tests. Meanwhile, one of the nurses had tried to take a blood sample from Rube's fingers, that needle he'd always been dreading, and she couldn't do it. She couldn't get the damned needle through his skin. The skin on his index finger was too tough, and the needle broke off. This surprised the hell out of her, and she asked the doctor to have a look. He couldn't believe what he saw.

"The tissue on his finger wasn't alive anymore. It was hard as a rock, especially on the inside surface." He pointed to the side of his index finger, right next to the nail. The exact spot that a perfect knuckleball would slide off a pitcher's finger. The exact spot where any friction at all might start that ball spinnin', on its way to getting knocked out of the park. It didn't make sense, at least not yet, but all of a sudden I started feelin' sick to my stomach, like I had some idea of the awful news that was comin'.

"Same thing on his pinky finger," the doc said, pointing to the exact spot on that finger where the ball would need to slide right off, too.

"But that might just be callouses, right? I mean, you throw ten or twenty thousand pitches off those parts of your hand, you're gonna toughen up that skin, arent' you?" Brickyard asked.

The doc sighed. "You're gonna toughen it up, but not kill it. This is something different. This isn't a baseball rubbing against the skin. What I'm worried about is that this might be the other way around."

Brickyard and I looked at each other, and all of a sudden it made awful, horrible sense to me. The whole season made sense to me. Rube hadn't killed his fingers from pitching. He'd killed them for pitching.

"Sweet Jesus," I said, and Brickyard figured it out at the same time. "He plasticized his fingers. Oh, sweet Jesus." I slumped back into my chair and I suddenly felt like I was going to throw up for real.

The doc grimaced. "That's what I think, anyway. He had access to the right chemicals in the plant. It would have taken him a long time, months, maybe, but the test results would be consistent with regular immersion in a polymerizing solution."

No one said anything. We didn't have to ask the next question.

"Those solutions are incredibly toxic. It would have made the surfaces of his fingers smooth—smooth enough to pitch off of. I think that's how he was able to release those pitches so flawlessly—but it would have killed the skin and muscle on those two fingers and toughened the tissue so there wasn't any opportunity for infection or gangrene to set in. That's bad enough, but the real worry is that it diffused into his bloodstream, or lymph nodes, and once that happens the body doesn't have any way to break that complex chemistry down. It would have built up in the liver and the kidneys and slowly but irreversibly plasticized them, too. The prognosis..." he paused and took a slow, measured breath, "the prognosis is pretty bad."

Tammy buried her head in Brickyard's shoulder and quietly sobbed. The doctor put his hand on her back and just stood there quietly. Freddy put his head in his hands and stared at the floor. No one could say a word. Finally the doc said he'd let us know if there was any other information, but that we needed to find Rube's family and tell them they needed to come to Chicago.

None of us could speak. We sat there in shock, and I couldn't stop thinkin' about how desperate that must have been for Rube to plunge his hand into those chemicals for the first time, experimenting with something he must have known would give him that perfect friction-free knuckler, but that would also hurt him real bad. Maybe kill him. He must have known it was poison, he must have known that it was going to be a race against the clock to see if he could get a few good weeks out of

151

his damaged, dead fingers before the chemicals caught up with him and started breaking his body down. He must have known, and still he stuck his damn fingers in there. Then I thought of that stupid lucky glove he always wore and how that must have hidden what he'd done to himself and that did it for me. I ran to the men's room, and I sat there puking my guts out and feeling just cold and numb that someone had done this to themselves, and for what? And even more horrified that I'd been so taken in by this, by what he'd done. I felt like I'd somehow taken part, or encouraged this. Not even knowin' it, just by fieldin' the team and bein' out there, and it even bein' possible had made him do this. That was all too much. All too damn much. I took about half an hour in there and finally pulled what I could of myself together, washed myself off and rinsed my mouth out, and went back to the waiting room.

Freddy said he had to get back to the ballpark. The season was wrapping up and we understood that there were two big days to have up at Wrigley. The three of us, Bricky, Tammy, and I, made an odd trio, that's for sure, but we were there for each other and for Rube and we promised each other we'd wait it out together, good or bad. They let us go in and let him know we were there, but he was completely out, and with more tubes and wires stickin' out of him by the hour, it seemed.

That afternoon the Cubs lost, their third in a row, and they were tied with St. Louis with one game left, an afternoon one on Monday. Freddy called to say that he was going to come down to see how things were. I told him not to worry about it, but he came anyway and took us back to our hotel and got Tammy back to Rube's apartment. There was one message for me, from the plastics plant, that they'd tracked down Rube's sister and she lived out in Seattle now, but they'd left her a message to call me when she could. I checked my phone but there weren't any messages from her, and I wondered whether I ought to start callin' directory assistance out there and finally I decided I'd do it in the mornin'.

This is tough, talkin' about that Tuesday, but I'll try. What a day. What a goddamned day. It starts off with a message from the desk, sayin' I need to call Harry back in Keokuk. So I call him up thinkin' that he wants to know what the hell happened to Rube and can he help at all, but what he tells me is that me and Brickyard and Hobie are all fired. Gone. He knows the timing is awful, and he knows this ain't the day to tell me, but there's some contractual thing about lettin' staff go before the major league season ends and he's doin' it. He's sorry, but he just can't stand another losing season and he's talked with the organization about makin' some changes and they're gonna start with the coaching staff and work from there. I tell him I understand how this business works, and

I've been fired from much better teams in my day, and it's his team. But then I tell him that I don't give a damn about my job or about Keokuk or about baseball right now, and I'll call him back and let him know what I really think when my mind is clearer. He says don't bother and hangs up.

Brickyard and I took a cab to the hospital and I told him we was fired. He handled that pretty well, said he'd sort of expected it but thought maybe he'd made some good connections up at the big club. Anyway, he said, none of that matters, and we got to the hospital and went up to Rube's floor. The nurse there looked at us like there was somethin' she didn't want to say and I asked could I talk to the doc on duty. She came out and I asked her about Rube, and she said he'd had a rough night. His kidneys had shut down, and that combined with the liver damage was makin' it tough for his other systems to work. They were also worried that the chemistry had damaged his heart, and they were seein' things on his EKG that were pretty frightening in their own right.

"Did you find his family?" she asked me.

"Not yet."

"Hurry," was all she told me, and she walked away.

I looked again at my phone, but there was nothin'. I called the plastics factory and told them I needed that woman's phone number, I wouldn't tell them how I got it, but I needed to talk with her *now*. The secretary there told me she'd do it, but only because she was a Westerns fan, and I was tempted to say *fuck the Westerns, I don't work for 'em anymore* but instead I told her that Harry would probably give her tickets, hell, Harry might give her *season* tickets, if she gave me that number.

I dialed the Seattle area code and the number she gave me. The phone rang a bunch of times, and then a woman's voice picked up.

"Is this Mindy Tyler?" I asked.

"Yes it is. What do you want?" she said. Her voice was raspy and hard.

"This is Orval Sheckard. I was Rube's manager down in Keokuk."

"His manager, you mean at work?"

"No, ma'am, on the baseball team." She didn't say anything and I wondered if she knew anything about what had happened to her brother over the last couple months.

"I'm in a hospital in Chicago. He's sick. Very sick. The staff out here told me to—"

"Let me stop you right there, Mr. Sheckard. I ain't talked to my brother in fifteen years. We didn't have what you might call an all-

American upbringing, and our family wasn't close. In fact we've sort of gotten as far from one another as we could. Is he gonna die?"

"Maybe."

"What do you need from me?"

I was taken aback. "I don't know, exactly. I thought you might want to come out here and be with him."

"I can't see that happenin'. I ain't got the money for a plane ticket, and I stopped carin' what happened to him years ago."

"You know he's been playin' baseball," I asked her.

"Nope. But it doesn't surprise me. All he ever talked about. All he ever cared about. Might be that he'd be something today if he'd been able to think about anything else."

This wasn't going the way I'd thought. "Well, the hospital really needs next of kin," I told her. "I'm gonna give you a number here and ask you to call them and sort out any sort of legal issues they've got."

"Fine," she said. "Can I call them collect?"

"I'm sure you can," I said. "Do you want me to call you if anything happens to him?"

"Yeah," she said. "I guess I oughta know."

"OK," I said, and just hung up.

We got in to see Rube around lunch time. He was in and out of consciousness, and pretty delirious. He asked about me, and asked about Brickyard, and we both told him we were there. He asked me when his next start was, and I told him he had a couple of days, and rest up, don't worry about it. He pawed at Tammy a bit and asked how she was doing, and she held him for a while. After a while I couldn't stand it and I walked out back to the waiting area. The head nurse had a radio and I asked her if she could put the game on and she said sure. The others trickled out and we sat there, shell-shocked, listenin' to the game and lookin' out the window. The Cubs put up a good fight, but their relief broke down and they ended up losin' 7-5. The season was over for them, too. They weren't going to make the promised land this year either, despite Rube's best efforts.

Around dinner time there was a lot of alarms and commotion, and a couple of the nurses went runnin' for Rube's room. About ten minutes later the doctor on call came out and told us that his heart had stopped, and they'd got it started again but that it was time. We filed in to his room as the nurses was cleanin' up the equipment from getting him back among the living. Rube was moaning and sort of moving back and forth, and I went over to him and held his good hand, and told him we were here, that his friends were here and he had nothing to worry about. He whispered something, and I didn't really make anything of it

154

at first, but then he grabbed my arm and said it again, and I leaned in close and asked him to say it one more time and I will never forget what I heard him say then. In a quiet, fadin' voice, he asked *"did we win…did we win…did we make the playoffs…"*

Right then a million things ran through my mind. Do you lie to a dying man? Does it matter? And how much would it really mean to him one way or the other? Nothing in my life had prepared me for this, nothing at all let me figure out what was goin' through his fading mind, or what he wanted to hear. Did he want the truth? The truth was that all his efforts, even him killin' himself by making his chemically enhanced knuckleball fingers, had been for nothin'. The Cubs had lost. Their season was over, and Rube would be a footnote, for sure, maybe even a hero in some kind of twisted way, but he wasn't going to be the team's savior, he wasn't going to be the one who had gotten them to the promised land. It had, by that measure, all fallen short, and here he was, dyin' away from home, for a pipe dream that had fallen just short.

But at the same time, he wasn't going to be around to know that. He wouldn't be there no matter what had happened, whether they'd gone to the series and won it all or not. And maybe he was alright with that, though I'm sure that when he hatched this plan he'd seen himself pitchin' and winnin' game seven.

Anyway, I did what I had to do. I made a decision, and maybe you'll agree with it or maybe you won't. But until you're put in a spot like this, don't judge me. I leaned down, put my lips right next to his ear, and I said this:

"Hell yes. Hell yes you won. You did it, Rube. You got 'em there."

The truth was, he'd gotten us all there.

He smiled. He used his last bit of energy to smile at me, even though he couldn't even open his eyes anymore.

"Goddamn," he said. *"Maybe I'll get to pitch in the Series."*

And that was it. He held on for another hour or so and we all sat around him but he didn't say nothin' else. The doc told us that what they was startin' to see was different parts of him shuttin' down. His stomach had stopped workin', and next they said would be his lungs and his heart and then it'd be over. Rube never flinched. He squeezed Tammy's hands every so often but pretty soon that stopped too. Finally the machines all started goin' off and the doc just turned 'em off and left us with him for a while. None of us said nothin'. I just laid my hand on his head and I wanted to say somethin', to say goodbye, but I couldn't think of nothin' and I just walked out and stood in the waitin' room lookin' out at the city.

Brickyard walked up to me and put his arm around my shoulders. "You alright?" he asked.

"I'm alright," I said. "But fuck this game."

I called up his sister and told him he'd died. She asked me what it was and I told her best I could.

"Figures," she said. "All that ever mattered to him was baseball. Doesn't surprise me at all. He never did nothin' else. Never worked in school, never thought about college. He wasn't stupid, but he threw a hell of a lot away just playin'."

I told her now look here, he'd been a hell of a pitcher for us and that I had been proud to know him. She asked if he died happy and I said yes I guess he did and then I figured I'd done the right thing. I wanted to find out more, I had a lot of questions about Rube and about why he did what he did and wondered whether it was maybe his dad that pushed him into it or somethin', but she cut me right off.

"Mr. Sheckard, I appreciate you're keeping me informed. But like I said, I ain't talked to him in years. I got my kids to pick up at the nursery. So I gotta run. I just got one question for you."

"Yes ma'am?"

"Did he leave a will?"

"I don't know. We ain't..."

"'Cuz if he didn't, and I can't imagine he would have thought of that, I'm thinkin' maybe I oughta get me a lawyer. He make a major league salary?"

"The minimum. For a couple of weeks. I don't even know if it's worth it."

"Hell it isn't. Anyway. Thanks for callin'."

"I'm sorry, Ms. Taylor."

"I ain't."

Well, he didn't have a will, but the documents he was able to sign was enough to give power of attorney to Tammy. Freddie showed up and he said they was plannin' a nice funeral for Rube back in Keokuk, that he'd talked to Harry and Harry was gonna make sure that there was a good crowd and a preacher and all that, and there'd be a memorial out in center field, just like Yankee Stadium, and did I think I could get the team together for a nice tribute before it got too cold out? And I thought, you cold-hearted sonofabitch. You and Harry just fired my ass, and Rube just threw his life away for your team, your sport.

I looked at Tammy, and she looked at me, and we both said "sure."

But what we did was Tammy told the hospital to cremate him. And they did, and we drove back to Keokuk together wonderin' what the

156

hell we were gonna do with him. Tammy reckoned we ought to just give him to Freddie and Harry and let them do whatever the hell they wanted, but the thought of him goin' back in that ballpark pissed me off, and I wanted to be there to say goodbye to him but I sure as hell didn't want to put on a show with them assholes who fired me. We didn't talk much about it on the drive, but when we got to Peoria we stopped at a diner and I asked her whether she and Rube had ever talked about his life, where he came from, and what he wanted to do if he made it in the bigs.

"You know, what's funny is that first night, the night you all came to the club and he took me home? We never even got it together. All we did was talk. All night. Drunk as hell, but he sounded like he'd been waiting for years to tell his story. And he did. I ain't gonna share everything. You can guess what his childhood was like. Not too pretty. But he did say he didn't think he had long in this world, and he was bound and determined to, what were his words, 'kick the shit out of life' before it did it back to him again."

"You reckon he was happy?"

Tammy didn't say anything for a while. She held her cup of coffee with both hands and looked out the window at the parking lot and the highway. Then she sighed and said "Nope. I don't reckon he was. I know he enjoyed the ride he was on, and he enjoyed bein' on the teams he was on, and he appreciated the time you and all the coaches took with him. But he wasn't happy. He was nervous and scared and worried that it was all gonna be over too quick for him to enjoy it. I thought he was worried that his arm was gonna give out, or them hitters was gonna figure out how to hit his pitchin'. Now I guess he must've known his time was runnin' short.'

I didn't say nothin'. I looked down into my coffee. Tammy's eyes welled up and she wiped at 'em with her other hand.

"He once said the only place he was really at peace was when it was just him, throwin' in the back yard. He seemed like once he'd gotten discovered it had maybe been a big mistake. That he loved havin' that trick pitch but he hated givin' it up."

"Givin' it up?"

"Givin' it up to them hitters. To you. To the ballclub. To the fans. To the TV and magazine and newspaper reporters. It wasn't his anymore, once he showed it to you all that night in the parking lot."

I must have bit my lip.

"I didn't mean it like that, Orval. Like I said, he respected you and he knew he owed you a lot. But, really? I think the man was

157

happiest in his own back yard, with a six-pack of light beer, callin' them games in his own mind."

We looked at each other and smiled. I paid for our coffees, and we drove the rest of the way down to Keokuk and stopped at the Frog in the Hole and got a sixer to go. Then we drove over to Rube's place.

When we got there was already a crew there gettin' his trailer off its foundations and a repo man hot-wiring his car. Tammy gritted her teeth. "He talked about that bitch of a sister, too," she said. "Fuck her, she can have all this. She ain't gonna get him, though. Freddie and Harry ain't gonna get him, and neither is Keokuk and neither is baseball."

And with that we went back to the tree out behind his trailer, and stood by the Johnny Bench Batter Up, all torn up and held together with elastic bands and string and rusted like hell, and together we walked the 60'-6" to the spot he'd worn down in the grass. There was a carpet of green shoots comin' up on account of Rube hadn't been wearin' through them for a few weeks. Tammy started cryin', and I choked up, too, and we scattered him there, with a six pack of Oldie, on his makeshift pitchin' mound where he watched his dream take shape and where he knew that he was dyin', but that he was gonna be a major league pitcher even just for a few days. And where he must have made his peace with that, even as he was pissin' blood and coughin' himself awake at night and maybe—I guess, anyway—figurin' out that some dreams are better left unrealized because they cost too goddamned much. I dropped Tammy off back at her place and then I went back to my trailer and called Tug. I packed all my shit up in a duffle bag and I left that fuckin' town and I never, not once, looked in the mirror drivin' north.

About the Author

Hank Owens grew up a Red Sox fan but married into a Cubs family, and he now lives in central Iowa, where he works on old buildings and writes about them. He bats and throws left for a beer league softball team, and despite years of trying has never been able to master a knuckleball.